Wide Boys
Never Work

Wide Boys
Never Work
Robert Westerby

With an introduction by Iain Sinclair

LONDON BOOKS CLASSICS

LONDON BOOKS
PO Box 52849
London SW11 1SE
www.london-books.co.uk

First published 1937 by Arthur Barker
This edition published by London Books 2008

The publisher wishes to thank Elizabeth Westerby
for supplying information used in the production of this book

A catalogue record for this book
is available from the British Library

ISBN 978-0-9551851-5-1

Printed and bound in Great Britain by
CPI Antony Rowe

Typeset by Octavo Smith Ltd in Plantin 10.5/13.5
www.octavosmith.com

TO
JAS.
NARROWEST
OF THE
WIDE BOYS

INTRODUCTION

Wide Boys Never Work. We want to witness those letters in smoky light bulbs, fusing in the rain, on the side of some red Alhambra: a pastiched Hitchcock tracking shot. Robert Westerby's title has an ersatz immortality – but the author, along with all his other books and film scripts, years of Hollywood servitude (and loot), vanishes: absolutely. Charity-shop scavengers, over-the-collar hair lank with hard-travelled sweat, belted torpedo coats reeking of buses, amphetamine froth salt-white on chewed and blistered lips, would lean over my Camden Passage stall to whisper: '*Wide Boys.* Ever seen a first – in jacket? Let one go in Cecil Court, mint mint mint. O man, they stitched me up. I'll never see it again.'

Even the most memory-coshed runners have certain titles on the tips of their furred tongues – *Café-Bar, The Lowlife, Wide Boys NeverWork* – while the authors are completely forgotten. This subterranean, word-of-mouth London is a bibliography of items that are always on the point of being republished, newly promoted, decades after the originals have disappeared and the poor hacks responsible, drudging for a pittance, have been banished to oblivion. Cremated in Kensal Green. Buried alive in Willesden. Misquoted in a blizzard of pseudonymous blogs on some well-intentioned website. The act of 'rescuing' lost titles is the only restitution we are prepared to make for a condition of cultural amnesia, reliance on the lazily established canon of the broadsheet reviewers and their academic sponsors.

Robert Westerby is the antithesis of all this. He types on your eyeballs with a hot needle. His language is unvarnished, stripped to essence. He has a voice you learn to trust, the tale will tell itself: damaged men in damaged times. A prose version of photojournalism. Reportage, significant detail, snappy dialogue. Attitude without editorial intervention. Seedy characters frozen in the blinding flash of Weegee's ambulance-chasing camera. Murder scenes before the bad thing happens. Nothing to sell beyond its own occasion. Every published story a rejected film script.

So few people succeeded in locating a copy of *Wide Boys Never Work*, Westerby's September 1937 novel, that its status remained inviolate. The title defined a period; it enjoyed a life of its own, independent of author and the circumstances of original publication. A cultural virus, the book lodged in the private collections of later writers who made it their business to retrieve and remember. Schlepping about town as dealer in used books (libraries of the lost), I learnt that key works were scattered in musty bedrooms, heaped corridors, boxes under the stairs. Ownership was the initiation into a secret society open to all. A confederacy of gossip, rumour and mis-information: a cache of inscribed Gerald Kershs found in Morecambe by Martin Stone and sold to Michael Moorcock. Or traded for lavishly annotated Moorcock typescripts. The respected London historian, Jerry White, showed me a pristine copy of *Wide Boys* on his shelves. When I expressed my admiration, and asked him where on earth he'd found it, his reply was shocking. 'I bought it from you. Along with all those Mark Benneys.'

Ken Worpole, I'm pretty sure, had another copy. His pio-neering study of working-class authors and readers, *Dockers And Detectives*, name-checks Westerby, without proffering any further information. Worpole points out that Valentine Cunningham's 'definitive' account of British writers in the 1930s makes no mention of *Wide Boys Never Work*. The novel-ist, film-maker and serious collector of submerged London literature, Chris Petit, acquired so many copies in variant dust-wrappers that he was able to pass on his 1948 *Wide Boys* reissue (from John Lehmann's Holiday Library). Which comes with a nice little introduction by the author and a few tweaks and revisions. He now regrets his generosity in selling me Westerby's hard-boiled second novel, *Only Pain Is Real*, with the presentation inscription to 'Mr and Mrs Hall'. Who remain, as with so much in this story, properly mysterious.

The term 'wide boy' is a local pejorative, coming out of defensive middle-class sensibilities, to sit alongside the far uglier 'Jew boy'. Westerby's precursor of the post-war spiv, whatever the man's age, is socially immature, shirking responsibility, open to any racket. A threat to decency. A non-working, working-class bum with wop tailoring and American dreams. Padded shoulders, chicken legs. Permanent fag, cut-throat razor in deep pocket. Simon Blumenfeld published *Jew Boy*, an East End right of passage, in 1935. A lot of people have read that title, very few have braved the novel. The 1930s were a great period for crime fiction, melodrama, vampiric spectres of film noir. The blackshirt in the pinball arcade. The storm-trooper in the fun-house mirror. Gabardine reps, pipes primed, trade politics and smut on smoky trains.

Puffing heroically, as they return to the capital, the salesmen offer a grudging endorsement to the British fascist leader: 'Now, old Mosley. I don't like him much, but he's got the right idea about the Yids.' Westerby's protagonist, Jim Bankley, despite that subliminal 'bank' in the name, is anti-political, rather than apolitical. A disenchanted lout: 'muddy with poor food and chronic constipation . . . surly and anxious'. It takes Westerby a quarter of this slim novel to get his man to London. Where he will trade muscle for initiation into the tricks and subterfuges of the 'wide' world of dog tracks, clubs, car showrooms – before returning, having 'tasted blood', to the constriction of the terraced home from which he set out.

*

Robert Westerby shares a birthday, July 3rd, with Franz Kafka. That is one of the few facts the internet has to offer. Born: 1909, England. Died: 1968, California. Around a dozen books published by Arthur Barker between *Wide Boys Never Work* (1937) and *In The Money* (1952). After that it was the usual deliriously prodigal West Coast career, movie scripts for everything from *The Fighting Prince Of Donegal* to King Vidor's *War And Peace*. Vehicles customised for Peter McEnery, Richard Attenborough, Audrey Hepburn. *Wide Boys* was filmed in 1956 as *Soho Incident*.

Sketchy autobiographical material can be extracted from the Westerby memoir, *A Magnum For My Mother* (1946). The title was not a reference, as Americans thought, to a handgun: no potential Don Siegel option here. The book is episodic, shaped anecdotes from a childhood spent somewhere on the fringes of London (no specifics revealed), name and rank only. A Richmal Crompton world of respectably feral kids with eccentric relatives, servants and followers, weary mother and preoccupied father (something in the City). Pointers to the author's earlier realist fictions are available to those who are prepared to dig. One of Westerby's brothers is called Jim: the first name of the protagonist of *Wide Boys*. There is a standard *Just William* episode that warps from social comedy into remembered (and unassuaged) pain. A small boy, the son of an artist, a 'queer chap' with a dead wife and 'a spectacularly violent temper', is coerced into attempting feats of daring beyond his means. He falls from a tree and dies. He is called Eric Bankley. This unusual surname is inherited by the would-be wide boy of Westerby's most celebrated novel: the provincial labourer seduced by Jewish hustlers, motor traders from minor public schools, hard men, whores and professional losers. By London.

'The tragedy of Eric Bankley upset us all . . . It was easy to assess its effect on us children, because we never discussed it . . . The real shocks are absorbed, and comment on them has to be excavated. We never spoke of Eric again.'

Names migrate from the actual into the fabulous, bearing their karmic burdens. Chris Petit told me that whenever he was struggling for the name of a character in one of his thrillers, he fell back on the roll call at his prep school. Jim Bankley, surrogate brother and lost child, arrives on the pages of *Wide Boys Never Work* in a complex interweaving of autobiography and invention: a suitable vessel for inarticulate anger, furious energy and jaw-snapping boredom. Hours on a narrow bed waiting for the call to action. Awkward in his body, with 'very wide shoulders', hair 'tightly curled, almost like a negro's', Jim watches smoke rings climb towards the flaking yellow plaster of the ceiling. His imagination pricked and flayed by *Spicy Yarns*, a soft-porn shocker on whose lurid cover an unconscious blonde is 'sprawled backwards over the arms of a big tough mug'. Without self-love, the crab's claw, there'd be no love at all.

Wide Boys Never Work, in structure, is a traditional moral tale, an unsentimental education; the 'bad' brother quitting his home, with its narrow horizons, in search of the easy money and loose women of the capital. A quest for language and a new cast of characters: 'tarts, touts, ponces, louts, bookies, ex-pugs, petty gangsters, perhaps a stray newspaper reporter trying to feel tough and Metropolitan'. Westerby, as guide to the labyrinth, a detached insider with the lowdown on clubs and scams and off-limits locations, is a model for the future career of Robin Cook (Derek Raymond), another privately-miseducated malcontent of enormous charm and strategic erudition. Cook's novels of the Sixties, as lexicons of period slang, a blend of lowlife and bent establishment, were more useful than any timid researches undertaken in Wigan by patronising Cambridge Marxists under the guise of the Mass-Observation movement. Westerby prefigures Cook's performed identity as a toff in disguise (beret and clip-on Gauloise): a bar-room fixture sopping up dialogue and narrowly avoiding violence. Or incarceration. The narrative punch of *Wide Boys* echoes Cook's as-yet-untold anecdotes. That fiver peeled from a rubber-banded roll at the dog track. The chat. "Lo, Mory. How you doing?' Westerby achieves the rancid edge of those Derek Raymond 'Factory' novels: a posthumous nightmare, a city where it is always twilight and the dead greet the dead over curled seagull-grey sandwiches at the White City track.

Sexual encounters are arid, juiceless, necrophile. Like prizefights without the sponge and bucket. Bodies press together, half-aroused in lustful hatred, and all too conscious of damp wool, rotten armpits, sour breath, cigarette smoke saturating tangled hair. The pubic curl in carbolic soap. The exploding geyser in the shared bathroom. Congress is urgent and instantly forgettable.

Westerby is very good on smells. Small, sick men unbalanced by Freudian cigars. Attractive whores, face powder like cheap cement, have rabbits' teeth: black lips, blue smiles. Distracted women, on handkerchief-sized dance floors, wrestle with men who don't dance: they carry too much of the street indoors. They jerk neurotically, half-asleep, conscious of their blisters, to the shriek of a queer saxophonist. There is a forensic bite in Westerby's prediction of cancers flowering beneath lardy complexions. His pre-war London, balancing social and racial prejudices with authoritarian fantasy, stinks of the mob. Shaved monkeys in chalk-stripe suits scratching their privates. Consumptive Welsh boxers with anthracite underwear. Subhumans, conscientious objectors in the class war, incubate treachery and anticipate random acts of violence with masochistic relish. When razors flash and teeth are spat into sawdust, there will always be some clerk from the suburbs rutting under the table. 'Jim saw that the woman on the floor had no under-clothes on. The man with her was blubbering with fear and shouting something about the police.' This is Charlotte Street imagined by George Grosz or Otto Dix. A traumatised interval between global conflicts, *Palais de Danse* dissolving into concentration camp.

The motherless Jim Bankley is a reflex misogynist, attracted to a homosexual sub-culture that also repels him. Louie Franks, his Jewish mentor, is a gay man who indulges his gauche protégée: as disposable rough trade. Jim's motor-trade boss, Graham Swing, has been expelled from his private school after 'a rather strange episode with a smaller boy in the dark room of the photographic club'. Modernist art, when it appears, is a badge of decadence: screaming queens and inane cocktail-party chatter (acid as early Eliot). 'Tony shrilled with laughter. "My *dear!*" he said. "Too *Nazi!*"' The evening ends with a failed seduction, Bankley beating the man with the nice wallpaper to an ecstatic pulp. Jim Thompson meets Francis Bacon.

Moving the narrative from a motor-manufacturing town, somewhere around Birmingham, to the London of wide boys, gamblers, queers, working girls, suggests a disenchanted leftist perspective. *Wide Boys* is a product of its time, of the Spanish Civil War, thugs attacking synagogues, Oxbridge 'pylon poets' heading off to Berlin in search of the zeitgeist (and handsome blonde hunks). The assembly line is both a moral value for those like old man Bankley with his 38 years on the shop floor and a symbol of alienation that survives in English culture right through to Karel Reisz's 1960 film version of Sillitoe's *Saturday Night And Sunday Morning* and the cacophony of Jean-Luc Godard's visit to Cowley for *British Sounds* in 1969. But Westerby comes at his class drama from another angle, by way of American hard-boiled crime. His 1937 novel, *Only Pain Is Real*, is faux James M Cain, pulp Steinbeck: the road, labour riots, boxers and grifters. 'I've lived pretty hard, Van, and that's the way I'm dying.' Arthur Barker issued the book in pinkish cloth with vertical red stripes, to look exactly like the English edition of Horace McCoy's *They Shoot Horses, Don't They?*

Westerby's style is dynamic, influenced by early exposure to, and fascination with, cinema. As he reports in *A Magnum For My Mother*, 'the torrid entertainments we saw may easily have affected my growing mind . . . Theda Bara's death scene in *Dope* . . . *Cabinet Of Dr Caligari* (which gave me nightmares for a week) . . . And what happened to Sylvia Breamer? And Blanche Sweet? Barbara La Marr? Or Nita Naldi?' *Wide Boys Never Work* opens to the piston rhythms of Auden's lyrics for *Night Mail* (1936). 'Blackened chimney stacks, belching untidily like recently-fired rifles, pointed skywards.' The set pieces at the dog track, the drinking club, the boxing ring, become standards of low-budget British cinema. You can cast the thing for yourself: Gordon Harker, Googie Withers, Jack Warner, Herbert Lom, Diana Dors, Stanley Baker. 'The youth's name is Perce, and he looks as if it would be. His face is the colour of a dirty plate, and no one has ever seen him without a half-smoked cigarette drooping from his mouth.' The young Anthony Newley with his pleading and lizardly ancient eyes? Narcissism and melancholy.

There is a process that happens with the best writing when the author's considered and well-executed synopsis is over-whelmed by the heat of place, the savage ventriloquism of invented characters with a mythic force far beyond anything plotted in advance. It can't happen with film in the same way, you never get more than is there: the indifferent set, the inar-ticulate objects. In *Wide Boys Never Work*, Westerby's seething city of collisions begins to set its own agenda – and prose, which was urgent and effective within the conventions of genre fiction, takes on the vertiginous rush of Louis-Ferdinand Céline: the poetry of chaos. Nobody has written better about criss-crossing London, on foot and on buses, in the delirium of alcohol and electricity, exile and madness, than the shrapnel-in-the-skull race-crazed French medic. *Guignol's Band. London Bridge* (of which, scandalously, no edition has been published in England). And like Céline, by whom he appears to be influenced (without perhaps having read him), Westerby abandons orthodox grammar for the flicker-cuts of single frames separated by ellipses.

'He could see the lights on the grass, the movement, the black stirring of the crowd, the excitement of everything . . . the car . . . the girl in the taxi . . . the faces here at the party . . . pale, flaccid faces, bright eyes . . . the smell of perfume and drink . . . cigarette smoke curling bluely from the ashtray . . . London seemed far away . . . like death . . .'

Hallucination. Sickness. Vision. Truth.

My introductory notes for this book were unresolved but concluded, when I got the e-mail from Robert Westerby's widow, Elizabeth. I had thought the finish might be the discovery in *A Magnum For My Mother* of a character called Sinclair, a school fellow of Westerby's, who 'read a lot – under the sheets with an electric torch; it gave him permanently red eyes.' But Elizabeth's eye-witness report trumped all that. Robert Westerby, it seems, was working at Pinewood Studios on a Disney movie, *Three Lives Of Thomasina* (1963) – Patrick McGoohan, Susan Hampshire, a 'family' picture about a cat – when Walt invited him to come to Burbank to do some rewrites. Westerby loved California: 'the sun, beaches, playing tennis, dining, theatre and movies'. And he stayed. Lacking a green card, he chose to return once a year to England, to his 'large manor house' in Pinbury Park, Sapperton Valley, in the Cotswolds. The rural idyll. The place where John Masefield once lived.

Westerby covered a Joe Louis championship fight in Chicago in 1937 for Paramount News, but he was not a regular at the ringside and he never talked about boxing (an activity that features so much in his fiction). He relished the West Coast good life, playing table tennis with the violin virtuoso Jascha Heifetz, socialising with Eric Ambler and King Vidor and entertaining 'people from the studios': thereby proving that there are second acts in English lives. Those of us who are left behind, in our imploding city, in the weather, have Westerby's early novels, crafted by a man transformed, as windows into that vanished pre-war world.

Jim Bankley, drifting aimlessly down Charing Cross Road, pauses at Foyle's window. 'What did people want so many books for, anyway? Probably only the mugs who write could tell the answer to that one.'

Iain Sinclair

WIDE BOYS NEVER WORK

The sun broke feebly through the clouds. All over the valley hung a thick pall of dirty smoke. A forest of blackened chimney stacks, belching untidily like recently-fired rifles, pointed skywards. Huddles of mean streets, hideous in geometrical uniformity, primly dead in front, stragglingly despairing at the back. Row after row of them, grey and flat in the early morning light; rain-shiny streets; uneven, ragged fences dividing defeated gardens of trodden, bare earth; a large, derelict piece of waste ground, its edges littered with torn paper and old cans. Beyond that, allotments, pimpled with untidy sheds. The Town was waking, and the sun blinked feebly through at it. At this home of thirty thousand souls, hard-working, unimaginative, being beaten – beaten by something they didn't understand. Only the young ones still with any fight, and not all those still with hope.

The streets began to fill up as small groups of men, drably clothed, their faces pale with the pallor of those who seldom get the sun, straggled forward in the morning tide of workers towards the factory – towards one factory in particular – Chantrey's.

Chantrey's, the home of the Chantrey car, that ubiquitous piece of middle-class furniture, that bringer of blissful pride to the Man In The Street. The Chantrey car, for the possession of which many little sums had been, and still were, scribbled on the backs of envelopes. All over the country the hoardings screamed it blatantly, in countless periodicals the advertisements cooed it cleverly – '*You* can afford a Chantrey.' Screamed it even from the walls of the factory, 'The Home of the Chantrey – the Car *You* can Afford,' and to the men who worked there it hardly seemed ironical because they never looked at it any more. Chantrey-Six, the de Luxe Economy car, £195 *ex*-works, or by instalments. And these shiny, pressed-steel saloons, bright with paint, sleek of line, were vomited up in their thousands every month. Acre after acre of workshops, glass-roofed and clean, miles of roadway, of corridors, of offices, growing every year, swallowing manpower inexhaustibly. Splendid monument to Organisation and Big Business – Chantrey's.

* * * * *

Lark Street, Number 6. The same as Number 16, as Number 60, alike as the balls in a bearing, but not so clean. In a long row, set back ten feet from iron railings.

The light inside the house was poor, and old Bankley, stumbling down the stairs, had to peer closely at the clock which hung in the hallway before he could see the time. It was seven o'clock.

He went into the kitchen, scratching his grey head and yawning. Then he put the kettle on the stove and went back to the foot of the stairs.

'Hey!' he shouted. 'Hey! Ernie! You up? Give Jim a call, boy! Hey! Ernie! Ernie!'

'All right! I heard you,' Ernie shouted back, and the old man downstairs listened for a moment to make sure the boy was really getting up. These boys were a bloody nuisance. They would be sleeping till noon if someone didn't wake them.

Twenty minutes later there was tea and toast and dripping on the table, and, silently, old Bankley began to eat his breakfast. If those boys didn't come when it was ready, it was their own bloody fault, that's all. He looked at the clock.

Five minutes later, the boys came down.

'Come on, Ernie,' old Bankley said, 'I told you about bolting your grub. If you came down and ate slowly instead of filling yourself up like a snake in two minutes, before you rush off, you'd not have that indigestion.'

Ernie shrugged his shoulders. He was a tall, fair boy, about twenty years old. Thin and pale, with fine grey eyes and a weak mouth. He was in the drawing office at Chantrey's. Already he considered himself a step up from his father, who was a charge hand in the machine shops. He meant to get on, Ernie did. He meant to get out of all this, and he made himself clean and neat, and saved his money, and worked. He could see all round him men who were licked by life, who had been knocked around until there was no fight left in them. But he was different. He was going to get away. He ate his breakfast, saying nothing, looking at the clock.

Old Bankley glanced sideways at the other boy – at Jim.

They had had an argument the night before, he and Jim, and Jim was sulking. So old Bankley looked at him carefully, his eyes amused, comparing him, admiring him.

People talked about Jim, and plenty cursed him. He was a hot one all right, this boy. People kept on his right side, or kept away. There were plenty of hot ones in this town, but none of them came any hotter than Jim. Old Bankley grinned and wagged his head.

Jim, his eyes on his plate, chewed toast and drank sickly-sweet tea moodily. He was of medium height, and looked short. And this was because of his very wide shoulders. His hair was thick and black, tightly curly, almost like a negro's. His face was broad, square in the chin, sulky-mouthed. His eyes were dark blue, and very bright, the most remarkable things about him. But now they were heavy with sleep, and his face was muddy with poor food and chronic constipation. He was surly and anxious for something to grumble about.

Slyly he glanced at his brother, taking in the neatly slicked hair, the clean hands, the blue shirt and dark-red tie.

'What the hell are you wearing a red tie for?' he said. 'You're no bloody Bolshie.'

Ernie flushed and said nothing. He didn't get on with Jim. Jim was a hooligan.

'Hey! Clurk!' Jim said. 'Are you deaf or something?'

Ernie put down his cup. 'Leave me alone,' he said.

'What the hell d'you mean?' Jim said. 'I asked you a . . .'

Old Bankley got up from the table and took out his pipe.

'Shut your gob,' he said. 'That's what. You're looking for trouble again, boy. Leave Ernie alone, see?'

Jim scowled. 'Ah, shut up,' he muttered.

Old Bankley went slowly towards the door. 'I'm off,' he said. 'You coming, Jim?'

Jim wiped his mouth with the back of his hand and pushed his chair away from the table.

'Yes,' he said, 'I'm coming.'

Ernie opened the newspaper that was on the mantel-piece, and opened it noisily. He was on the office staff, and started work half an hour later. This half-hour meant a lot to him, it was the dividing line.

Old Bankley and Jim went out along the passage and through the front door. Jim slammed the door hard. He knew Ernie would hate it.

Though Mrs Bankley had been dead only two years, already it seemed that she had never existed. Poor, coughing Mrs Bankley, who had worked so hard, who had tried so desperately to fight off disappointment, her hatred of the house, the street, the whole world she lived in. She had been licked from the start. She seemed more futile even in death than in life, and was gone almost unnoticed. Three super-egoists in the house, warring one against the other, had slaughtered first her hopes, then her life, now her memory.

The woman who came in every day from the next street,

and 'did' for them, made the place habitable, prepared all the meals except breakfast, and kept out of the way. They asked no more, and, except to eat and sleep in, their home meant nothing at all . . .

The two Bankleys trudged on in silence, joining the few stragglers going to the works. It was early.

Jim began talking to some of his own crowd, boys from the running sheds, dashingly technical young toughs who did the road tests. And old Bankley walked alone.

Nodding to the gatekeeper, old Bankley strolled over to the shops. This was the time he loved, when the great place was almost empty.

He wandered slowly in and through the doorway. There was no one about. Putting his pipe away, he went inside the shop, glancing round at the silent, leashed-in power all about him. Long avenues of machines, forests of shafts and belting, the dim light of the early morning filtering through the glass roof, swerving off sleekly-oiled metal to drown in the dull blackness of the floor.

His footsteps echoing loudly, a man walked slowly through the shop towards the door. He nodded when he saw old Bankley. 'Hullo, Ted,' he said. 'Seen Mr Whitcher?'

Old Bankley shook his head. 'No. Just come in.'

'— him!' the man said, and turned away.

Old Bankley laughed.

'And — you, too!' the man called out, looking round.

Old Bankley didn't say anything. He took off his coat and walked through the shop to where he was working.

There were men coming in now. First in ones and twos, then in large numbers, talking, laughing, arguing, their white, peaky faces in violent contrast to their greasy overalls and work-scarred hands, grained with the dirt which no soap would ever move.

From somewhere high above the roof, like the voice of God itself, came a deep-throated roar of sound that rose, whining through two octaves to a shriek. Sullenly, with steadily-growing rumble, the huge diesels in the power-house started under the kick of the compressed air, and protestingly, spreading from its heart, spreading quicker and quicker, the whole place woke to life. Shaft after shaft, the belting squealing wildly for its grip, spun into movement. Belt after belt, pulley after pulley, until the entire forest hummed and twinkled with movement, movement and power. From the far end of the shops the mad clamour of the stamping presses crashed staccato, like gunfire. From somewhere in the roof two men started riveting, the automatic gun firing intermittent bursts of sound that split their way through the general uproar like a razor slash through silk.

Old Bankley watched it all, as he had watched it a thousand times, the growth of this great world of machine power, and he smiled. It was his own world, his life. Ernie was a fool to sit on his behind all day long in an office, and Jim, too. They both missed all the magnificence there was in all this.

Maybe old Bankley was something of a poet way down underneath the mediocrity, for he looked around the shop and nodded his head wisely. 'Bloody fine,' he said.

* * * * *

In the corner of the running sheds a small group stood round Jim.

'Just saw your brother come in,' one of them said, a little wiry man, sleeves rolled up over thick muscular arms, clean white overalls matching the pallor of his face. Working mostly in the open air seemed to be the only thing keeping him alive. His name was Tom Richards.

Jim grinned. 'Little Ernie?' he said. 'Bet he didn't speak to you, Tom.'

Tom made a grimace. 'Speak? No, not him. He didn't speak. He was with the little Wilson girl – the one in the office.'

Jim looked interested. 'Was he? I didn't know he . . .'

'Didn't know he – what?' Tom said.

'Maybe he doesn't,' someone else said, and they laughed, nudging one another.

'Not a chance,' Jim grinned. 'Not old Ernie. He's too cautious – even if he knows what it's all about.'

'Not like you, Jim – eh?' Tom said. He was half-scared of Jim, always trying to be on his right side, always trying to please him.

'Me? I ain't the time,' Jim said. 'I've got ideas about things.'

'Go on!' the others jeered, and Jim flushed and grinned again, mighty pleased with the aura of imaginary exploits conferred upon him.

'Well, anyway, I ain't talking,' he said.

From the doorway, the foreman came briskly towards them. His eye automatically fastened on Jim. It was better to pitch into him direct, instead of having his side remarks cutting in on another's argument.

'What the hell d'you think you're doing, you little runt,' he said. He called everyone 'little'. He was a big man and liked you to realise it.

Jim didn't say anything.

'And another thing,' the foreman started, 'I told you to take that . . .'

'I took it,' Jim said. 'Just got back. Temperature's okay now.'

The foreman cooled off for a second. Then he scowled.

'Okay,' he said derisively. 'Why do you talk like that? Why can't you say "all right", eh? All this American rot you talk, you silly young baskets! When you talk to me, you talk English, see?'

'Okay,' Jim said, and his face was like a mask.

The foreman looked at him, his face red. He hated the boy, only tolerated him because of his father, even though he was good enough at his work. There was something about the boy that made you mad every time you looked at him.

He took a deep breath. 'We'll finish this later on,' he said. 'Now listen. Mr Chantrey's coming round. He's got a party with him. He'll be due here inside a quarter of an hour. Everything's got to be absolutely straight, see? And you, Bankley, if you don't watch yourself . . . and look, if anybody asks you any questions, make it civil, and don't try to get funny. Right? Now get busy.'

The group broke up, and, in ten minutes, had the cars in line, engines running – a fancy-dress parade.

One of the men from the foundry went past the door, glanced over his shoulder, and came in.

'His Nibs is here,' he said. 'Got some tarts with him. All *right*!'

Jim jeered. 'Go on, get out!' he said. 'The heat in that foundry's been getting to work on your imagination.'

The man grinned at him. 'Okay, chauffeur, maybe you'll get the job of taking one of them for a trip,' he said, and went out.

Then the visitors came across the yard and filed in through the doorway. People looking round was nothing new. There were visitors all the time; solemn, half-scared rubber-necks, asking stupid questions; pompous, knowing men; keen men, soaking up information like sponges; foreigners and school kids. But the Boss only came a few times a year. He was an event.

The party walked briskly in. Chantrey did everything briskly. He was a short, dark man, very neat and dapper in a grey suit. His eyes were bright behind pince-nez spectacles, his small, dark moustache close-clipped. Behind him were three other men, elegant nonentities, and two young women. The women were good looking in a chromium-plated sort of way, but looked as if they needed more exercise.

'Running sheds,' Mr Chantrey said. 'They go from here . . . morning, Mr Phipps,' he turned to the foreman. 'How are you?'

'Very well, thank you, sir.'

'Everything all right?'

The foreman stared. 'Everything all right!' He wouldn't be here if everything wasn't all right. Chantrey knew that. If there was anything wrong he would have been told at the offices! 'Everything all right!' Good God!

'Yes, sir,' he said.

Chantrey walked along the line of cars, talking energetically and technically, his party trailing behind him. They had all come from a house party in the neighbourhood. Chantrey as well. None of them looked very interested, and one of the girls was smoking.

Opposite Jim's car Chantrey stopped suddenly, his eyebrows drawn down in a frown. 'Hey, you,' he jerked. 'Yes, you, come here, will you?'

Jim left the car and walked nearer. Beside Chantrey he looked very tough. His eyes were cold, and he looked his employer in the face.

'What was it you said just then?' Chantrey snapped out.

Jim just looked at him without answering.

'Come on, man!'

'Well,' the boy said, 'maybe I'd better not speak, Mr Chantrey.'

'Why not?'

The boy half-smiled. 'Your friend – the lady – she's smoking,' he said quickly. 'It's dangerous – in here, sir.'

Chantrey went red. 'Wait a minute,' he said. 'Who are you?'

Jim scowled. 'Bankley, Mr Chantrey,' he said. 'I ain't

meaning to be rude – but it ain't fair, sir. Smoking's dangerous in here. We have to work here, sir.'

Chantrey looked at the foreman, and at the girl beside him. He was in a spot. His passion was for rules, rules and discipline. The foreman's eye was as cold as the girl's. But the girl was a Special Guest. She was important to him.

'What are we waiting for?' the girl said quietly. Her eyes were on Jim, flicking over his broad figure and tousled hair, hating the insolence in his face.

Chantrey straightened up. Discipline had won.

'Your cigarette, my dear,' he said. 'Smoking isn't allowed in here. Very strict rule.'

The girl looked at him, saw the resolution in his eyes, saw that he was forced to keep his face before his men. Just for a second she hesitated, then shrugged her shoulders and threw the cigarette to the ground.

She looked at Jim again. 'Feel better now?' she said in a mocking voice.

Jim half-closed his eyes, his mouth smiling one-sidedly.

'Yes, miss,' he said.

The girl turned away. She could have hit the lout.

She followed Chantrey through the sheds, not listening to what he was saying. That grinning, insolent hooligan! At the far door she glanced round again at him. His face was expressionless, indifferent.

As soon as the party had gone, Jim flopped on to the running board of the car and laughed helplessly. His face creased up as he laughed, and he slapped his hands on his knees.

The others came over and admired him. Old Jim, he was a bloody marvel! 'Caw! I thought old Chantrey would have kicked you out,' Tom said. 'And that girl! Was she wild!'

'Flashy bitch,' Jim said. 'I bet I showed her!'

'You showed her! You certainly showed *me* something, anyway!' the foreman said, pushing through them, glaring down at Jim. 'You showed me that your blasted insolence is equal to anything! You showed me that you want a kick in the slats, and if I'd been Chantrey I'd have given you one!'

Jim stood up. His eyes were cold now, and he looked at the foreman for a long moment. 'You?' he said. 'No, not you. I don't think you'd kick me in the slats, Mr Phipps.'

The foreman put his hands in his pockets and glared. 'You go to the pictures too much, kid. Get on with your work.'

He walked off down the sheds, ordering the others what to do. But at the doorway of his office he mopped his face and swore. 'That young bastard's crazy,' he muttered. 'And I'm damned if I like it.'

* * * * *

The hands of the big clock above the office buildings moved from 5.29 to the half-hour. Away at the back of the shops the hooter screamed out, rising out shriller and shriller, cutting through the roar of the machinery, drowning the rumble of the assembly line, stilling the chatter of the typewriters, like a charm.

From every doorway and shed, every corner and corridor, men and women poured out. An army of cyclists shot for the gates in a solid bunch, magically immune from disaster, from collision. A dense crowd filtered across the yards out on to the roads, halting traffic, a thick, dark river of humanity . . .

Old Bankley opened the door of Number 6, and stumped through into the back room. Mrs Snell had left the tea ready for them, but had gone. She was like a poltergeist – doing things, and remaining invisible. The Bankleys saw her rarely, and then only by accident as it were, for if they did she would whisk out of sight again as if playing some sort of a game.

Old Bankley looked at the table. Tea, bread and butter, cold meat and tomatoes. He grunted, looked at some letters lying on his plate. Two of them were bills, and he picked them up and tucked them half behind the mirror over the mantelpiece. The third letter was important. It was his football coupon, and would need careful study, intellectual co-operation with Ernie. It was an Important Thing, the possible key to Escape.

Within a few minutes of one another, the two boys came in and joined him. They hardly spoke all the time they were eating the meal, and as soon as he had finished Ernie got up.

'Going to help me with the coupon, Ernie?' old Bankley said. 'I see some chap in Aberdeen won ten thousand quid last week in the big pool. Ten thousand quid!'

Jim jeered, and Ernie went to the door. 'Later on, dad,' Ernie said. 'I got to go out until ten o'clock or so. I'll do it before we go to bed.'

'Before *who* goes to bed?' Jim said. 'You and Betty Wilson? A hell of a fine time to start talking about football, just before . . .'

Ernie scowled and went red. 'Shut your dirty mouth,' he said fiercely. 'You leave Betty Wilson alone, see?'

Jim looked up at him and roared with laughter. Old Bankley leaned across and punched Jim in the chest. 'Shut your gob, boy,' he said, grinning. 'Leave Ernie alone, can't you?'

Ernie went out of the room, slamming the door behind him, and stamped upstairs, muttering angrily. They could hear him moving about in his room, washing, opening and shutting drawers. And when he came down again his hair was slicker than ever, his face more shining, and he had changed his suit. He walked through the back room, without speaking, on his way out to the privy.

As they heard him lock himself in, there was a knock on the front door, and Jim got up, grinning. He signed to his father and went outside to bang on the privy door.

'Sounds like your girlfriend, Ernie,' he shouted. 'Shall I show her in?'

'Yes, of course, you fool,' Ernie snarled back at him.

'But there won't be much room, will there?' Jim said. 'I think you'd better come on out.'

'I mean into the front room,' Ernie said. 'You know damn well what I mean.' He was blustering with anger. 'Why don't you go away, you vulgar swine.'

Jim laughed, and went to open the front door.

'Evening, Miss Wilson,' he said politely. 'Come in, will you?'

'Thanks.'

Betty Wilson was small and slim. Her eyes were large and pale blue, her hair soft and thin, carefully water-waved and set. Her lips were really thin, and quite pale, but looked soft and shapely with the lip salve she had on them. Dressed in a brown face-cloth coat with rabbit collar, over an art-silk dress of light blue, she looked just Ernie's type, neat, lady-like, and quiet.

As she stepped inside the house she looked sideways at Jim. Ernie had told her something about him already, and she had heard a few other things besides. Jim was hot stuff and not nice for a girl to know, but she hoped in a funny sort of way that he would not go away just yet. He didn't.

She went inside the small, over-furnished front room. It was stuffy in there, airless, and smelled as if no one ever went in there. And that was natural enough, because no one ever did.

Jim lounged against the doorpost, looking at her. She wasn't bad, in a pale sort of way. She had nice breasts, too. Jim always noticed that. Breasts were very important to him.

'Will – will Ernie be long?' Betty said suddenly.

'Dunno,' Jim said. 'Depends on what he's doing.'

'Why, where . . . ?' Betty began, but the clangour and

swoosh of the cistern out at the back checked her, answering her question, putting a horrid suspicion into her mind. She looked at Jim's expressionless face, and, her own face a fiery red, sat on the arm of a chair. Imagine a boy saying things like that to a girl!

'Do you like Ernie?' Jim said suddenly.

'I . . . Why, yes – I like him.'

'What for?'

'I don't know what you mean.'

Jim grinned sheepishly. 'Well, does he give you a good time? Does he – well, you know – kiss you, and that?'

The girl stood up, glaring at him. 'Jim Bankley! You've got no right to talk to me like that!'

Jim smiled. He was getting that tight, hollow feeling inside him. He always got it when he made himself say things that shocked people. It was funny, but it made him feel good afterwards. 'I'd want to kiss you if you were my girl. You're pretty,' he said softly. And, still smiling, he went out of the room.

Outside the door he bumped into Ernie.

'Look out, you clumsy lout,' Ernie said viciously.

Jim prodded him lightly in the stomach and grinned.

'Go to it, cock,' he said, and went into the back room. He thought Ernie was a fool, but he was half-jealous of him. After a minute or two he heard the two of them go out.

All the way down the street Betty Wilson was thoughtful. She hardly heard what Ernie was saying to her. Imagine Jim Bankley saying things like that to a girl! She thought about him, about what he had said. 'If you were my girl I'd want to kiss you. You're pretty.' Cheek! She felt her face glowing red. Jim looked a hot one, like people said. Perhaps he . . . then her mind closed with a snap. Jim Bankley was no good, everybody knew that. He was no gentleman. It wasn't any good even thinking about people like that. It was wrong.

Sighing, she held Ernie's arm a little tighter.

* * * * *

Back inside the house, old Bankley was standing in front of the mirror, his face pulled taut by his free hand, going through the agonising gamut of expressions of one who shaves hard stubble from a sensitive skin. He looked round when Jim came into the room, and paused.

'You going out, Jim?' he said.

Jim stood beside him, putting his tie on, staring carefully at its reflection in the glass.

'Yerce.'

'Where to?'

'Mind your own business. I don't ask where you go to.'

'Because you know, that's why. Otherwise you would. I'm going to the Conservative Club.'

Jim laughed sourly. 'Conservative Club, eh? Thought you were a Socialist,' he said.

Old Bankley went on shaving, talking in a strangled voice as he stretched the skin of his throat. 'What d'you mean? "Thought I was!" You know bloody well I am.'

'Well, why do you go to the Conservative Club, then?'

'Why?' Old Bankley laughed. 'There's a billiard table there, that's why.'

Jim grinned. 'Is that why the others go?'

'I expect so,' old Bankley said. 'Why else should they go?'

Jim straightened his tie out, pulled his coat on, and picked up his cap. 'I'm going to the dog track,' he said.

'And lose all your money?'

'Well, it's my bloody money, ain't it? At least I spend it on myself instead of taking cold little tarts out, like Ernie does.'

He glared at his father and stamped out of the house. Outside on the street he dug his hands into his trouser pockets and scowled. Why the hell did the old fool have to say that? It was unlucky, talking about losing before even getting there. If he had a bad night he would have a thing or two to say when he got back.

He walked on, away from the town, thinking about the two 'tips' he had heard for the races; thinking about what he would do if he won some money, forgetting about the last time he had gone . . .

The dog track was new, a small one, but good. It was a little way out of the town in the centre of a bare piece of land which had been for years derelict. Two big, silver-coloured corrugated-iron-backed stands flanked it, and at each end was a bank, like at a football ground. Already there was a lot of people there, and more going towards the gates, a constant stream of people, silent and preoccupied.

Jim put down his money and went in. He was on the far side from the winning post. The overhanging floodlights, glaring down on the track, made the grass unnaturally green, the white paint of the starting traps and hurdles unnaturally white.

He looked down at the race card in his hands. Nothing in the first race, or the second. The tips he had were for the third and the last races. He looked idly at the parade of runners as they came out from the paddock. Skinny little pups. They wouldn't be any good, they were too green, not worth wasting money on.

A name on the card caught his eye. 'Sweet Betty'. Sweet Betty, eh? And in Number 6, too! He laughed. Bit of a joke if she was to . . . He looked quickly at the betting . . . Six to one, shortening to eleven to two . . . why not? He hesitated a moment, thinking fast. 'Chuck it,' he muttered. 'Don't be a mug. What a bloody way to bet, picking 'em like that. Like some old woman. Go on, chuck it!'

But all the time his mind was uncertain, and he looked hard at the bitch as she was led past where he stood. As he watched her she stopped, and, crouching in that hideously apologetic way dogs have, excreted at the side of the track.

Jim grinned slightly as an old racing superstition flashed into his mind – 'If they do that it means two lengths up.'

He laughed and snapped his fingers. Why not? Yes, why not try a couple of bob? Couldn't be much harm in that, after all. Yes, why not?

He went straight down to the bookies and laid his money. Eleven shillings to two, Sweet Betty.

As he went up into the stand again the bugle went, and the kennel men shoved the dogs inside the traps one by one. The lights in the stands went out, making the grass still more brilliant under the arcs. Down below him, the layers wiped the prices from their boards and the hare rumbled round the outside circuit. 'These dogs must be bloody unintelligent,' Jim thought vaguely. 'That thing looks about as much like a hare as I do.'

The traps flew up as the hare went past, and the six streaks of whipcord muscle flashed out onto the track. The bitch in Number 6 broke clear, and swept into the first bend holding the rails and a two-length lead. Their feet puttering on the grass, the dogs flew along the back straight with their order unchanged, and went into the third bend. The bitch was still in front, and Jim watched her, sweating, his face expressionless, his heart pumping. She led all the way round the curve and into the finishing straight. And suddenly a black dog from Trap 1 moved up on the outside, challenging her in a powerful finish. The bitch was in front still, but fading, and together the two of them raced for the line. Jim clenched his teeth hard and sweated worse. He stared closely at the beam as the dogs flashed across it at the finish. The black dog was a head in front.

With silent savagery he tore up his ticket and threw away the pieces. Blasted fool! Wasting money on an 'old woman's bet!' Bloody fool trick that didn't deserve to come off. Moodily, he slouched across to the refreshment bar. For a trifling subscription he had joined the 'Club' on this, the cheap side. The Club itself was a long, wooden-walled room, with half a dozen tables and a bar in it. Bookies, their clerks and runners, a few habitués, hangers-on, these were the people who used it; silly talkers, for the most part, mean men and toadies, lookers-out for cheap money. But Jim thought it useful. You sometimes heard things there.

The place was full tonight. There was an Open Invitation Race on the card, and some London dogs were in it. All along the bar was a line of men talking. Jim looked at them, shrugging his heavy shoulders, and leaned in the doorway. From a table just behind him he could hear someone talking urgently. He kept quite still, staring out at the crowd, his ears stretched.

'. . . wait until they push it out, see? They're bound to do it, and then you and Louie step in,' the voice said. 'You ought to get threes, maybe fours, but get all you can. Plaster him all along the line, see? And keep your bleeding mouths shut until you've done. We're all right over on our side.'

Jim waited for a few seconds, and then went outside. He looked round casually as he went away, fixing his eyes on three men at the table by the door. One of them got up and went over to the bar, and another came out into the stand, and as soon as he moved Jim made up his mind what to do. He'd follow this man, keep close to him all the time and do what he did. The other tips could go to hell. This thing looked like the goods, and these bastards were Londoners, and they hadn't come up here for their health, had they? So he smiled knowingly and kept close.

The man in front of him was short and plump, almost fat. His head, round as a ball, was covered with thick, crisp hair, and, as he moved away into the crowd, he pulled on a blue, small-brimmed felt hat, jerking it well down over his right ear. He had a grey, pinstriped suit on, with a Charing Cross Road cut to it, and wide trousers which made his short, plump legs more than slightly absurd. As he pushed his way through the crowd he looked resolute and tough.

Jim saw him go up the stand until he was at the top step, and signal to another man farther away. He seemed quite indifferent to the race in progress, and Jim just kept an eye on him and waited. There was plenty of time.

The race ended, and the pay-out began. Then the new cards were pinned to the stands, and Jim watched the layers chalk up the prices, watching each other as the prices went raggedly along the line. Immediately they had finished, the market was swamped. One of the London dogs, Sunset Bay, was being backed down hard to evens. Jim glanced sideways at the man in the blue hat. He was moving down the stand towards the layers, and, elbowing through the crowd, Jim stood behind him. The prices were being chalked up again, and the other London dog had eased out to fours.

Suddenly there was another scramble, all along the line, and the little man in the blue hat pushed forward, a bundle of bank notes in his hand.

'Eight pounds to two, Molly's Boy!'
'Eight pounds to two, Molly's Boy!'
'Eight pounds to two, Molly's Boy!'

He darted along, getting fours three times before the price dropped. Jim pushed in excitedly, getting on the right side of the little man. He pulled out a pound note. It was his father's money, not his own. It was to pay off the woman who 'did' for them, but he hardly thought about it. In the last scramble before the price dropped, Jim got £4 to £1, just beating the little man to it.

The gamble seemed to have gone right round the place, and there was scuffling over on the far side, in the five-shilling ring.

Jim backed away, his ticket in his hand, and felt someone grab his arm. He looked round quickly, and saw the little man with the blue hat grinning up at him.

'What d'you know, kid?' the little man said. 'What are you doing, eh?'

Jim said nothing.

'You're a smart boy, aren't you? You got the last of the fours, didn't you? Eh?' the little man went on.

'Why not?' Jim said. 'This place ain't your bleeding property, is it?'

The little man stopped smiling. 'Listen, kid,' he said, 'I'm soft-hearted, see? I don't like trouble, so I'm not making any. But you better watch out for yourself, that's all. You're liable to get mixed up in something unpleasant, see?'

Jim jeered down at him. 'You don't scare me, mister,' he said. 'I'll kick the daylights out of you if you start anything with me.'

The little man narrowed his eyes. 'We'll see,' he said. 'I was only tipping you off for your health's sake, kid.'

Jim shook off his hand and moved away to the top of the stand. The bugle had gone, and the dogs were being pushed into their traps. He was still ruffled at what the little man had said to him, and, as the hare went round for the first time, he began to think about the money, wondering what he could do if he lost, knowing the God-awful row there would be about it. There was a hard, cold feeling in the pit of his stomach, and sweat on his forehead as he stood watching.

On the far side of the track the traps shot up, and the dogs flashed into view. Molly's Boy was black, in the pale-blue jacket of Trap 5. He broke badly, losing four lengths on the whole field to the first turn, and Jim swore. But the leaders bumped, throwing the third and fourth dogs wide, bringing the fifth to his knees so that he spun over sideways, rolling out across the hare trail to the wire fence. But the black dog kept in close to the rails and made ground. All the time they raced along the track straight Jim was shouting. Sunset Bay, the favourite, was in front, but the black dog was still pulling up on him. Into the third bend he reached the shoulder of the leader, drew level, running stride for stride for twenty yards, and passed. The hard feeling in Jim's stomach was getting worse.

'Stay there, stay there! For God's sake – stay there!' he muttered, and clenched his hands hard, rocking himself up and down on his toes.

From somewhere below him in the stand he heard the little man in the blue hat shout with laughter. 'No danger! No danger!' the little man yelled out. 'What a beauty!'

The black dog was pulling out with every stride, and passed the beam at the post six lengths to the good, while the crowd went crazy. The dog had been backed from fours to twos, but Sunset Bay had been carrying the money, and Sunset Bay was beaten. And where a crowd's money is, that is where you find its heart.

Jim pushed his way down and collected his money. He felt almost light-hearted with excitement, and his mouth was dry. He saw the man in the blue hat going down the line in front of him, collecting a small fortune, laughing with someone who was with him.

Jim glanced round at him, as if for the last time. Stuffing the money into his pocket, he turned towards the gates. He had had enough, and knew when to stop, and he wanted to get home and talk big about it, but from the other end of the stands there seemed to be some sort of a commotion going on, and he turned to stare at it. From all parts of the stand people were pushing towards the trouble, and Jim elbowed his way with the rest. Any sort of uproar drew him like a magnet.

It seemed at first to be just an ordinary skirmish, when all at once, apparently without warning, it started in earnest, and got rough.

A dozen men rolled on the ground, hitting madly at each other, thumping, shouting, tearing clothes. A small, struggling group, locked together, crashed backwards into one of the bookies' stands, upsetting it, sending a cascade of money over the ground. The bookmaker screamed out something, and dived for it, but all around him people were wrestling to pick up this manna from heaven, and he was hurled backwards into the fence.

In the middle of it all, Jim saw the little man. He was grappling wildly with a big tough in a dark-blue suit and a cap, and, behind him, another man was preparing to kick him in the back. Jim took one look, and ran in. He banged his left up into the rearguard-action's face, slinging him back into the mob, with a split lip. Then he turned round. The man in the cap had begun to use his feet, so Jim used his. Grabbing the big man by the neck, he bashed him on the side of the knee with a heavy boot, and the man fell, screaming, rolling over to disappear in the writhing forest of legs behind him.

'Razors! Razors!' someone yelled, and Jim saw a man stagger towards him, his face half-hidden behind a curtain of blood. There were nearly fifty people fighting now, and somewhere there were police whistles blowing. Ironically, overhead the loudspeakers were blaring out 'I'll be glad when you're dead, you rascal you.'

Backing away from a couple of the fighters, Jim felt a tug on his arm. It was the little man, and he looked scared. 'For God's sake, kid, let's get out of this,' he shouted. 'Quick!'

Jim nodded his head, turned round and charged through the crowd, swinging his fists viciously, ploughing a way through the jostling, fighting mob until he was clear, the little man stumbling wildly behind him. Running as fast as they could go, they made the gates and raced through into the car park.

Jim went on, making straight for the road beyond, thinking only about getting away, but the little man shouted after him. 'Hey! C'm'ere!' he yelled. 'Wait a minute, will you?'

Jim stopped and looked round at him.

'This way, quick,' the man said, and opened the door of

an old American car near the gates. Hardly thinking any more, the boy clambered in beside him, and the car shot away, tyres spinning in the mud of the roadway.

They drove in silence, and in the centre of the town the little man stopped the car and sighed.

'We're staying at the Red Lion,' he said. 'I better wait. The rest of the boys ought to be here in a minute. You better wait with me.'

Jim stared at him. 'Wait? Why the hell should I wait? I don't know your bloody friends. I've had enough trouble.'

The man grinned and looked sideways at him.

'You're a friendly little bastard, aren't you?' he said.

Jim scowled and said: 'Maybe, but I've had enough trouble.'

'You're a mug, boy,' the little man answered. 'But I kind of like you all the same. Come in and have a drink. We've just about got time.'

Jim shrugged his shoulders and followed him inside.

The Red Lion was seedy and out-of-date. A dusty palm in a battered brass stand smirked drunkenly in the hall. An improbable stuffed fish hung over the hat stand, looking uncommonly like the bored girl at the reception desk. The whole atmosphere was dim and depressing, and just going into the entrance hall you knew what the entire place would be like.

The waiter would be old, with bad feet and a worse suit. The beds would rattle as the lorries rumbled past in the night. The bells in the bedrooms wouldn't work properly. There would be only one bathroom, with a dull, spattered mirror in it, steamed over, and nearly as damp as the mat on the floor. The bath would have long tongues of rust hanging below the faucets, and pubic hairs sticking to its rough, painted sides. The food would be poor and unimaginative, the service disobliging, and the whole place depressing. And the establishment would be recommended by the motoring organizations.

But Jim had never been there before. It was almost a taste of high life to him. And he took his cap off and followed the little man into the bar.

The little man ordered two whiskies, paid for them, and carried the glasses over to a table in the corner of the room, jerking his head for Jim to follow. Then they both sat down.

'Well, kid, bottoms up!'

'Bottoms up!' Jim said, and thought it was a pretty funny joke to crack a smutty remark before having a drink. Then he swallowed some of the drink. It hurt his throat a bit, but he held his breath and said nothing. He had never tasted whisky before, but he wasn't going to let this man see anything.

Suddenly the little man leaned forward and grinned at him.

'What do you do around here, boy?' he said.

'Me? Oh, I'm in the running sheds at Chantrey's.'

'Chantrey's? Oh, yes. Yes, their works are here, aren't they? So you can drive a car, eh?'

Jim jeered. 'Drive a car? No, I don't drive a car. What do you think? I take 'em out and push the bloody things!'

The man laughed. 'You're a touchy young bastard, you are,' he said. 'What's the matter with you?'

'Me? Nothing. I'm all right.'

'Look; call me Louie, see? Louie Franks, that's my name. That was my cousin's dog you saw tonight. Molly's Boy. We came down here to plaster it.'

'You mean you came here to back it? From London?'

'Sure,' Louie said. 'We cleaned up on it. And we upset the Gisberg mob's gamble on Sunset Bay. That's what the fight was about.'

Jim looked thoughtful and took another sip at the whisky.

'Listen, kid,' Louie said. 'I like you. You did me a couple of good turns in that shemozzle at the track. I'd like to . . . '

'Ah, shut your gob,' Jim said, and grinned.

'How old are you, boy?' Louie said.

'Twenty-one.'

'Yes? You look more'n that.'

Jim looked pleased. 'No, really?'

'Sure. You look twenty-five at least. What's your name?'

'Jim Bankley.'

'Live here, do you?'

'Yes. With my dad and brother. My mother's dead.'

'What's your dad do?'

'He's at Chantrey's same as me. Machine shops he's in. Only he likes it.'

'Don't you like it?'

'Me? Not likely! Would you like getting up at seven every morning, and working every day until half-past five for three quid a week? Talk sense!'

Louie looked thoughtful and stared slowly at the boy in front of him. Then he took an envelope from his pocket and scribbled an address on the front of it.

'Look, Jim,' he said. 'Any time you want to come to London, you look me up. You're a likely boy, and you've got guts, and I could do you a bit of good most likely. Here's where you'll find me, or it's where I sleep mostly, anyway. Can you read it all right?'

'London,' Jim said. 'I've always meant to go there. But what could I do? I've got a job here, and I couldn't get one in London, I don't suppose.'

'You just come with me, Jim,' Louie said. 'I owe you a thing or two, and I'm no bloody piker, and I'll tell you something else. I've got a God-awful fear of razors, and when that Gisberg mob began pulling them tonight I got so scared I nearly puked. If you hadn't come and pulled me out of it when you did I'd have got hurt most likely. Might have got my face cut up and spoiled, and God! I'd have hated that, Jim boy. Some people think I'm not bad looking, you know.'

Jim looked at him sideways. Caw! the chap was serious! He really thought he was good-looking! Jim looked at him, at his round head and curly hair, his black eyes wide apart under thick brows, his red, curving mouth and blue chin.

'How old are you, Louie?' he asked.

'Me? Thirty-two. Why?'

'Oh, nothing.'

Someone looked in through the doorway and whistled softly at Louie, and then went out again.

Louie got up quickly. 'Hey, come on, Jim,' he said, and gulped down his drink and made for the door. 'That's the boss.'

Jim followed him, without really knowing why, and together they went into the hall. There was a man there waiting for them, a man with a face like a horse, a big man.

'Hullo, Bill,' Louie said. 'You got away all right, then? Say, we had plenty of trouble on our side. There was . . .'

'Shut up,' the big man said. He looked at Jim coldly. 'Who's this?'

'Oh, he's all right. He's a good kid, and he's no mug. He's a friend of mine. Got me out of that razor fight up there. Saved my bloody neck, most probably. Name's Jim Bankley. Jim, this is my cousin, Bill Franks.'

'Hullo,' the big man said.

'Hullo,' Jim said.

'Come on up, I want to see you and the boys,' the big man said. 'Come on, Louie.' And he turned on his heel and went upstairs, Louie and Jim behind him. They went to a room on the first floor. There were three other men there, and a fat man lying on the bed. And this fat man had his hands bandaged up, and was lying there cursing softly all the time.

'Hell!' Louie said. 'What's happened to Benny?'

'He's got his hands slashed,' the big man said. 'They cut him bad with a razor, blast 'em! It was the Gisberg mob.'

'Did you get your dough all right?' Louie said.

'Yes, we cleared about a hundred and twenty odd quid. There wasn't any trouble on our side at all.'

One of the other men in the room looked up. 'We'd better get out of this dump, hadn't we, boss?' he said. 'There might be trouble. Why don't we get farther on the road and sleep somewhere else? I don't like this bloody place, anyway.'

Louie nodded. 'Sounds good to me,' he said. 'Come on, Bill. Why don't we?'

The man who had spoken before looked sideways at Jim.

'Hullo, seen you before. You were up there tonight, weren't you?' he said. Then he turned to the others. 'Kid fought like a bloody rattlesnake. I saw him. He a friend of yours, Louie?'

'Yes. Name's Jim Bankley. He's all right.'

Then the big man snapped his fingers. 'All right, we'll clear off,' he said.

All the others looked pleased, and the fat man on the bed sat up. He was completely bald, with a round pink face. 'I'd better see a doctor with these hands,' he said. 'I'm bleeding like a pig.'

'Well, if *you* don't bleed like a pig, who will?' the big man said, and laughed. And when he laughed the others all laughed as well. Then the whole crowd of them went downstairs together, and Louie paid the bill to the surprised girl in the office. Then they went outside, and there was another car out there at the kerb, besides Louie's, a big new Buick.

Louie turned to Jim while the others were climbing into the first car. 'Well, so long, Jim boy,' he said. 'And don't you forget to look me up any time you want to. You're all right, see? And I can use you. And you were right about working, too, kid. Only mugs work. Remember that, will you? Only mugs work. Well, so long. And don't forget.'

'So long,' Jim said.

The two cars accelerated away into the darkness, and Jim stood quite still, watching the tail-lights until they had gone from sight. Then he shrugged his shoulders, and his fingers clenched round the money in his pocket, and he grinned slightly, comparing the amount won in thirty seconds with his wages every week. He thought about Louie, with his dark, confident face, and quick eyes, and he laughed. 'Only mugs work,' he said. 'Caw! He's right.'

He turned away and wandered slowly down the street. There was hardly anyone about, and the streets were shining wet, reflecting the neon signs outside the cinema, distorted and trembling lights across the puddles as he walked along towards them.

And Jim stopped at the cinema and looked at the stills inside their glass case on the front walls. They had pretty girls in those film towns, in Hollywood and that. Look at that one. She was a hot-looking girl all right. Take a lot of money to get a girl like that, wouldn't it? But that's what he'd do if he had a lot of money. He would get girls like that one. And he stood there thinking about it, turning vicious thoughts over and over in his mind. That chap Louie. Bet he had some girls. There were some pretty hot-looking girls in London, he'd seen them when he'd been up for the cup final. All hanging about Regent Street at the corner there looking at you, and their eyes bright, brighter than anybody else's eyes. And they stared at you, half-smiling, and muttering things you could never quite hear, and it made you feel queer and hollow in the pit of your stomach, even though you were half-scared of them. But they were the cheap ones, compared with this girl in the photo. The others would be better, easier, if you had the money.

Jim clenched his fists and turned away from the cinema. One day he would know. So he walked slowly along the pavement, whistling through his teeth, feeling depressed and bored. But as he turned into Lark Street he quickened his pace and felt better, realising that he would have an audience for his story, knowing that Ernie would be jealous of him, jealous of the money he had won.

He went inside the house and listened for a moment, and then he smiled. Ernie was home, then, he could hear the voices talking in the back room. He and the old man would be doing the football, probably, silly asses, fiddling about with their Homes and Aways the same as they had done for years, and without ever winning anything.

Jim opened the door of the back room and swaggered in. But neither Ernie or old Bankley looked up, even after he had closed the door behind him. They were leaning over the table, poring anxiously over newspapers, 'competitors' hints', and Pool lists, their foreheads creased with concentration and indecision. Ernie was sucking a pencil.

'No, not Bury, dad,' Ernie said. 'They won't do it, not away. Listen what the paper says . . .'

Old Bankley snorted. 'Paper me eye! I wanted to do Bury last week, and the Arsenal too, but your bloody paper said no, and I didn't do it – and they both went and won!' He looked up at Jim. 'Hullo, boy,' he said. 'You just got in?'

Jim scowled. 'Yes.'

'Lose all your money?'

'No, I won a bit,' Jim said, and he could hardly keep the triumph out of his voice.

Ernie laughed. 'My, my!' he jeered. 'Aren't we clever! So we won a bit, eh? How much?' He still kept his eyes on the papers in front of him.

Jim took a deep breath. 'Four quid,' he said.

The two Pool students looked at one another, and then turned round on Jim.

'Four – quid?' Ernie said slowly.

Jim flopped into a chair. 'Yes, four quid. There was a big gamble on a London dog there, and I got in on it. There was a fight up there after the race, too. Razors and everything. Gor, you should've seen it. I got my money all right, and I cleared off bloody quick when they started getting excited, and before the police got into it. But there were fellers all over the ground, bashing one another, and one of the bookies got his money pinched when they upset his stand. I never seen such a fight, it was bloody terrible.'

Ernie sniffed. 'A fine place that track is,' he said. 'Still, I expect you enjoyed yourself. You seem to try and get into any bit of trouble that's going, if you ask me.'

'Well, I'm not asking you. I'm not asking you anything. I'm just telling you,' Jim said sourly.

Ernie shrugged his shoulders and turned to the table again. Jim was just impossible, he was no more than a hooligan. Fighting, and hanging around with that dog-track crowd, he hadn't any self-respect at all. And he would like to know just what he had said to Betty, too, because she had been funny all the evening, not paying attention and all that. Ernie scowled at his coupon, trying to get his mind back to the peregrinations of League Football.

Old Bankley puffed at his pipe. 'Well, you got away with your money, did you?' he said to Jim.

Jim nodded. 'Yes, I got it here.' He fished out the roll of notes. They were all ten-shilling notes, and he was glad. The money looked more that way.

Old Bankley narrowed his eyes. 'You've still got old Ma Snell's money, haven't you?' he said evenly.

Jim flushed and nodded his head. 'Yes,' he said.

'Well, let's have it back, then. I'll leave it on the table for her in the morning.'

Jim peeled off two ten-shilling notes from the roll, and as he did so he looked quickly at his father's face and away again.

The old man said nothing, but his mouth was half-smiling as he held out his hand. And Jim cursed him, knowing that he had seen everything, knowing that he realised just how much of a gamble it had really been. But old Bankley just put the money on the mantelpiece and smiled. Silly young idiot, taking risks like that, he had better watch out for himself, or one day he would be sorry.

Jim got up and went to the doorway. Somehow his news had fallen flat, nobody seemed either interested or pleased about it. Muttering 'good night,' he slammed the door viciously behind him, making Ernie jump.

'Blast him,' Ernie snarled. 'Why the hell does he have to do that? He knows I hate it.'

'You boys are like a couple of Kilkenny cats,' his father said. 'I've never seen anything like it, the way you're always fighting and quarrelling. Fair makes me sick.'

Ernie scowled. 'Well, can you wonder at it? Jim just goes out of his way to be a tough. He thinks it's clever.'

Old Bankley said nothing, shrugging his shoulders. He bent over the football papers again, puffing thoughtfully at his pipe, trying to concentrate. He envied Ernie his memory for records and form, his application to the job in hand, and sighed heavily.

Ernie pencilled in his selections, full of hope. Nothing could damp him – even years of failure. He was convinced he would win one day, convinced he could buck the system and win out. He didn't know the odds against it, didn't realise he was trying for a chance in forty-seven million, and even if he had known it he would have gone on just the same. He never for a moment would admit the futility of it, not even to himself. He was willing to go on trying for ever, for he knew, yes, *knew*, that one day he would do it . . .

And upstairs, Jim leaned his forehead against the frame of the open window. Below him, the garden straggled down to the fence. Dim in the moonlight, and beyond the rows of roofs which stretched away in deadly parallels, raised high on an embankment, the lights of the railway winked back at him.

It was quiet, the town asleep, and there were few lights to

be seen in the houses, but up there, where a train panted stertorously out on its journey northwards, where a shunt engine groaned, and jinked the buffers of the freight trucks, the sound running quicker and quicker down the line until it was lost, up there was the way out. Up there you could get a train and go to London, you could get away from all this. From dad, with his talk about work. From Ernie, with his whiney, gentlemanly manners. From . . . everything . . .

Jim sighed and scratched his bottom as he turned away . . . 'Something seems to have happened to me, tonight,' he muttered. 'Oh, blast everything! And I bet thinking about all this will keep me awake.'

He climbed into the creaking bed and lay down. The murmur of voices from downstairs filtered up to him, indistinct and distorted, like listening to an unknown language. And within three minutes he was asleep.

* * * * *

All the next day Jim was sulking, keeping to himself, snarling and rude if anyone crossed him. And the whole time he was thinking about London, growing more dissatisfied with his job. He began noticing the older men at the works. Mr Phipps, his foreman; ten years ago he had been foreman, and ten years from now he would be foreman still. He had worked for that, maybe for years, struggling, keeping his eyes open, waiting. And then he had won it, won what he wanted, and stayed. It was the irresistible force creating the immovable object.

Other men, too; men in the machine shops, grown grey at their work; men in the drawing office; men in his own department – they were all the same, complacent, asking no more than they were getting, or, if they did ask, asking merely as a kind of principle, scared of 'getting above themselves', expecting nothing.

Jim turned it over and over in his mind. He was not going to be like that. He wasn't, and that was sure. He wasn't going to kick his heels here half his life. It was no good waiting for opportunities, you had to get them for yourself – the way Louie Franks did.

He slouched into the running sheds, thinking about it, scarcely looking where he was going, until an electric horn peeped close behind him, making him jump round, sweating.

The radiator of a car was close to his back, and, inside the car Tom Richards grinned at him, grinned like a fool.

'Hey!' Tom shouted. 'You wanting to get killed?'

Jim turned on him fiercely, red-faced and angry. 'Silly bastard! Playing games like that! You're not safe in a bloody car. You ought to . . .'

But he touched the other on a raw place, for driving ability was almost a religion with Tom. He was the oldest of them, and the only one with a completely clean record.

'What the hell's driving got to do with it?' he said. 'It's you walking about like a ghost, not me!'

Jim scowled, and seized on the weakness instinctively. 'Nuts!' he said. 'There was plenty of room each side of me. You don't watch where you're going half the time. You drive like an old woman!'

'Oh do I? Is that so?' Tom got out of the car and faced up to Jim, scowling.

'Yes. Everyone knows you do.'

'What! Why, you clod, I could drive you . . .'

'You could drive me crazy! You can potter about on test, and I'm not saying you can't. But what the hell do you know about driving? You know about as much as a school kid!'

Tom began to get really angry, losing all the caution he usually remembered to use with Jim.

'You silly sod,' he shouted. 'I could . . .'

'Well, what? What could you do?' Jim jeered at him, and

laughed suddenly as an idea came into his head. 'Look here, then, Malcolm Campbell, why don't you prove it? I'm going out in ten minutes. I'll take you on round the Wakefold circuit, and show you the way to do it. What about that, eh?'

Tom steadied down. 'In a works' car? You're mad. You can't smash up a works' car just to settle an argument!'

'Smash up?' Jim said. 'I don't smash up a car if I drive it fast – if you do!'

Tom swallowed hard, pride conflicting against the fear of losing his job. He glared at Jim, glanced round and saw some of the others watching him, waiting for him to back out, and he decided quickly.

'Right,' he said evenly. 'You get your car out and meet me at the corner by the White Hart. Talk to me about driving! I'll show you a thing or two about that! Driving!'

Jim went away, glad for something to have taken hold of his mind, glad to have a vent for his depression. Tom Richards, eh? He'd show old Tom how it went.

And half an hour later he drove up to the meeting place and met Tom there already. They both had the same kind of car, Model R of the Chantrey range, light-six saloons, sparkling and new.

'All right,' Jim called out. 'I'm ready when you are. We'll go from here across to Fukely, round the common and back, right? One of the others is keeping an eye on old Phipps in case he wonders what the hell we're doing, but we'll have to be bloody quick about it.'

Tom nodded. He was still angry, and knew the whole idea was crazy, crazy and dangerous, and he knew he would have to go through with it now, and he was afraid. He looked at Jim and saw the hard obstinacy in the boy's face, and he set his chin. There couldn't be any backing out now.

The road was quite clear, and they drew abreast of each other, running slowly at eight miles an hour.

'Go!' roared Jim suddenly, and jumped on the throttle.

Immediately he shot in front, jumping the start, but Tom could change gear like sliding a knife through soft butter, and after a hundred yards Jim was two lengths behind him. For a mile they shot down the road in line, not going too fast, both of them instinctively saving their engines, neither of them sufficiently warmed up to it yet to get reckless.

Nose to tail they flew into Fukely, rocking round the squalid circle of the village green, Tom swerving wildly to avoid a dog, Jim passing him on the inside. A rush and a hum of exhaust, and they were gone, leaving astonishment and anger behind them.

As they shot out of sight along the road, a man in the Post Office telephoned to the works, speaking indignantly . . .

Jim glanced in his driving mirror. Tom was ten yards behind him, and he laughed. A hundred yards ahead was the signpost where they turned left, and he steadied the car to take the curve.

Behind, Tom snicked the gears through third into second, swinging over to the right, and, on the apex of the curve, cut in on the near side. He judged it to perfection, holding the slide, balancing the machine's weight with its impetus, forgetting nothing except the most important thing of all – the sort of temper Jim was in. For Jim saw what would happen, and pulled in, scraping against the other car, tearing paint off the wings, angry at being tricked, thinking about nothing except holding on to his lead.

For an instant as the cars scraped together both he and Tom went cold, seeing the damage. Then losing their heads, they gave the cars all they could take. Side by side they flew down the road, indifferent to everything else, blind to all thoughts, except one. Ahead of them, a mile away, was their finishing point, and Tom was slightly ahead still. He was grinning mirthlessly, his heart beating fast, watching in the mirror every few seconds to see if Jim was any closer. The cars were identical, and now he was in front Tom knew he would win. Both engines were at their maximum, and he knew Jim could not pull out any more to gain what had been lost. But all at once the oil-pressure gauge flickered on the facia board, flickered, wavered uncertainly, and fell; and Tom sweated. His instinct was to shut off, and for a half-second he hesitated, the engineer against the individual. But as he hesitated Jim drew nearly level, and Tom clenched his teeth, keeping his foot down, sitting hunched up behind the wheel praying for the engine to hold out.

For fifty yards they went almost side-by-side. Then there was a cough from the engine of Tom's car, the violent clattering of run bearings, and a spurt of oil dropped a trail in the road. Triumphantly, Jim raced ahead, laughing, jeering as Tom fell farther and farther behind.

And then, as he drew nearer the finishing point, reaction set in. At the corner by the White Hart he braked the car to a stop. There were two other cars there waiting for him, works' cars, and in one of them was someone he recognised, and the sweat rolled down his face as he stared across the road. Phipps! Caw! someone must have told him . . . Phipps . . . hell, now there'd be a row . . .

* * * * *

Together with Tom he came out of the office building.

'Pedalled, eh?' Jim said. 'Fancy the swines not even listening to the excuse.'

Tom's face was white, his eyes worried. He was trying not to wonder what his young wife would have to say about him losing his job. Only two months to go for her, too. God, what a mess. He turned on Jim with all the futile anger of the weak man roused. 'It was your bloody fault,' he said bitterly. 'It's you that ought to get the pedal, not me. You don't even care about it, but I do. How the hell do you think I'm going to find work in this place again, eh? How the hell do you think

I'm going to get a living, you swine? It's your fault, Jim Bankley, and what are you going to do about it?'

Jim laughed uncomfortably. 'Oh, shut your gob,' he muttered. 'It's the same for me as for you. It was just bloody bad luck getting caught out, that's all there is to it. What the hell do you think I can do, eh? Bust out crying and take you home to your missus?'

Tom went red with anger, his mouth working, his eyes narrowed. 'You're a proper berk, Bankley,' he said. 'And one day someone's going to kick the guts out of you. You think you can go on messing up other people like you do now – but you can't, and one day you're going to get what's coming to you. You're just a . . .'

'Ah, shut up, will you?' Jim snarled. 'Go home and work that off on your wife. Leave me alone, or I'll poke you one, see? Go on, leave me alone, will you?' And he stuck his hands in his pockets and walked off across the yard.

Behind him, the huge plant hummed and roared, pulsating with energy and life. An insignificant component had been thrown out and the machine of Production went on undisturbed. Unheeded and forgotten already, Jim went through the gates and into the road. Behind him, iron jaws chewed up raw material, the forest of belts vibrated, the lathes whined, the assembly line rolled forward steadily, moving, moving, always moving . . .

Jim looked back at it all, and spat viciously. 'Bloody good riddance,' he said, and walked on.

* * * * *

He walked home slowly, his mind turning and turning on the same point. Variations on a theme.

He ought to go back and try and get Tom's job back for him. He ought to go after Tom and say he was sorry about it all. He ought to go to Tom's missus and see her; give her some money. They were going to have a kid, weren't they? Caw! life was a proper bastard, wasn't it?

Even as he thought all this he knew he would never do it. He was a tough guy, wasn't he? Like those blokes from London. Caw! if they knew he thought this way they would laugh at him. You've got to be tough if you want to get on. It wasn't any sort of sense being soft, was it?

He swore bitterly, trying to convince himself he was right, trying not to feel ashamed. Well, it was too late now, anyway. He'd have to do the best he could. He'd have to study Number One. Tom and the rest of them could go to hell. He was the Tough Jim Bankley, and he was going to make a pile of money, and he was going to . . . oh hell! hell! hell! Life was a bastard – and he was a bastard as well.

* * * * *

Well, all right. You don't like Jim Bankley? You don't like the effect. But look for the cause. He is born into a family which cannot really afford him, for a start. His mother is far too busy washing, cleaning, polishing, shopping, or cooking – if she is respectable; talking, gossiping and slopping around, if she isn't. She has her time taken up too much, anyway, to pay much attention to the boy in his formative years. He sits with forty-nine other little boys in the infants' class at the Council School, under a harassed teacher. After the teacher has inspected the ears, hands, and faces of some of the grubbier urchins, listened to the lies of yesterday's absentees, and taken today's roll call, she has little time or patience left for imparting knowledge or character-building information. There were few playing fields when Jim was a boy, except the streets and a stony yard. He released his surplus energy screaming and fighting, playing raggety games with a string-bound paper ball. His reading consists of 'bloods' – lurid tales of murder and muscular violence, carnage and priggishness, all in some mysterious way trying to prove the superiority of action and callousness. A sprinkling of the salt of the Public School principles comes from the *Magnet* or the *Gem*, from the immortal Bunter, the poor-boy's Falstaff, and the young white sahibs of Greyfriars College.

As he gets older, the boy finds school more and more dull. He envies his friends who have left to take jobs in factory, shop, or warehouse – they are wage-earners, they are free, even if only free to loaf about the streets towards the slack times. All the time is this longing for escape, through the pools, through the tote.

If Jim Bankley is tough, unsympathetic, and callous, well, it's just a damned shame. The sooner the national conscience worries about teaching, and gets around to giving all children an equal chance to learn something and do some good with it; to organise a present exciting enough to switch the desire to escape from it into some crazy dream world of easy prosperity, the sooner the Jim Bankleys are going to disappear.

You still don't like him? Then watch.

* * * * *

He had finished his tea when his father got home, and was sitting reading the paper in an armchair.

Old Bankley stared. 'Hullo,' he said. 'You're early, boy.'

Jim didn't look up. 'Got the pedal,' he said.

Old Bankley stared for a second or two. Then he sat down heavily. 'You've been sacked?' he said slowly.

'Yes.'

'But – what for?'

'Oh, your bloody old friend Phipps will tell you, I expect. I'm not sorry, anyway, I'm glad, see? Yes, I'm glad.'

Old Bankley shrugged his shoulders and began pouring out the tea for himself. 'Yes, but that's all very fine, Jim. But what are you going to do? Where are you going to find work?'

Jim put down the paper. 'In London,' he said.

'London? Who do you know in London?'

'I know someone who said he would give me a job, and a better job than driving those tin cans of Chantrey's about.'

He got up and went out of the room. He didn't want to have an argument about it. His father was obstinate and cautious. He would talk about it all the evening if necessary, go on and go on until someone was rude to him and made him angry. To hell with families, they never would leave you alone. They had to put their oar in all the time, to offer their opinions when they weren't bloody well wanted.

He changed his clothes quietly, washed and went softly downstairs. In the back room he could hear his father and Ernie talking away like old women. Bet old Ernie's getting a kick out of it, silly ass. Jim smiled savagely, seeing Ernie's prim face, imagining the speech he would have ready for delivery. Yes, Ernie gets a kick out of it, and I get the boot, Jim thought and laughed. That wasn't bad, that was pretty funny, really. He gets the kick, and I get the boot. Ha, ha, not bad, not bad.

He went up into the town and had a look to see what film was showing at the cinemas. *Mr Deeds Goes To Town*, eh? That was sort of funny, when he was going to Town himself. Yes, that was funny all right.

He paid his shilling and went blinking into the smoky darkness. It was a bloody silly film though, after all. This young chap who inherits twenty millions, he does all the damn silliest things with it, and even gives it away in the end. All that stuff about money making you unhappy. The people who wrote plays, and who made films about that, had never had to be without money probably. God almighty, if he had twenty millions in any sort of money he would show them a thing or two. This chap in the film could have had any girl in the world, or all the girls in the world, with the amount of money he had. And the fool didn't have any, except that he was going to marry the blonde at the end. And who the hell wants to get married if he has twenty million in money? God, it was just silly, that's all, just silly.

When he got home it was late, and he went straight up to his room. Ernie called out something or other as Jim shut the door, but he didn't shout loud enough, and Jim just blew a razzberry at him and went into his room and shut the door.

He stood looking out of the window for a moment or two, listening to the trains on the embankment, and suddenly an idea came into his head. He stood quite still for a long time, turning it over and over in his mind. Then he sat on the bed and counted up his money. With the money he had been paid off with and the money he had won last night, he ought to be able to get along for quite a time, if he met Louie Franks, even if he didn't get a job right away.

He went over to the door, opened it and listened. By the noise of snoring, both the old man and Ernie were asleep.

Jim hesitated, pulling thoughtfully at his lower lip. From the distance a train whistle shrieked out twice.

Bending down, he pulled a battered suitcase from under the bed . . .

* * * * *

Clatter, and the banging of doors, voices which echo hollowly under the dirty-girdered roof. A shrill whistle which screeches out hideously, going through the head like a needle stab, boring into the eardrums to murder thought. Slow panorama moving past the windows. Green-painted slot machines, a row of dusty railings, the iron-shod stairs sinking below the platform, diving out of sight. A newsboy, tired and white-faced, mouth opening and shutting like a fish, soundless, his puny shout drowned in the roar of muscular steam-power, sliding oil-smooth pistons. Two porters, aimless and bored, jauntily-hatted weeds, personalities drowned in uniforms, leaning on trolleys to stare disinterestedly. Refreshment bar. Grim oasis for jaded travellers, badly-lighted, dusty windows, dull and cheerless, shrine of too-strong tea and the dusty bun.

Goodbye, barmaids, bored and leaning slackly on the counter top, weary to death of standing, of listening, of trains, of steam, of frocks that are going under the armpits, of cheap stockings, of travellers with dirty jokes, of bad wages and poor food.

Goodbye, booking clerks, pale and ill-looking, shiny buttocks perched on stools, huddled in dense fog with tickets for companions, tickets and boredom. Goodbye Iron Jelloids, goodbye Oxo, goodbye Maples, Guinness, Bovril . . .

Rhythm of wheels, slowly growing tempo; going away, going away . . . wheels nicking over the metals, wheels hammering it into your head . . . going away . . . going away . . .

Passing the sidings, grime-streaked coal trucks. Two fantastic gnomes, flare-lit, working on the coal banks, turning to stare, teeth and eyeballs white in black faces. Glitter of rails, twining, writhing like snakes past the eyes. The local train, bright-lit and empty, with its dumpy, out-of-date engine panting and pushing it from behind. Platforms slide away and slip from sight, lights from the town twinkle up through the smoke and haze, and there, in the valley, a few furnaces flaring. A glittering cascade avalanches down a grey mountain of man's creation, vomit from Industry, excretion from Production . . . Goodbye to the dark houses and boredom, the steamy pubs, rank with human smells, *homo sapiens* at close quarters. Big pubs and little pubs, bitter contradictions to electrically-lighted promises of cheer. Sliding away into the darkness, to be swallowed, swallowed by space, darkness, and memory . . .

Ninety-two wheels thundering over the metals, pistons sliding, cranks whipping over too fast for the eye to see. Rocking round curves, flanges whining, long plume of smoke from squat funnel, ripped and torn away by the wind. Glare from the furnace like an orange flag fluttering in the darkness. Irritated shriek from the whistle. Lighted windows flashing through surprised wayside stations. Hundreds of people, hundreds of tons of metal and woodwork, racing through the night at sixty miles an hour, eating up space, eating up time, splitting the darkness . . .

* * * * *

Jim pressed his forehead against the window, watching the last lights of the town fade from sight, and he sighed heavily as if a load had been lifted from his mind. Well, there they went, and that was that, and a damn good riddance.

He turned and stared round the compartment. There were four men there besides himself, and three of them at the other end were having some sort of an argument. They were all of a type, middle-aged and heavily-built, red-faced, dressed in blue suits, unbuttoned gaberdene raincoats, silver watch-chains stretched across stomachs. They looked superficially so much the same they might have been more than just brothers under the skin. And they talked and laughed in the same whisky-oiled voices. Jim had seen plenty of their kind, and thought them awful. Just talkers, that was all they were. Other men did the work, and these fellows went around talking and trying to sell it. Just hot-air machines on legs, though maybe it wasn't so much fun for them all the time, even if they did get so hearty.

The fourth man was a little dried-up person in black, bald and pale-faced. He was asleep in the corner, huddled up, his mouth open loosely as he snored wheezily. Jim stared at him carefully, trying to place him. Schoolmaster, probably, or something like that. Looked a miserable little bastard, anyway.

The talk of the three travellers, which had paused when Jim had got in and settled himself, started up again. And one of them, a tightly-fleshed man with thick sandy hair and fat hands, was holding forth, modulating his voice, exaggerating his intonation in an irritating way all the time, as if he were imitating someone. And Jim listened to him idly, staring at the floor as though thinking of something else.

'Well, I've been there,' the sandy-haired man said. 'And I thought they were getting on fine. All those young fellers and girls stepping out on their parades, and all the smartness and keenness. It was a damn good show, old man.'

One of the men opposite him was tapping his hand impatiently on his knee, waiting for an opportunity to interrupt. Suddenly he broke across the sandy-haired man's talk.

'Oh nuts, old man,' he said. 'The thing just can't work much longer. There may be plenty of outward signs that everything's going on all right. But it can't last.'

'But look, old boy, there's morale, and – and discipline and purpose there. And when the people . . .'

'Morale? Purpose? Maybe there is, old man. But that don't do so much good as a square meal every day. People get sick of purpose, and get to wishing their stomachs were a bit more full of grub, after a time.'

The third man, who was fat and half-bald, gave a loud, whisky laugh. 'Ha, ha,' he guffawed. 'Sausage mit sauerkraut mit plenty beer, eh? Good old German sausage, what, old boy?'

The other two took no notice of him at all, but he went on chuckling to himself until he met Jim's eye. Then he stopped. Jim was staring at him, looking him over coldly. Fat old fool, thought he was bloody funny, didn't he?

The sandy-haired man went on talking in his exaggerated voice. 'But, look here, old boy, the shortage is only a temporary thing, you know. Why, in the *Daily Mail*, I saw that . . .'

'Temporary?' the second man said. 'And what about the other things, are they temporary as well? Don't you think the people are sick already of being spied on and frightened by having to salute every young plug-ugly in uniform that looks 'em over, and sick of being afraid to say what they think? No, old boy, they're only foreigners, but I hate to see 'em like that, all the same. I hate to see anyone with the pants scared off him all the time.'

'Well, anyway,' the first man said. 'It's a dashed sight better than the Bolshies' way of doing things, old boy.'

The half-bald man looked solemn and leaned forward. 'Yes, we don't want the Bolshies, or the blasted Yids. Good thing your pal Hitler's giving them both what for, in my opinion.'

'Well, I don't know about that,' the second man said. 'Seems to me he's gone a bit too far with the Jewish persecution.'

'Well, has he?' the sandy-haired man said. 'The damned Jews went about just asking for it, and still do. They'll be the ruin of the whole world, one day, just as they nearly ruined Germany – unless someone stops them in some way before they can manage it. Now, old Mosley. I don't like him much, but he's got the right idea about the Yids.'

'Ah, Mosley,' the half-bald man muttered. 'Clever man, that.'

'Well, maybe,' the second man said slowly. 'But I'm not so sure about it. And I don't think he's right in this case, because I don't believe he's sincere about it. A few years ago, you know, old man, he said he hadn't any quarrel with the Jews, and was as polite as you please with them.'

'The Yids are a damned nuisance anyway, and I hate them,' the half-bald man said. 'Why, only yesterday I got tricked out of an order by a little Yid in Birmingham. Absolute dirty trick, it was, too. You ought to . . .'

The sandy-haired man guffawed. 'Well, old boy, we're in the same cart there, all of us. If it isn't the Jews that get in ahead of you it's the foreigners. At least, it is in my line. I can hardly turn my back before some slimy little foreigner cuts in on my customers.'

The little man opposite Jim was awake now, and he sat up straight suddenly, so that Jim looked quickly at him. He looked ill, this little man, his eyes were red-rimmed and tired. And the sandy-haired traveller looked across at him, smiling apologetically. 'Sorry, old man,' he said. 'Did we wake you up?'

The little man in the corner sat forward on the edge of the seat. 'Yes, you did wake me up. I was listening to what you were saying, and, if you'll excuse me saying so, I think you've all got hold of a lot of wrong ideas.'

The half-bald man guffawed. 'Well, well?' he said. 'Then perhaps you'd better go back to bye-byes and try to forget about 'em?'

The little man just looked at him. 'Yes, just listening to you made me think quite a lot,' he said.

The sandy-haired man leaned forward, grinning. 'Well, what did it make you think?' he asked.

The little man looked at them, each in turn.

'All right,' he said. 'I'll tell you. It made me wonder what was the matter with you all, not only with you personally, but with everybody. All this talk, all over the world, all this continual talk. Talk about Germans and Russians and French and Jews and Gentiles. There's plenty of room for everybody, isn't there? All people want is food, comfort, warmth, and to get a little pleasure out of life. That's not so much to ask for, is it? What's the matter with all these professional heroes that they think it's necessary to dress up men, and even little children, in uniforms, and give them tanks, guns, and bayonets to play with? All their talk, all their highfalutin' nonsense – God! it makes me sick. Why, the things they are trained to fight for, the things they are told to sacrifice themselves for, don't exist. They just don't exist, I tell you. There isn't any 'National Honour' – only 'honour'. There isn't any 'Race' – only the human race as a whole. Why can't people just stop and think about that; think about each other a bit more?'

The man stopped suddenly, breathing hard. His face was white, and there was sweat on his upper lip. For a long moment no one spoke or made a sound. Then Jim laughed shakily.

'Hurray!' he said. 'What are you? Bolshie, or just religious, eh? I thought that was what we were in for when you started. Give it a rest, mister. You're talking a lot of tripe.'

The little man looked across at him. 'I'm sorry for you, boy,' he said. 'I really am. I'm sorry for you.'

Jim looked uncomfortable. 'You needn't be,' he said. 'I know what I want.'

The little man spread out his hands and shrugged his shoulders. He looked at the three commercials. 'You see?' he said. None of them said anything, so the little man got up and said: 'Excuse me.' Then he went out into the corridor and away. His face was very red.

The sandy-haired man leaned out of the doorway and watched him go. 'Chap knew he'd made a fool of himself,' he muttered. 'No wonder he pushed off. Silly ass.'

The half-bald man nodded and looked wise. 'Yerce, extraordinary chap,' he said. 'Bit of a crank, really. What? Eh? Don't you think so, old man?'

'H'm. What d'you think about it, young feller?' the sandy man said to Jim. Jim shrugged his shoulders. 'Barmy old coot. Didn't listen to him much,' he said.

The sandy man laughed. 'Where you from, young feller?' he asked.

'Been working at Chantrey's,' Jim said. Caw! this chap was a proper dumb-looking bastard, and nosey, too.

'At Chantrey's, eh? I've got a Chantrey.'

'Yeah?'

'Yes. Good cars, Chantreys, aren't they?'

'All right, I suppose.'

'Like to have a game of cards? What about you fellers, eh? What about a little flutter?' the fat man said. The half-bald man and the other one rubbed their hands. 'Don't mind if I do,' one of them said.

'Take a hand, boy?'

Jim shook his head. He felt superior to these fools. 'Don't play cards,' he said. 'Dog racing's my vice.'

'Dogs? Ah, don't you believe it. Don't you touch it, young feller,' the half-bald man said. 'Lose all your dough on the dogs, in time. I know, because I've had some.'

Jim went red. Who was this silly old bastard to talk about dog racing? Probably went along on sixpenny tips bought at the local newsagent's shop – punting in bob doubles, or something. Silly fool! 'Yeah?' he said.

'Yerce. It's a mug's game.'

'Any game's a mug's game if you play it like a mug,' Jim said.

The man sat up straight. He looked very angry and red, and Jim felt a little uneasy. 'That's no way to talk,' the man said. 'You keep a civil tongue in your head, young feller – unless you're looking for trouble.'

Jim swallowed hard. 'Because why?' he said.

'Because if you are I'll send for the guard,' the man said. 'I'm not going to stand any nonsense, I can tell you. Now then!'

Jim just looked at him. Fat old fool. Thought he could tell you off, didn't he? Thought he was bloody clever. Well . . . what was the proper line to take with a chap like this, anyway? 'I'm not looking for trouble,' he said sulkily.

The three commercials sighed heavily. Funny sort of chap this young feller. There were too many like him about nowadays.

Jim got up and went out into the corridor. He felt very foolish. He staggered down the swaying corridor to the lavatory at the end. When he was inside he slammed the door violently behind him, and swore. Uneasily, he sat on the seat, his elbows on his knees. The lurching of the train jogged him about as it went round a curve, but he hardly noticed it, and sat there thinking, and picking his nose.

Talk, talk, talk. Everybody seemed to talk too much. Everybody seemed to have some pet thing they had to say. Why the hell couldn't people quit it all and keep quiet? Why couldn't they just get on with what they wanted to do? All this talk! It didn't get you anywhere, so what was the matter with people that they had to go on gabbing and gabbing the way they did . . .

After a few minutes he went back to his compartment. The three commercials were playing solo when he got there, and didn't say anything to him as he came in. They just glanced up for a moment and went on playing. So Jim sat down in his corner and pulled his coat collar up to his ears. He settled himself down in the seat, folding his arms across his chest. The rhythm of the train, the rhythm of the wheels, sang into his brain, sang and sang until it seemed just a part of him, like the beating of his heart . . . Stations roared past the windows, dim lit . . . bridges changed the tone; points the rhythm. But, however checked, the steady nicking of the wheels over the metals regained the swing of it . . . going away . . . going away . . . going away . . . going away . . . rumbling on into the darkness . . . the darkness . . .

Night cloaks the landscape as the train rumbles past . . . Long black scars in the hillsides, slag heaps dandruffed with weeds and thin grass . . . long lines of quiet chimneys, smokeless, standing stiffly naked against the sky, in huddles over empty workshops . . . Wheel and pulley silent and rusted. Long deserts of useless, leashed-in power . . . forgotten, waiting hopelessly. Quiet. Quiet everywhere in these hills, in the dark-straggling towns, in the rotting yards down at the rivers . . . a generation of men unwanted . . . The darkness cloaks it decently, hides mysteriously the nation's shame . . .

Wheels rumble nearer, the engine shrieks, and those listening in the silent towns hear it pass them by . . . hear it as they hear life, promises, hope . . . hear it pass by.

Slowly the sounds die away in the distance, and everything is quiet again . . .

* * * * *

He woke with a jerk, the whining shouts of porters in his ears, the bustle and thump of bags being heaved down from the racks all about him. And he rubbed his eyes, irritated at himself for sleeping, and looked out of the window.

The train was sliding in along the platform. High overhead, the steel and glass roof was misty and vague. The white, blurred faces of the porters flickered past the windows slower and slower, and, with a slight jerk the train stopped. A man in the corridor peered out at the big clock hanging overhead. 'God! what a time to arrive,' he said.

Jim stood up and buttoned his coat and pulled his suitcase down from the rack, taking no notice of the others in the carriage. Then he opened the door and got out.

London. This grey platform, spit-flecked and dirty, this was London. These pale men, these porters, had their home here. London and Londoners. The biggest city in the world. That sounded fine, didn't it? The biggest city in the world . . .

The station was so big and dark it didn't have the same crowded hysterical air he always remembered. But coming up for the cup final was different. This was right and usual, and anyway people were mostly asleep at this time. Hell, what an hour to arrive, what a damned awful hour to arrive . . .

He walked the length of the train, his case swinging in his hand. The train looked different now, like something dead now all the movement was over. All its power was gone, all its sleek wild passage through the night finished and forgotten, its oneness, its individuality, all gone, and it was a dead thing, lying inert in a glorified greenhouse . . .

Jim stared ahead of him. The train had given him a headache, and his legs were stiff and cramped from the position in which he had been sleeping. Beyond the barriers at the end of the platform he could see a few people waiting about, looking tired and bored. And over at the suburban side there was a sulky-looking girl and a scared-looking young man arguing bitterly about having lost the last train home . . .

He went through the barriers, handing over his ticket to an insolent-faced old collector with a big moustache and flat feet, and crossed the booking hall to get to the street. There was a slight drizzle falling, and the street was dark and he felt lost until he got to the end where the traffic was. It was brighter there, and the streetlamps reflected dizzily against the shining roadway. The tramlines, winding at the bottom of Pentonville Hill, gleamed like silver.

He stared about him, walking slowly, and pulled up the collar of his coat. He suddenly felt alone and rather shabby, and his head was getting worse. There was a small hole in the sole of one of his shoes, and the wet seeped through, clamming his sock, making his foot squelch as he walked. But he went on, wondering dully what the hell he could do. All the glamour of the thing seemed to have worn off now.

Down a side street an electric sign hung over an all-night café. The place was small and probably cheap, and Jim turned down towards it, quickening his pace. Suddenly he realised he was hungry and cold.

Pushing open the door he went in and looked round. It was a small enough place, but bright. A counter piled with delicatessen was along one wall, a row of stools facing up to it, stools fixed to the floor. And in the back of the room were a few marble-topped tables. There was a grey-faced man in glasses behind the counter, and he looked up from the paper he was reading when Jim came in.

'Evening,' he said.

Jim nodded. 'Evening,' he said, rather too loudly.

He went over and sat down at one of the small tables in the back of the shop.

'Plenty of room at the counter,' the man called over to him.

Jim scowled and tucked his suitcase behind his chair. 'I'm all right here,' he said.

The man shrugged his shoulders. 'Well, what'll you eat?' he asked. 'Eggs and bacon, or sandwiches. We got all kinds of sandwiches, and . . .'

'I'll have eggs and bacon and a cup of tea,' Jim said. He sat there slackly while the man went and called down the chute for the food. The place was empty, and very quiet.

After a time the door opened, and a girl came in. She was a pasty blonde and sour-faced, her cheeks a faint purple under the powder with the cold. She was dressed in black, and her little hat was drooping a good deal with the wet. Her light stockings, above patent-leather shoes, were rain-spotted and muddy.

As she sat down at the counter, she glanced quickly sideways at Jim with shrewd, dark eyes, weighing him up. And Jim stared back at her, trying to get a smile out of her, pursing up his mouth knowingly, but she turned her head away.

'Eggs and bacon, tea. Here y'are, mister,' the counter-man said, and took the plate out of the chute.

Jim got up from his chair. 'I'll have it at the counter,' he said, and swaggered over and perched himself on the stool next to the girl.

While he was eating he kept looking sideways at her. She was smoking, and drinking black coffee, and seen close to, you could notice the tired sag to her skin, the dark roots of her hair. She was over thirty, and looked hard as nails, and smelled of wet cloth and cheap talcum.

'Doris been in tonight, Harry?' she said dully.

The counterman nodded. 'Yes, about half-hour back. Said to tell you "tomorrow", whatever that means.'

The girl nodded without saying anything, and sat slackly on the stool staring out at the rain-soaked street. After a time, she pressed out her cigarette into the saucer. Then she got up, wincing slightly as she stood upright on her feet. 'Well, good night, Harry,' she said, 'be seeing you. I'm going home.'

The man grinned ironically. 'Tired already?'

The girl turned and looked at him from the doorway. 'In this rain, and with the blister I got on me heel, I couldn't hook a drunk Welshman,' she said sourly. Then she went out.

'Nice girl,' Jim said.

The man looked at him. 'That's as maybe,' he said. 'And I saw you making up to her, young feller, too. And if I can offer you a bit of advice, it's this. I don't care what anybody does outside of this place, but no one's going to try anything on *inside*, see? The girls don't want any trouble while they're in here, and they respect my rules, and I don't want any trouble either.'

Jim flushed red and went on eating, but he didn't look up or say anything. He scooped the food into his mouth almost without tasting it, and when he had finished he got up.

'Got a phone here?' he said, and nodded as the man pointed to one in the corner on a shelf.

He went over to it, fishing out of his pocket the envelope Louie Franks had given him. It had been rumpled in his pocket, and the pencilled writing on it was smeared so that he had to peer closely at it. Then he made the call. Waiting for it, he got very hot and sweaty, and when he heard the receiver taken off the hook at the other end he could hardly speak. He swallowed hard and coughed, and jerked out at last: 'I want to speak to Mr Louie Franks. Mr Louie Franks. You . . .' But the voice at the other end was hoarse and angry. 'Who the bloody hell are you to ring up at this god-forsaken hour, damn your eyes? I don't care who you want, or what you want him for! You can bloody well wait till morning, see? Good *night!*'

Jim blinked, and hung up the receiver and went back to the counter. 'What's the time?' he asked thoughtfully.

'Just gone two,' the man there said.

Jim swore. 'Well, where the hell . . . I mean, where can you get a place to sleep at this time?' he said. 'I've just got here, and I'm tired as hell.'

The counterman looked thoughtful. 'Well, lessee. I don't know anywhere, unless you try the YMCA. They might let you in there, I should think . . .'

Jim thanked him, and paid the bill. Then he picked up his bag and went out. There was a cold wind blowing down the street, driving the rain in gusts. There was scarcely any traffic about, and less people, and Jim pulled down the brim of his hat and began walking.

It was very late when he found the YMCA, and he had walked the whole way and was wet through, and hated the whole world. But the clerk there was decent to him, and told him where to go, and in a short time he was bathed and in bed in a small room which looked out over some roofs. Just for a minute he lay still, turning plans over in his mind, then he sighed and curled up in the bed, and almost as if he were drugged, he fell asleep . . .

* * * * *

He woke early, and lay on his back in the bed for a long time, trying to make up his mind what to do. It wouldn't be much good trying to get hold of Louie Franks before evening, or before midday, anyway. And that left the whole morning to be filled in somehow, and that was a bit of a problem . . .

He climbed out of the narrow bed and scratched his head thoughtfully, yawning, and staring out of the window. 'Hell, this won't do,' he muttered. 'I better start moving.'

Time wasn't so hard to kill as he had thought, and at half-past eleven he was strolling along the streets, all set. He had checked in his bag at a tube-station cloakroom, had a shave and some breakfast, and felt fine. It was worth the whole trip just to be walking along Shaftesbury Avenue, looking at the people, looking in shop windows, realising that he was free to do what he liked and had money in his pocket to do it with. Thinking for a moment about Ernie, with his shiny-trousered backside perched on a stool, he laughed out loud. To hell with all that, it was a mug's game, and it was done with now; all over.

Just after midday he went round to the address Louie had given him. It was in a long, narrow street off the Marylebone Road, and took some time to find. The houses were severe and uniform, very strict behind low railings, but pleasant enough in the sunshine. Jim walked along slowly until he found the right number, and rang the bell.

After a minute, a drab little woman in a faded brown apron opened the door and peered out at him. She had bright eyes, like buttons in her sallow peaky face, and a wisp of hair that floated in front of her forehead. All the time she spoke she pushed this wisp away with the back of her hand, and all the time it flopped forward again, until Jim wanted either to cut it off, or scream.

'Mr Franks here?' Jim said.

The woman brushed away the hank of hair and looked interested. 'You're not the doctor, are you?' she said.

Jim grinned. 'No,' he said. 'I'm not the doctor, I'm a friend.'

'Oh, I thought you might be the doctor. Still, I s'pose you can come in, leastways Mr Franks never said as no one was to see him. And you're a friend of his, are you? Well, all I can say is I hope you're more of a friend than his other friends are. Been to see him only once, they have – a couple of young fellers, it was, and then they didn't stay long. Huh, I said to myself only this morning, it's nice friends Mr Franks has, and him up there all by hisself. Oh, plenty coming when he's well, and can give 'em drinks and all, but not now, oh dear, no. It seems to me it's nice friends what leave you alone when you want them, and no mistake.'

Jim stared. 'Wait a minute, Ma. Is he – is he, ill?'

'Ill? Yes, of course he's ill. Leastways, he's – er – not well, as you might say. I don't ask no questions, and I'm not answering none, owing to the way things are. And any gentleman living here can be sure that . . .'

'Wait a minute, will you?' Jim said. 'Don't talk so much. Look, I'd better see him, hadn't I? Where is he?'

The little woman brushed the hair from her face and looked annoyed. 'All right, come in,' she said, and, as Jim stepped into the hallway, she slammed the door hard behind him. 'Upstairs, Number 9, second floor,' she snapped out. 'And don't go making too much noise. Some of the people here don't like it – and I'm one of them!'

Jim went up the creaky stairs with their worn carpet. There were brass numbers on all the doors, and from behind one of them a man and a woman were arguing bitterly.

He paused a minute on the first landing, trying to hear what was going on, but it was too confused, and he went on up.

He stopped outside Number 9 and straightened his hair,

smoothing down his coat. Then he knocked on the door, heard someone call out, and went in. It was a small room, frantically untidy, and on a bed in one corner, lying amongst rumpled sheets and a plaid rug, was Louie Franks. The window shade was half-down, but even in that light Jim could see what was the matter. Louie had been beaten up. His face was almost black on one side, and swollen on the other. A badly split upper lip gave his mouth the appearance of a sinister leer.

'Hullo, Louie,' Jim said awkwardly, and went over to the bed and sat down. 'Thought I'd look you up. Remember me?'

Louie sat up in the bed and stared. 'Who the hell . . . ? How did you get here . . . ? Oh, *you*! Strewth! boy, I wondered who the hell it was. Jim, wasn't it? But, what are you doing here anyway?'

Jim grinned. 'Well, a lot of things happened, and I thought I'd come to London, like you said I ought to do – remember? And then I thought I'd come and look you up, because you told me that, too. And now, I'm going out to get you some fags and a paper, and anything you want. Then we'll talk. Right?'

Louie smiled painfully, holding his face. 'Say, that's fine of you, Jim. You might get some grub, too, while you're out, will you? God! my face hurts. Caw! I can hardly speak, boy.'

Jim went down and round the corner to a delicatessen, and bought sausage and bread, milk, butter, cigarettes, and newspapers. Then he went back again.

All the afternoon he stayed in the room, talking, and eating with Louie, and he told him everything, trying to make it all sound tough, and trying to make himself feel more confident. And all the time Louie watched him, following the broad-shouldered figure with his eyes, as Jim moved about the room, weighing up every possibility.

Then he began to talk. He told Jim about himself, about how he had got into a fight with some young bloods who were selling a Fascist paper and shouting a lot of stuff about Jews, in Rupert Street. There were two men with him, and three of the Fascist boys, and it had started as a joke and then got rough. 'Some bastard trod on my face,' Louie said bitterly. 'I wouldn't mind what else he'd done, I'd have taken it. But the bastard jumped on my face, and look at it, will you? I'll be stuck in here for a week, goddamn and blast his soul! Still we got away before the cops came up, and Sid, who was with me, gave one of them a hell of a fine split nose, and I blacked another one's eye.'

Jim laughed. 'But what was it about? I mean, what do these chaps do, or say, or what?'

'The Fascist boys? Oh, I dunno, a lot of stuff about Bolshies which makes it sound like the boys were raised on penny dreadfuls, and a lot of smut about us Jews. They talk about us as if we weren't English people at all. But I don't mind that, I never take no notice of them, and this time we only wanted to have a little bit of fun. But good Gawd, Jim, I wish I'd never opened me mouth, now. Just look at me, boy! I feel like hell, and look worse.'

Always he kept on talking about his face, almost crying with anger, but after a time he eased off, and in the evening the doctor came.

While he was there, Jim went and fetched his bag, and then, as Louie had suggested, went along to the agent's and took a room that was vacant in the same house, a small, cold room on the top floor. The previous tenant had left only the day before, but a few of his smells were left behind him. It was that sort of room. A small gas fire with a cooking ring over it, a single divan bed, a closet which smelled of mothball and mould, dull blue distempered walls and a small mirror over the mantelpiece, and a dim landscape picture in oils of the sort that people's aunts painted rather a lot during the last half of the nineteenth century – a nightmare in dirty greens with a tarnished frame. The room was small, and

74

looked lonely with all the loneliness of everybody that had ever been bored there. But to Jim it meant independence and security, just to be able to lock the door on himself was good enough, just to have a place where he could do as he liked, it seemed fine. And anyway, he felt better now he had seen Louie and had some definite place to go to, even if only to sleep. Louie being laid up in bed rather upset things, in a way, but Jim hardly knew what he had expected to happen even if things had been normal, and now there seemed to be only one thing to do. So he told Louie how much money he had to last him out, and asked what he had better do about it. And Louie looked wise and got out of bed and muffled himself up and went downstairs to the telephone. He spoke there for a long time, and when he came up again he went straight over to the bed. 'Well, I've fixed you up as best I can,' he said. 'I spoke to Bill – that's my cousin – and he knows a feller that's got a second-hand car place over in Willesden. Bill thought he remembered you, and I said I'd guarantee you, anyway, so he's going to tell this feller to give you a run for a few weeks and see how you do. He'll put you in as a salesman, probably, seeing as you know all about cars and that, and in the evenings there'll be something else for you to do – when I'm about again. But look, Jim, any bloody funny business while you're there is going to mean trouble, see?'

Jim flushed and felt fine about it all. 'That's damned nice of you, Louie,' he said. 'Caw! that's just fine. A salesman, eh? What money'll I get, d'you think?'

'Dunno,' Louie said. 'But not much, if I know anything about second-hand car places. Still, it'll be something, won't it? For a time anyway.'

Jim started walking about the room, thinking fast. Then he stopped, pulling at his lower lip thoughtfully. 'Why are you doing all this, anyway?' he asked suspiciously. 'What's your idea?'

Louie grinned painfully. 'It's an investment, boy,' he said. 'I can use you. You're going to be useful, see? And I want to keep my eye on you. We're not kids any longer, Jim, and you've got to realise that you can't get on unless you get what you can out of other people, even if you've got to help them along to do it. And if I seem to be doing the good fairy act with you, it's because I'm expecting to make it pay. Get it?'

Jim grinned back at him. 'I get it,' he said. 'And I think you're bloody well right.'

He went up to bed that night feeling on top of the world, swaggering up the stairs like the proper tough guy he intended to become . . .

Lying on the bed, listening to Jim's footsteps overhead, Louie Franks laughed silently.

'Silly young idiot,' he said. 'A first-rate mug. Now watch me.'

* * * * *

For a long time Jim lay sleepless. In the next room a girl's voice talked occasionally, and a man's voice answered her. And sometimes the bed creaked and there were long silences. Then, at eleven o'clock the man came out on to the landing and kissed the girl good night with a loud sucking noise before he tiptoed downstairs.

Lying in bed and listening to him, Jim began thinking. It seemed you could do what you liked in the place. That girl now, she had a man up in her room until this time, and no one to say anything. He remembered the fearful row there had been at a boarding house he and Ernie had stayed at in Yarmouth one year. A young man had been caught coming out of a girl's bedroom at ten o'clock one night. But people here seemed different, and more willing to let you alone. So as soon as he knew any people he would bring them up and make use of every privilege there was. And why the hell not? It wasn't any good living anywhere unless you had a good time. And for this sort of a good time there was every modern convenience, and not to make that useful – why, God, you might as well live at home!

* * * * *

When he woke it was eight o'clock, and he climbed out of bed quickly, shivering a little and scratching his head. He shaved and dressed and cleaned his teeth carefully, staring hard at his reflection in the glass when he had finished. He seemed to be looking extra pale, and his mouth was sulky as he looked himself over, but on the whole he looked good enough.

The best thing to do now was to get some breakfast, look in on Louie before he went out, and then go to the place Louie had said. And even as he stood there thinking about it someone knocked on the door, saying something obscure in a hoarse voice.

He went over and opened the door and the little wispy woman with the boot-button eyes was out there.

'Mornin',' she said. 'Seein' as ow you din order no brekfus, I thort as you might be wantin' some brort, but too fergetful to menshun it like, so here it is – and it's eggs and bacon and tea which will cost you extra at the end of the week if you're agreeable to payin' for havin' it brort up every day, that is.'

She paused for breath, and Jim grinned at her as he took the tray in. 'Thanks, Ma,' he said. 'You can bring it up every day. Suits me all right.'

He was just closing the door when the little woman leaned towards him, brushing the hank of hair from her eyes and winking, hoarsely gasping out a stage whisper.

'Any bother from Number 14?' she breathed. 'I mean

Miss Thomas, there. Any noise or anything? Eh? Proper stuck up Miss, she is, and I'd . . .'

Jim shook his head. 'No, I didn't hear anything.'

'Well, in case you should be . . .' the little woman said, but the door behind her opened and a girl came out.

'Would you mind holding your meetings somewhere else, Mrs Phillips,' she said furiously. 'And will you take a bit of notice when I ring my bell. And will you get my breakfast up. And will you please, please, *please* mind your own business a bit more?'

She went back into her room and slammed the door, and Jim got no more than a brief glimpse, a blurred impression of a pink dressing-gown, a mop of fair hair and a pale face, before the image disappeared from view.

Mrs Phillips clasped her hands over her stomach, cracking the joints of her fingers with hideous clicks.

'Well, of all the cheek! Why, Mr – er – did you ever . . .' But the door handle behind her twitched again, sending the little woman clucking away downstairs.

Half an hour later Jim had eaten, called in on Louie to say he was going, and was going down the stairs when he saw the girl again. She was dressed up now, in a brown costume, with a red scarf round her throat, and a felt hat pulled over one eye. Her face was carefully made up, but she looked tired.

Jim looked at her and smiled. 'Morning,' he said.

The girl looked right through him, and sniffed as she went along the hallway. Jim grinned sideways, watching the swing of her hips. God! but she was a fine bit. And just across the landing, too. A dozen little thoughts started dancing around inside his head as he went out and walked slowly along the street. God! with a girl like that . . . God!

He went on towards Baker Street, thinking about Louie's instructions. He went down into the station and found the right platform almost at once, climbing on to the train almost as it began moving. And thirty-five minutes later he walked for the first time into the showrooms of Graham Swing's – 'Over 100 for under £100' . . . 'Over 100 for under £100' . . . The slogan signs hung everywhere, leading up in size to the father of all signs, a two-hundred-foot board which hung the whole length of the place.

Jim walked in almost truculently, wandered through the front showroom and into the doorway indicated by a painted hand – a hand executed by one without any apparent knowledge of manual characteristics – a doorway labelled 'Office'.

Up a short flight of stairs, another door, propped half-open, its white paint marked with the dirty prints of many hands, said 'General Office'. And next to that a frosted glass door said 'Mr Swing. Private'. And from inside this last door came voices.

Jim knocked and was told to come in. There was a young man sprawling back in a chair behind the desk, his feet up. And facing him was another young man. The man at the desk was angry, and doing all the talking, the youth facing him, silent, and badly scared.

Jim blinked across the room from the doorway. 'Sorry, thought you said "Come in,"' he muttered awkwardly.

'So I did. Siddown, and shut up a minute, will you?' the man at the desk said, and then his voice changed again. 'And you, Clark, you poor silly bastard. You've bloody well got to pull your socks up. I'm getting tired of the way you and the other sods down there let people get away with it. What the hell do you mean by admitting liability to that old fool who brought that Rover back – eh? Liability my foot . . .'

'But you told me yourself that the guarantee on . . .'

'I told you nuts! What d'you think you're supposed to be, eh? You're a salesman, see? A salesman. And you damn well leave the rest of this business alone. Guarantee! God Almighty! Guarantee!'

'But what was I to say then . . . ?' the youth started.

'Listen; you say too much, if you ask me. Your only asset is an adenoidal public-school accent, and a striped tie. You've no brains, and damn little ability – and you know it. And unless you can make up your mind to do what I tell you – out you bloody well go! And that goes for the others, too. Now then. Anything to say? Eh?'

A girl came into the office while he was still speaking.

'Telephone, Mr Swing,' she said.

Swing turned round and stared at her. 'Well, why the devil don't you put me through then?' he said.

The girl sighed, and looked at her fingernails. 'Your receiver's off,' she said.

Swing grinned. 'Oh? Oh, is it? Yes, it is, isn't it? All right then. Switch it through. Who is it anyway?'

The girl strolled over to the door. 'The editor of the *Motor Car*,' she said, and went out.

Swing picked up the phone. 'Hullo? . . . eh? . . . yes, this is Graham Swing . . . yes . . . good morning . . . now, wait a minute, will you? . . . yes . . . yes . . . well, of course I did . . . wait a minute . . . You say this son of a bitch has written to you as a reader? And he says *what*? . . . yes . . . yes . . . oh, he does? . . . well, he paid me thirty quid for the bloody thing . . . what does he mean it was a fake-up? . . . No, I don't care what you say to him – or to me . . . eh? . . . oh, you do, do you? Listen; which do you care most about – my twelve quid a week advertising in your bloody paper – or this three-ha'penny-stamp fathead who has written to you . . . yes . . . yes . . . That *is* how it stands . . . No, I don't care, man. What? . . . well, do what I'd do if he came back here to complain – tell him to — off!'

He hung up, and winked at Jim. 'Editor of the *Motor Car*, my backside!' he said.

He turned to the young man standing in front of the desk. 'Well, want to say anything more?' he said.

The red-faced wretch facing the desk shook his head dumbly.

'All right then. Get out.'

When the door had shut again, the lounging young man got up and grinned at Jim. He was tall and extremely thin, with so much oil on his thick, fair hair that it looked grey. His eyes were prominent, with fair lashes and eyebrows, which made him look perpetually surprised. He had a good chin, but a thin-lipped, small mouth. And he looked hard and energetic – which he was – and looked like what passes in a good many places for a gentleman – which he wasn't. But whatever anyone else thought about him he didn't mind. He was twice as shrewd and keen as you could imagine anyone to be, and knew it.

Given up as a disgraceful disappointment by a family steeped in the best traditions of the Civil Service, he had been asked to leave school after a rather strange episode with a smaller boy in the dark room of the photographic club. At a loose end for a time, he had been finally pitchforked into the car business, and at once found his true *métier*. A year as a salesman gave him the measure of both allies and opposition. A borrowed twenty pounds gave him the impetus, and after that there was no stopping him. From the chrysalis stage of freelance touting to the possession of a large showroom of his own, from the tooth-and-nail possession of a battered Morris-Cowley and several debts to match it, to the complete ownership of a Rolls-Twenty, and a bank balance, was a short span of time. Three years of work, of relentless driving of his staff, of developing his already acute sense of bargain, had flashed by, and now he had what he wanted. He was known everywhere in the cheap car trade. Graham Swing – a hard nut to crack, and a good fellow so long as you watched out for yourself and let him see you were watching. He was a wide man, with an eye for a snip and a mug to take it that amounted almost to genius.

He looked Jim over carefully as he shook hands, and then patted him on the back. It was the sort of pat you gave to the dog at the house of someone you don't like very much.

'I heard about you from Franks,' he said. 'Good chap, Franks. Useful, too. D'you know him well? I suppose you do, don't you?'

Jim nodded. 'Yes, I know him. He's useful, all right,' he said.

They stayed there talking for ten minutes, and Jim got the idea with five minutes to spare. Swing thought he was using the Franks, and meant to do it as hard as he could. He had some idea in his head about it, and he was going to work it out. Jim was nothing. Give him a job as salesman – sure! Quid a week and a quid for every car he sold. No trouble – do it any time to please the Franks. That was the idea. Please the Franks – and keep in with them. If the boy had been at Chantrey's and served his time there he would be an engineer. He looked tough, too, and not unpresentable at that. Better than the striped-tied heroes down there in the sale rooms now, anyway. Give the kid a run for a month, and then look around and see what good had been done. No trouble to anybody, no trouble at all. A pleasure . . .

After he had explained what he wanted done, and how it had to *be* done, he told Jim to go downstairs and start work. 'You're bright enough to pick it up in an hour or two, Bankley,' he said smoothly. 'Just you watch the other fellers, and talk to old Clines in the garage. You'll be all right . . .'

Jim went down the stairs scratching the seat of his trousers thoughtfully. Well, he could try, anyway.

The whole of the morning seemed to be spent in listening to other people. First there was Clines. He was the 'fixer' – an unqualified mechanic, a cunning handyman of thirty years' experience, who received forty-five shillings a week and a bonus of sixpence for every car he saved from the breakers' yards.

The crocks taken in part exchange poured in in dozens. Some were resaleable after a mere lick of paint, a squirt of paraffin, and a 'tyre cut'. But others were wheeled out into the garage yard for Clines. And when Jim saw him, the little man was eyeing a ten-year-old Austin-Seven. The car was dead beat, and looked ashamed of itself, but Clines set about it at once. In thirty minutes he had patched up a broken wing stay with wire and insulating tape, plugged three body rattles with wet cardboard rolls, secured the battery box with string to the frame, and poured oil into the sump – oil which made up in heaviness what it lacked in cleanliness.

Jim grinned. This sort of casual trickery seemed very amusing and clever. 'How often d'you have to fake 'em?' he asked, and Clines scratched his grey head with a dirty finger. 'Dunno 'xactly,' he said. 'I s'pose abaowt noine outer twelve 'ave ter be faiked up some'ow. Ther's always loose bits ter pack up, an' things ter be woired up somewhere, y'know.'

'Still, makes the cars look a bit weary doesn't it?'

Clines laughed sourly. 'Well, if that sod Swing sells 'em for fiver ten pun', you don't 'spect 'em ter look spectakkler, do yer?'

The whole business was an eye-opener in a way. Used, as he was, to seeing thousands of immaculate machines roll off the assembly lines every day, Jim couldn't stop wondering at the fantastic decline in the cars' fortunes in so short a time. And here they were, just four or five years after being the pride of a first owner – the owner who had given place to that mythical person the 'Owner Going Abroad'. Now they slouched in line, whining of axle; groaning of gearbox; rattling of wings and body; slack of compression; torn of upholstery; their registration books covered, in some cases with name after name – four, five, six owners before the ramshackle wreck was wheeled out for the eye of Clines to sneer at, to take its last chance to escape the final degradation of the breaker's yard.

But that was only Class 3, as it were. Above that were the two- and three-year-old family tanks, little machines in fair order, their only real fault an incipient 'just-about-to-happen' complete breakdown due to bad handling over a long period. Five out of ten of them had doubtful axles, oval crankshafts, or some major fault imminent, which was going to cost someone plenty of money. But now they were polished up, the mileage on the speedometer dial reduced to a mere 10,000 by the simple expedient of running the drive backwards on a dynamo spindle for an hour or so and stopping it at the required figure. Or, more simply, by breaking the glass and forcing the figures with a screwdriver.

Then Class 2A, the larger machines. The third-hand Chryslers and Buicks, trusty, but voracious old tanks traded in by once-ambitious bloods who found the huge appetites of the motors for petrol and oil too much for them. These machines were heavy. Heavy to run, and heavy to sell off again. Apart from the extra bonus of a pound which was paid to any man who sold a car which had been in stock for more than four months, there was a special sense of triumph which went with the disposal of any of these leviathans. And it was well earned.

That left the cream of the collection, the dealers' caviare, the paving on the sidewalks to success – sports cars.

Brightly-painted little buzz-boxes, nicely pimpled with gadgets, chromiumed of lamps and fittings. Low-built little motor-cars beloved of the Blood. The tone of the loud-farting exhaust more important than the comfort of the seats. A maximum speed, a performance inferior to most of the large tanks in Class 2A, they relied for their appeal on resplendent names – 'marque' appellations fatuously reminiscent of the continental Grand Prix. Flat-folding windscreens with aeroplane screens behind – the invention of a genius who had weighed up the mentalities of his future customers so well. Cowled wind-scoops, fly-off handbrakes and the 'quick-action' filler cap. We salute you, my lord sports car!

Row after row of them, rakish little machines, already caned half to death by young people with indulgent parents.

Easy to fake up, these cars. Remove a baffle plate or two from the exhaust silencer, and let the noisy tone cover a multitude of other sounds; touch up the wheels and give the paintwork a polish; screw a Union Jack onto the bonnet; leave on some badges which look so fine even if they mean so little; advertise subtly this little motor as being '24-hour race type', or 'Grand Prix type', 'fast and reliable', 'the fastest of this make on the road': fold down the windscreen and push the thing into the showroom. There's no need to do any more – you'll knock 'em cold.

Forty cars a week were sold at Swing's. Forty cars every seven days, right through the year. And over this little robber's cave of plate glass and polish smiled the patron saint of the industry – Saint Hire Purchase . . .

* * * * *

When Jim met the other salesmen, he withdrew a little into his shell, conscious all at once of his provincial accent. These young men were not a kind he was used to. Loud-mouthed young rascals with oil-slicked hair, loose-lipped and prone to spots, they were astonishingly of a type until you realised they were *trying* to be. Check sports-coats and grey trousers, or even lounge-suited, they had always two characteristics in common – an Old School Tie and a drawling voice which hardly sounded Cockney at all. Highly-polished shoes and vaguely-polished manners, a persuasive and inexhaustible flow of technical slang apper-taining to 'buses', 'revs', 'con-rods', 'remote-control boxes'; an astonishingly vacant mind, a small intellect contrasting with a shrewd eye for a customer – these seemed to be their hallmark. Their interests outside their work seemed kin as well. And at Swing's the sole topics of idle conversation were vague references to sport (with some sort of unstated notion that 'Rugger' was somehow a more socially desirable game than 'Soccer'), and an almost passionate interest in sex. Hour after hour, day after day, they were always ready to stand about in little groups and discuss the 'crumpet' of the night before. It seemed to Jim that the moment they could get away from work they would shoot off in their rickety motors to Hampstead Heath or Wimbledon Common, looking for Girls. Social misfits, for the most part, utterly incapable of managing any job other than the one they were in, the perpetual appetite for 'crumpet' with Girls was the most definite thing about them. 'Crumpet' – and Beer. 'Grend Stahff – Beeah!'

To Jim they all behaved about the same. They were helpful, but distant. Ready to exchange a little gossip and ask questions about him, even to tell a smutty joke or two. But he was never one of them. He was not a Public School Man.

Graham Swing had been like that once. He was cast in exactly the same mould, but a genius for seeing himself objectively had pulled him out of it. One pound a week, and a pound for every car sold. The others thought it fair enough, but Swing thought another way. He had pulled himself up, but he was one of the Tribe still. He knew the weaknesses, the fatal desire to keep the job because it was not hard work, even if the hours *were* long. And he played on that, choosing his men carefully, slinging them out at the first signs of discontent, the first hint of intelligence other than that required for a sale. Like most people that have made good, he distrusted almost everybody, hated almost everybody who worked for him. No hypocritical sentimentalities about 'The Working Man' for Mr Swing. 'The Working Man,' he would say, 'God! I hate the bastard. Never knows when he's well off.'

* * * * *

Jim stuck out the week, fighting against boredom. And boredom seemed to be the keynote of the whole job, the continually encroaching weariness of hanging about.

He watched the other salesmen, watched the way they gathered in lounging groups, gossiping, tirelessly describing sexual exploits, scattering eagerly when a customer came in. He listened eagerly to MacRay, the tallest, spottiest of them, watched him fascinate a young man who came in looking for a sports car, watched him lead the youth towards one the firm had bought in that week for £40 – and which they intended to sell for £95. And MacRay had it taped from the start.

He was a born liar, an effortless blackguard with the invaluable gift of more than half-believing his own lies even as he made them up. Listening to him, you just had to admire his quick summing-up of his customer, the way he adopted his tone to suit his ends, the lightning decision of which line to take.

'Oh, this one?' he said easily, glancing quickly over his shoulder. 'Funny you should notice it, you know. It's a bit of a different proposition from the others. As a matter of fact, Mr Swing himself is rather keen on it – said something about nabbing it for his missus. Oh no, no, no. Rather not . . . Customers first, old man. Just take a look over, will you? See? Reinforced thingummies here . . . spring-gaiters; these large dummy brake-drums – they're to assist cooling as well as appearance, you know. And the engine has extra-high compression . . . polished ports, and that. Damned hot stuff. Just take a look at her. Only had one owner, and he had it chauffeur-kept . . . You see, it's really . . .'

Easily he discussed the racing successes of the make, reeling off a string of results, famous names dripping from his lips until the customer became convinced that here was a pure-hearted enthusiast.

A young man, this customer, fresh from school. A conscious wise guy, and cautious with it. He thought he knew what he wanted. Thought that the lesson he had learned from the *Autocar* articles had put him one jump ahead of the other fellow when it came to buying. The points in 'What To Look For When Buying A Second-hand Car' became jumbled inside his head, jumbled hopelessly as he listened. MacRay had him taped and hog-tied. He had discovered that the boy was going to pay cash. And after finding that out – nothing could have stopped him. Still with 'maximum revs', 'straight-through changes into third at speed', 'remote-control gates', 'hot plugs' and the like drooling from him, he led the boy into the office for the final kill. Axiom 1 of the Swing's Salesmen's Creed had been carried out – 'Never give a trial run if it can be avoided' . . .

'How good is this little machine?' Jim said to Clines when the little man was filling the car with petrol in the yard.

'Oh, not bad,' Clines said. 'It'll go all right, treated reasonable. But ther's somefin the matter with the oilin'. If you rev the bloody thing up high for any length er toime it runs all the bloody bearin's. The mug we bought it from 'ad run sixteen bearin's in two munfs. 'E was the sort what never learns, I s'pose.'

'But it's got a four months' guarantee. Cost more than fifty quid, and that means the guarantee comes in, doesn't it?' Jim said doubtfully. 'Isn't that of any use?'

Clines sneered. 'Well, I c'n on'y fink of one plaice where it'd be of any use,' he said.

Jim laughed and went into the showroom again. He was feeling more confident now, and when, two hours later, after having been forced to take the car for a trial run, he had sold a Chantrey-Six to a commercial traveller, he felt better still. The customer had been obviously impressed with Jim's connection with the works. He had swallowed all the bogus maintenance advice he had heard. It was a cinch.

But even with this to fillip his spirits, the prospect of being there until 9pm every night was bad enough, and by the Saturday evening he was brooding about it when Swing sent for him.

He went up to the office and found the boss ready to leave. It was six o'clock.

'Hullo, Bankley. You've done all right this week, haven't you? Good. Now listen. I've just had a phone call from Franks. We're going to meet at the White City tonight. And he asked me to bring you along. So you'd better get your hat and we'll beat it right away.'

They left the place together, and, sliding smoothly towards the West End in Swing's Rolls-Twenty, Jim began to think. He had the thing figured out almost instinctively. Swing was going to be plucked.

He glanced sideways out of the corner of his eye. Yes, this bloke wasn't Franks' kind. He was a hard nut, and no fool, but he hadn't their sort of callousness. He was ready to go to almost any limit, but the Franks would always go further. Swing probably drew the line just above robbery with violence. The Franks didn't.

Jim had enough common sense, too, to realise that his own position in the game was like the balls in a game of tennis. And Swing seemed to think he was a useful unit, for some reason. And Franks had some sort of idea as well. They all thought they were being smart, didn't they? Well, all right. Let them. Every man for himself. That was fair so long as everyone was ready for it. Every man for himself. That was the only way to get along.

They met Louie Franks outside Schmidt's in Charlotte Street. He waved at them as soon as he saw them coming, and stepped into the road. He leaned in through the window at Swing's side and began to talk.

'Hullo,' he said. ''Evening. Bill sent me here instead of coming himself. He's gone to pick up one of the boys to go over to the White City. I said I'd go along with you. Me and Jim, see? Shall I get in the back?'

Swing nodded shortly. He didn't think so much of Louie. 'Yes, you get in. But look, here, what about food?'

'We can have some food when we get there,' Louie said.

The Rolls sighed its way westwards, Louie and Swing talking casually, neither of them taking any notice of Jim at all. They were early, and as they swung in through the gates of the car park at the White City there were only a few other cars there.

When they had parked, and stretched their legs, they walked across towards the gates. Louie paid, and then led the way into the old Club Entrance. And to Jim, after the track back home, this maze of walks, this huge structure of steel, concrete and glass, the polite attendants, the carpeted stairs and diffused lighting – Caw! it was an eye-opener.

He stared round quickly, trying hard not to be impressed. Up in the barroom, with its polished counter and glistening array of glass, its soft carpet and softer lighting, its glass and steel-tube furniture, he began to feel uneasy. Gawd! this was posh enough for anybody.

Louie led the way to the bar and ordered drinks and sandwiches. His manner was a little quieter and less flamboyant now, and he seemed to have one eye on Swing and the other on the door.

Down at the far end of the bar was a small, sad-looking man with a dead-white face. He was so frail and thin, his eyes were so dead and fishy, the fact that he was smoking a huge cigar looked like an irreverent joke. He looked up as Louie passed him and spoke.

''Lo,' he said. 'Seen the card?'

Louie shook his head. 'No. Not yet,' he said. 'Don't think there's anything, though.'

The little man shrugged his shoulders, smiling mirthlessly. 'So *you* say,' he muttered, and turned away.

'Good God! Who's that?' Swing said.

Louie grinned. 'Him? Name's Ike Gisberg. He's hot stuff. His brother runs a gang of boys at a lot of the tracks. He's behind a lot of the bookies all over the place. He's worth a packet, too. And bets like a maniac.'

Swing looked along the bar at the frail little man, noticing his poor clothes, his cheap shoes, the greasy rim of his hat. 'Looks flat broke to me,' he said.

Louie shrugged. 'You think so? Well, I tell you he could put all *you* got inside his waistcoat pocket and forget about it. Broke! Wish the bastard *was* broke. He gets in the way too much. Half our time we have to be watching him.'

'What are we going to do tonight?' Swing said.

Louie looked at him, and then at the door again. Then he said: 'When Bill comes you'll know.'

They ate and drank for half an hour while the place filled up and the lights went on outside over the track. Jim wandered out through the doorway. Below him, the huge, perfectly-kept stadium looked fine.

Then Bill Franks arrived with another man. He came over and said something to Louie, and was very jovial and shook hands with Swing. When Jim came back Bill nodded to him almost absent-mindedly. The young man, whom he introduced as 'Mick', was much younger than he was. A short, broad-shouldered young tough with fair hair and eyelashes. His eyes were very pale, and stared straight at you, under a perpetual frown. His mouth was hard, and drooped sideways when he spoke – which was seldom. He looked as if he had a grudge against life; and he had.

After the second race, Swing and the two Franks went outside, and Mick moved up closer to Jim, eyeing him.

'You come here a lot?' Jim said.

Mick smiled sourly. 'Off 'n on,' he said.

'Bets pretty heavy, Franks, doesn't he?'

'You never can tell,' Mick said coldly.

'Anything on tonight?'

'You can't tell that either.'

Jim gave it up. Conversation with this bloke was heavy going. 'Well, I'm wondering what the hell I'm here for,' he said.

Mick gave a short laugh. 'So 'm I,' he said.

Jim scowled and turned his back. He ordered another drink.

'I drink too,' Mick said, watching him.

'Well, go ahead. You've got some money, I suppose,' Jim answered sulkily.

Mick scowled. 'You being funny, kid?' he said. ''Cos if you are – I'm not bloody well laughing, see?'

Jim looked round at him. 'You can go and — yourself,' he said. With drink inside him, he felt he could knock the swine's face in.

When the bell went they both went outside to watch the race. 'Got anything on this one?' Jim said.

Mick said nothing and looked away. The shouting down below at the layers' stands died away, and the lights went dim. The hare was rumbling round the outside circle, gathering speed. It swung round the bend, whipped past the traps, and in a second the dogs flashed out after it.

A brindle in Trap 3 broke three lengths clear and held the lead the whole way.

'That's the way. Trap to line, and no bleeding mistakes,' Mick said. 'That's the boss's dog. He's the one for picking 'em all right.'

In a few minutes Swing came up the steps and led the way back to the bar. He was looking very excited, and ordered a whisky, grinning all over his face. 'By God! I won sixty quid on that one,' he said. 'And didn't miss a heart-beat. Marvellous! Have a drink, you fellers.'

Jim grinned. 'Got one,' he said. 'Have one yourself.'

Swing pushed the first drink he had ordered across to

Mick and asked for another. He was feeling pretty good.

'Is the boss doing anything more?' Mick said suddenly.

Swing shook his head. 'No. He said there was only one tonight. There's two at Wandsworth, though, tomorrow.'

'Does he fix these races?' Jim asked Mick.

'Fix them?' Mick said. 'Don't be a sap! How could he fix them? Eh? He just waits, that's all. He knows just what every dog is doing, what every dog can do – from every trap – barring accidents. If it's going to be tight, if there's too much chance in it, he passes them up. If he feels sure, he has a go. Why, the boss studies form like a professor – dogs' form, and men's form. Most information costs money, and the boss pays off to the right people – and gets what he wants. He knows every blade of grass the tykes are going to put their feet on. But he can't do any dirty business – here. Caw! they almost take a bloody dog to pieces here before they'll let him run. But there's ways and means at some of the dirty little Flapping Tracks, even if they're on the level at this place.'

The bar was full now, people drinking and talking, people eating at the tables; a mixed crowd. Bookies and their women, impermanently jewelled; a few people in evening dress; a crowd of youngsters in good clothes; all sorts, all with one idea. The management provided the setting, the comfort, the luxury, the sport. Society, or civilisation, or what-you-will, provided the rest. Two thousand Mugs to every Wide Boy; professional gamblers, basking in temporary opulence; hangers-on and rabbit-faced tipsters, noses sniffing after the dirty stink of dirty money. A crowd of people to whom dog racing had begun as an enthusiasm, worked through to being a craze, and ended as being a habit. Night after night of it, winning, losing, winning again, meeting the same people, talking the same talk, losing all sense of values. Some of them hold out longer than the others, but they all get licked in the end. You can't buck a mathematical certainty however much you try.

Just as the Franks came in again, Gisberg moved away from the bar and made for the door. He nodded to Bill, his face like a mask. When he had gone, Bill laughed.

'What's the joke?' Swing said.

'Old Gisberg. He lost eight tenners on the last race,' Bill said. 'His bitch came in third.'

Bill was in fine humour now, and gave Jim a pat on the shoulder. 'Well, boy,' he said. 'How d'you like selling cars?'

Jim grinned. What a bloody silly question. 'Oh, I'm doing all right,' he said.

'That's the idea,' Bill said. 'That's fine.' He turned to Swing. 'Nice of you to fix the kid up, Swing,' he said. 'You satisfied with him, old man?'

Swing nodded absently. His thin, shrewd face was very flushed. 'Sure,' he said. 'He's doing all right as far as I'm concerned. But listen; about tonight. You'd better subtract your cut before you send me along the cheque when you collect – all right?'

Bill shook his head. 'No. You'll get the cheque, and you can send me along my share when you like. I told the bloke to pay you, anyway.'

Swing grinned. 'Fine. That'll do all right. Well . . . can I give any of you a lift back. I'm going through to Maida Vale.'

Jim opened his mouth, but Louie jerked him by the sleeve, and he closed it again.

'Thanks all the same,' Louie said. 'But we're going on to a party after this. We'll see you tomorrow. Better meet the same place in Goodge Street, at the corner – *you* know.'

Swing nodded, and stood up. 'Right-o. Well, cheer-o, and see you tomorrow.'

As soon as he had gone, Bill buttonholed Mick and drew him along the bar, leaving Jim and Louie together.

Louie ordered a drink. Then he said: 'Well, has it got you guessing, still?'

Jim shrugged his shoulders. 'I don't know anything. Why the hell did I have to come here? I haven't done anything the whole evening – except eat and drink.'

Louie grinned, and ran his fat fingers through his crisp hair. 'No, and there wasn't any need. You had to meet Micky, see? Well, and did you see *him* doing anything? He draws a regular wage for not doing anything. So did all the boys that had his job before him. Bill pays them to see there's never anything to do. I told him you were a tough boy – in fact he knows you are. And Mick seems to pass you okay, too. You see we have to be careful, boy, and sometimes people get rough – get it now?'

'You mean I've got to look after you and Bill, is that it?'

'Well, in a way, yerce.'

'Well, why the hell do I have to go to Swing's place and sell his rotten cars, eh?'

Louie shrugged his shoulders and winked. 'Werl, you'll find that out. It's just an idea, really. Bill's up to some dodge with that young Smart Aleck. You'll know in time. But Bill never talks till he's ready. But if he says you work at Swing's – well, you just bleeding well work there, that's all – see? You got to learn not to ask any questions. Bill does all the thinking, and we do the rest.'

'Will I get any dough from Bill, Louie?' Jim said.

'Depends. Depends how things go,' Louie said.

They sat there slackly until they had finished their drinks. Through the doorway they could hear the crowds milling round the layers' stands outside. The parade for the last race had started. Suddenly Bill turned round.

'Hey, Jimmy, I want you,' he said.

'What?' Jim said.

'I think you're going to be a useful boy, so long as you use your loaf. But you got to remember two things. You got to hold down that job at Swing's until I say so – that's one. And you got to keep your trap shut – that's two. See? You

95

show me you're willing to be a useful boy that don't talk, and we're going to get along fine. That's always been the bleeding trouble with the boys I had working for me. They either thought they was too Wide, or they just flapped their big mouths all over the place.'

Jim just looked at him. 'I don't talk, boss,' he said. 'You can depend on that.' Silly old cock, he might be a hell of a tough guy and a gambler, but he lapped up this line like a fool. God! he had 'em all fooled, all except Jim Bankley. Jim looked at Mick for a second. Well, all except Jim Bankley – and Mick.

'Werl,' Bill said. 'That's fine. Now I guess you'll want some pocket money, won't you? I'm paying off now.' He took a bundle of money from his inside pocket. The notes were mostly white. It was more money at one time than Jim had ever seen in his life. Something made him think of the way his father used to finger the ten-shilling notes the day the rent man called. Thirty bob seemed like a tidy sum then. Thirty bob! Caw! And Bill Franks had two or three hundred quid in his hand.

Bill fingered the wad and peeled off seven one-pound notes from the inside of it. He pushed them across the table, steering five of the notes to Jim, and two to Mick. 'Might be a good idea to have a bit on Satan's Baby in this race,' he said casually.

Jim got up and started for the door. The air outside in the stadium seemed cold after the heat inside the bar, and the noise was very loud. The bookies were laying five to one about Satan's Baby.

When Jim came back, Bill and Louie were sitting at one of the tables. Bill said something to Louie and laughed. Then he looked at Jim.

'What price d'you get, Jim?' he said.

'I took twenty-five quid to five,' Jim said.

Louie narrowed his eyes. 'Did you put the whole bloody lot on, boy?' he said. 'Strewth!'

Jim said nothing. He was playing a hunch. He sat quite still, his face dead. Then Mick came in and told them Satan's Baby had come in fourth.

As the dogs were led back into the paddock, Bill burst out laughing. 'Well, I was wrong,' he said. 'Bad luck, Jim, boy.'

Jim grinned. 'Can't be helped,' he said. 'You're the boss, and if you don't know – well, I don't.'

Bill laughed again and looked pleased. He leaned back on his chair and put one finger in the armhole of his waistcoat. He looked like a conceited schoolboy, all puffed up and pleased with himself. 'That's fine, Jimmy,' he said, and laughed again. 'That's what I want. You do what you're told, and we'll get on fine.' He pushed two pounds across the table. 'Here, catch hold of these – and look after them a bit better this time.' And he laughed again, slapping his knee. It didn't seem to be difficult to please Mr Bill Franks.

Jim picked up the money and pushed it into his pocket. The hunch had come off.

And later, when they were going towards the car park, he nudged Louie and said: 'You know, I bet I could have bluffed old Bill I'd put the whole of that fiver on the damned dog. I bet he'd have been bucked about it just the same.'

Louie looked at him sideways. 'Don't be a mug, Jimmy,' he said. 'Mick was tailing you. If you'd tried on anything funny, he'd have said so. Bill's no baby – and Mick's grown-up!'

Looking across at Mick, noticing his wide, powerful shoulders and big hands, his cold face and mouth, Jim chewed his lower lip. He didn't like this blond young man. For the first time in his life he was afraid of someone.

They found Bill's Buick, and Bill said would Jim like to drive it, and Jim said would he not! He drove beautifully, his judgement and control good to the point of genius, and he pushed the big machine hard, pleasing and interesting even the blasé Louie who was beside him.

As they rolled slowly along the shining wet streets and turned into Tottenham Court Road half an hour later, Bill suddenly spoke. 'Turn up here, Jimmy,' he said. 'That's right, Goodge Street. I want to get into a poker game at the Quarter Club. I'll tell you where to stop. You drive bloody well, boy, don't you? Might come in useful one day, you never know.' And he laughed throatily, nudging Mick beside him.

They parked the car at the kerb, and Bill got out and rang the bell at a shop which was jammed between a delicatessen shop and a restaurant. It was some time before the door opened, and it opened mechanically, because there was no one in the passage when they all went inside. Then Bill led the way upstairs.

The Quarter was just a club, one of those mushroom growths that spring up and are gone in a few months. It had been open seven days now, and was in full strength. There were three rooms on the third floor, and another room on the fourth. Bill went through to the top room, and went alone. The other three stayed in the Club improper.

Most of the people there were under forty, though some of the men looked more. The girls were for the most part tarts. Some were there on business, the others relaxing with their gentlemen friends and protectors. There was a lot of noise, and the air was thick with cigarette smoke, the smells of drinks, cheap scents and armpits.

To be on the safe side in future, Louie introduced Jim to the manager, a little, baby-faced man called Harry Craig. 'We don't need no register, Jimmy,' Harry said. 'Once I see a feller I don't never forget him. Harry's got a good memory, Jimmy, and Harry never forgets a face.'

Most of the time they were there, Jim sat in a corner with Mick, who sneered openly at everyone there. He told Jim that whilst Bill was in his poker game upstairs they must stay sober. 'You lay off the drinks, boy,' he said coldly. 'You've had enough for one night, anyway. And you can keep your eyes off the tarts, too.'

'Because why?' Jim said, going dark red in the face. Who the hell was this chap to tell him what to do?

'Because we're here on business – and not their business. And anyway, all the fun you'd get with those bitches would be to catch something you don't want. You know much about tarts?'

'Werl, no, not much.'

Mick nodded. 'Well, I do. And I say either watch your step or lay off. Playing around with tarts gets you nowhere. See?'

Jim nodded and said nothing. He still didn't like Mick, and was wishing to God that Louie would appear again and talk to him. He could see Louie standing in the doorway talking and grinning with a boy there, a boy with long, curly hair and powder on his face.

Half an hour dragged past slowly, and then Harry Craig appeared with a message from Bill, telling them to go home, saying that he would put the Buick away himself.

So the two of them went out together. Louie had disappeared, and Mick and Jim separated mutually at the door of the Club.

'S'long,' Jim said. 'See you tomorrow.'

Mick just nodded and walked away. And Jim looked after him. 'Bastard,' he said, and turned for home.

He walked the whole way, and was tired when he got in, but it was a long time before he was asleep.

* * * * *

MICK. In a crowd of misfits, he was the worst misfit of them all. But he would have been out of place in any society. He was cold and dangerous, more dangerous than any of them, because he had brains. None of his acquaintances knew much about his past, few of them had much to do with his present, and none of them had any hope for his future. He was morose, spoke seldom, in a quiet, bitter voice. Occasionally he smiled, and hardly ever he laughed. Short and powerfully built, his arms and shoulders were almost freakishly developed. Habitually he walked slowly, his shallow, almost dead, grey eyes staring straight ahead of him. He looked absent-minded sometimes, but he missed nothing. His fair hair was smooth and well-brushed; his thin lips, against the unnatural pallor of his face, very red. The long, white scar of an old razor slash went right down his face from left ear to corner of his mouth.

Born in a decent, respectable middle-class family, he first went wrong at the age of twelve. His family could do nothing with him, neither could anyone else. And two short doses of prison between eighteen and twenty-four gave a polish to the already hardened surface of his outlook.

In a tight corner he would fight with hideous, cold-blooded ferocity. Sober, he was sardonic and bitter, a poor enough companion. Drunk, he was the devil himself.

Even Bill Franks, basking in the image of himself that he had created; Bill, the pseudo Al Capone with his two strong-arm men, was more than half-afraid of him at times, handling him with care.

Mick watched every opportunity, because he wanted to get on. Nothing else was half so important as his Ambition. The other mugs could blow all their money on tarts and cards, on getting tight and that – but not him.

Every once in a while he would go through periods of lust. And even the three or four girls at the Quarter and Greek Joe's, girls with a reputation for lasciviousness, were appalled by his insatiable appetites – appalled and fright-ened. Usually indiscriminate, and strictly business-like with his women, once he had met and been interested in a girl apart from just using her. And this girl had run out on him, hurting his vanity more than he cared to admit, even to himself.

He was a hard case, and cared for only two things in the world – Himself, and Money. He was careful about both of them, and distrusted everything else.

His full name, so usual as to make everybody he knew believe it assumed, was Michael John Smith.

At twenty-five years of age he had not a single friend in the world. But, as I have said, he had brains.

* * * * *

The days went slowly. Long hours at the showrooms; talk. Talk with the salesmen; talk with the customers. Just talk, talk, talk, day after day. Nine till nine, and alternate Sundays.

At the end of the third week Jim nearly gave in and told Bill Franks he was fed up with it, but each time he got to the point where he led off, each time he steered the conversation round to his job, something checked him. He was making money, even if he wasn't spending it. All day long at the showrooms; four nights a week picking up Mick and following Bill Franks about from Club to Club. Just sitting about and talking again, every rotten Club they went to it was the same. Louie he hardly saw, except on Sunday mornings when it was his day off from Swing's. And then, as likely as not, Louie had a head on him after a booze-up the night before.

For another fortnight the boredom dragged on. And then Bill showed his hand a little.

It was a Friday night, and Jim had gone back to his room at Number 22, and was lying smoking on his bed, reading a shilling sex-novel – central heating for his erotic imagination. It was his evening off.

At ten-thirty, Mrs Phillips came up and said there were two gentlemen downstairs who wanted to see him.

The gentlemen were Bill Franks and Mick, and they came up together: Bill, calm and impassive; Mick, staring curiously round the room as soon as he had shut the door.

'Hullo,' Jim said. 'Sit in the armchair, boss. It squeaks a bit, but it's not bad.'

Bill nodded and sat down in the wicker armchair. Mick leaned back against the mantelpiece. He was picking his teeth with a pin. Then he looked at the book Jim had thrown down when they had come in. 'What's that?' he said.

Jim looked uneasy. 'Book by that chap Louie told me about. Hot stuff,' he said.

'Why don't you read something decent, if you've got to read anything,' Mick said.

'I read a book once,' Bill said thoughtfully. 'Called *The Sheik*, I think it was. Didn't like it, though.'

Mick laughed shortly, and then went on picking his teeth. For a short time the three of them were silent. Then Bill pulled a cigar from his pocket and lit it. When he had it going properly he leaned forward and tapped Jim on the knee. His long, horse-like face was very solemn.

'Well, I've got a few questions to ask you, Jimmy,' he said, and paused. 'Getting fed up with your job in the car business, eh?'

'You're the boss,' Jim said slowly. 'When you say I'm fed up – I am.' He knew just how to handle Bill now. And out of the tail of his eye he saw Mick smile sardonically. The bastard! He didn't miss anything!

'Good!' Bill said. 'That's fine. Now listen. Did you do what I said, and keep your eyes open?'

'Well, I know how much money Swing takes every week, if that's what you mean.'

'Well, how much *does* he take?'

'He sells about forty cars a week, cheap stuff, you know,

and banks about eleven hundred quid. The overheads are about two hundred; the ads about seventy-five quid and a bit; outlay for buying – I dunno. He lives in Shepherd's Bush, with a judy called Iris Jewell. He runs the Rolls, goes out a bit, and that's about all. The bastard's lousy with money, and thinks he's the smartest thing this side of Kingdom Come. I reckon he pulls in a clear two thousand a year.'

Mick stopped picking his teeth. 'Not bad – eh, Boss? Strewth! Didn't think you had it in you, Jimmy boy.'

Bill laughed throatily. 'Naw, not bad. Say, Jimmy, got anything to drink here?'

'Beer,' Jim said. 'I got a bottle somewhere.'

'Good, let's have some. My tongue feels like someone's done a dance on it in woollen socks.'

Jim got up, and fished out a bottle from under the bed. He poured out three glasses and handed them round.

'Ah! that's fine,' Bill said. 'Now listen. No, sit down, boy, and listen to what I got to say. Right. Now, I'm not taking that bastard Swing round because I like his blue eyes, see?'

'No. I guessed that,' Jim said.

'Right. I met him on a train coming home from Brighton races last month. Showed him how to rig the three-card game – you know how you get to talking to fellers in a train. Well, he seemed to me a smart boy – but only smart in his own game. Oh, he's smart enough in the car racket, and I'm not saying he isn't, but he's not so bloody smart as he thinks he is.'

'No, couldn't be,' Jim said, and laughed, looking from Bill to Mick. Neither of them thought he was funny.

'Now then,' Bill said. 'You saw him pick up sixty nicker at the City the other night – remember? And he picked some more the day after. I've been taking him around now for some time, and he's gone up and down, see? At the moment he's over two hundred nicker up – and I've got him going.'

'Well, what about it?' Jim said.

Over at the mantelpiece, Mick grunted impatiently. 'For Gawsake shut up, boy, will you? Listen.'

Bill went on slowly. 'Right. Listen, Jim; I didn't know how he stood, and to get him going proper I had to find out. That's where you came in, see? 'Smatter of fact it was mostly Louie's idea, all this. And now we got Swing on the heat. He's ready to start laying the big money. Caw! I coaxed him into laying an even sixty, day 'fore yesterday. And the schlemihl can't bet anyway. I'm handling his dough and getting a point better every time.'

'How d'you mean – a point better?'

'What? Well, look; I'm just betting for nothing. I can't bleeding well lose, see? Swing gives me the dough. I lay it, with my boys, and get a price. He beats the SP price – and I beat his. Get it now?'

Jim grinned. 'Oh, I see! But . . . but why not go on that way. I mean ter say . . .'

Bill shook his big head, screwing up his dark little eyes. 'Naw, not enough to it. I got a better idea, see? I bought a dog last week, one from Ireland. It's a good 'un, real smasher and all. Now, you got to tell Swing about it – confidential, see? You're double-crossing me, see? That sort of stuff. I'm sending you flapping with the dog, see? Over to the little track you went to with Mick here. All you got to do is collect the dog and go there. Everything's fixed up. Phoney name for the dog, all worked out with the racing manager. Proper job, see? You show Swing how much dough you're putting in.'

'But . . .'

'Wait! I'll give you a hundred, and you go up to these two bookies,' and he scribbled the names on the back of an envelope. 'See? Benny's one of them, and Jake's another one of my boys, too. Now, these two blokes lay a false price, see? Then Swing can have his bit, and he'll have it with these two because they'll be a point over the odds, see? Then we got him.' Bill stopped and laughed. Then he finished his beer and belched.

'And then?' Jim said.

'And then the dog is given a drink of water and comes in bleedin' last.'

Jim grinned and rubbed his hands on his knees. 'Fine. That's easy. I can do that all right.'

'Yeah? But that ain't all. You're scared, see? You're scared because you've lost, and you tell the bastard that I'm wild as hell. And then you go off to the Flapper at what's-its-name – near Nunhead, *you* know, next night, see? And you do the same again – doubling up to win, see? I'll have all the dope fixed there as well, and then we can trim him for a packet both nights – and he can't bleedin' well murmur.'

Jim looked puzzled. 'He can't?'

'Naw. Course he can't. It's the double-cross, see?'

Jim stood up and scratched his head. Gawd! these blokes were hot stuff. Caw! must be fine to be like that. That was the bloody way to live – fooling the mugs. Caw!

When the other two had gone he sat on the edge of the bed and thought it out. Things were going fine, now. He didn't look as if he would be at that showroom much longer. Caw! Only mugs work.

* * * * *

He went to work in the morning, and at lunch-time, with a show of secrecy and wideness, told Swing about the dog. He dangled the bait well enough, because Swing took it straight away and let him leave work at seven o'clock to pick the dog up. They met later on at the track . . .

At eleven o'clock Jim went to the Quarter and asked to see Bill. Bill was in a poker game, but when Jim came up he stopped playing. He put his cards into his pocket, told Mick to keep an eye on his money, and led Jim into a corner. His face was rather flushed.

'How'd it go, Jimmy?' he said.

Jim grinned. 'Easy. The mug put up sixty quid. Thirty he laid with Benny, and the other thirty I stood myself. Here's Benny's thirty. The bleeding dog came in fourth and looked unlucky.'

Bill laughed wheezily, and smacked Jim on the shoulder with a flabby hand. 'Fine! That's first crack to us, eh?'

'You're telling me,' Jim said, and looked cocky and pleased with himself.

'Well, where's the other thirty?' Bill said. Jim pulled another roll out of his pocket and handed it over. Six fivers.

'Thanks,' Bill said. 'You done all right, Jimmy.'

Jim grinned and said nothing. Too bloody sure he'd done all right. Swing had given him thirty-five. He was getting as wide as the rest of them, by God!

* * * * *

With the knowledge that he was outsmarting Swing every so often, Jim took more kindly to working for him. A few weeks in London, contacts with the salesmen at the showrooms; with the Franks; with Mick; keeping his eyes open and being naturally imitative, he was gradually smoothing off the rough edges. He found himself copying more and more the speech of the Franks crowd; more and more the cocksureness of Mick. The salesmen at Swing's who had made fun of his provincial accent, his way of saying 'aowt' and 'abaowt', the burring of his Rs now found the superimposed Cockney language easier to listen to. They were always rather frightened in case they sounded Cockney themselves, anyway. A lot of people in the car business are.

Swing was still polite, but getting uneasy. He was losing a lot of money. When he went to the dogs with the Franks and played their tips he won money. Not so much money somehow, but money anyway. When he went flapping with Bankley he lost. Yet if Bankley went without him the little bastard came back with his pockets stuffed full of money.

The thought never entered his head that he was being given the run-around. Swing was that sort of man.

But on a Friday afternoon, four weeks after the first 'trimming', he discovered what it was all about.

Jim was backing a car into the garage, a car which had been to the 'tyre cutters'.

Clines came up to him as he got out and switched off.

'Get 'em done? Good,' Clines said. Bending down, he looked at each wheel in turn.

Tyre cutting is a fine art, and consists of slicing worn-out covers, trimming off the jaded rubber, and making a new, clean-looking, if very thin tread. What you think of this idea, considering that eight times out of ten the dealer doesn't mention it to you – preferring to rely on his advertisement's 'good tyres all round' – or what you don't think of it, depends very much on the sort of person you are.

'Werl, he's done 'em all right,' Clines said.

Jim grunted, and began to comb his black hair. This was a new habit he had picked up from Louie. Jim was getting particular. After pressure from Louie, and a few good nights with Bill, he had been smartening himself up. The serge suit he had left home in was gone, and now hanging in his room were three new suits, natty affairs which would have gladdened the heart of any Astoria or Corner House boy. The suit he worked in was a little subdued, but his shirt was a shade too bright, a shade too tight in the collar, his tie too striped – and in the wrong way. Jim was one of the Wide Boys, and liked to look the part.

'Going to get a cupper tea,' he said to Clines.

The little man nodded absently. Suddenly he snapped his fingers. 'Oh, I siy. Knoo I meanter tell yer som'p'n,' he said. 'Feller in Swing's orffice. Bin there 'arf hour. Looks like oner yore pals. You know, proper flash boy, an' all.'

Jim put his comb away. Louie had come, maybe. No, wouldn't be Louie. Clines knew him by sight. Better go and have a look-see. Scratching his behind thoughtfully, he went upstairs to report himself back.

As he reached the landing, the office door opened and a young man came out. Just for a second he and Jim looked at one another. Then the man went quickly downstairs and out into the street.

He was one of the Gisberg boys.

* * * * *

At eleven-thirty, the bar at the Quarter was waking up. There were a lot of people in the Club. A few were dancing, but the majority were in the barroom. There had been a big fight at Harringay, with Tommy Farr topping the bill. The West End was full of Welshmen. Gala night for every tart west of Holborn.

Bill Franks was there, drinking miserably at the bar. He was in a bad temper, because he had had a losing night at the City. Both his Good Things had come unstuck most unluckily. He was on the lowest wave of Manic Depression.

Louie had gone off with one of his boyfriends. Mick was working a pin-table in a corner with Benny and Benny's son. Benny's son was a brilliantined, bullet-headed young man with a spread nose. He had been a boxer, and was still considered to have been the best actor who ever entered a ring. But after he had taken a dive once too often, the Board of Control – who show a narrow-minded intolerance towards fight-gambling in general, and giving a boy a few quid to be obliging about the result in particular – decided that the noble art could get along all right without the pride of the Bennys. Since that time he had done nothing.

Jim was dancing. He was wearing a grey-striped suit, suede shoes, and a cocky expression. He was slightly drunk. The girl he was dancing with was pretty, with nice eyes and a soft-looking mouth. But she didn't smell so good.

Split up as they were, none of the Franks crowd saw Swing and his party come in. They came in noisily, and they were looking for Bill. There was Swing, MacRay, Williams, and Johns, from the showrooms – all swathed up in old school scarves and ties. They were all fairly lit-up with whisky, and all ready for trouble, as Bloods should be. Behind them were two of the Gisberg boys.

As the music came to a stop, Jim began to clap his hands. Someone tapped him on the shoulder. Mick.

'Hey, quick! There's going to be a row,' Mick said.

Jim turned round and saw Swing and the boys. Grinning happily, glad to show that snooty swine MacRay that this was *his* territory, Jim swaggered across to them.

'Hullo-ullo, Mac, me old cock,' he said. ''Lo, Mr Swing.'

'Hullo yourself, you crooked, twisting little swine,' MacRay said. 'Been looking for you.'

Jim stopped smiling. 'Why, you Scotch ponce,' he said. 'What the hell are you talking about?'

MacRay's face went very red. Without saying anything more, he swung his right fist into Jim's mouth. Jim went back on his heels, too surprised to feel anything.

MacRay did it again. Jim's mouth felt woolly and wet, and he dropped to the floor. Swing went across to Bill Franks, pulled him away from the bar and hooked him hard in the stomach. 'That's what *you've* been asking for, berk,' he shouted.

Shouting with enthusiasm, the other supporters of the visiting side charged at Benny *père* and *fils*. Several of the Welsh boys joined in, and there was a good deal of noise. After a frantic appeal from the barman, the music began again in the other room. It made hardly any difference.

Jim found himself on the floor with the Williams boy on top of him. Then Williams got up and began weaving and sparring. He was a Public School Man, and fought fair, bless him. Jim scrambled to his feet and swung a left hook at Williams's head. Williams swayed out of distance and rapped Jim over the eye. Jim grunted, and missed with his right cross. Williams jumped in and banged him on the ear. Jim went down and rolled into the corner. He wasn't hurt, but this thing was getting too tough. The best thing was to stay out of trouble, and, besides, he had a new suit on.

Williams was feeling fine. There was nothing to these rotters, after all. He looked round for someone else to clout, and chose Mick. He squared up to Mick and lefted him twice in the mouth. Click, clack – lovely. Just like that. Mick bored in and banged Williams in the stomach. Williams uppercut Mick before he could get clear. Smack! like that. Mick went down. Williams grinned savagely. That made two of the swine. As he stepped back, Mick reached up and grabbed him by the vitals. Williams screamed and collapsed, writhing. As he fell, Mick rolled back and kicked him in the face, flinging him clean across the room like a sack. Williams slumped down against the wall, curled up, holding himself in with both hands. He looked in pretty bad shape.

Bill Franks was handling the two Gisberg boys. He had pennies jammed in between the fingers of each fist, and when he hit – he cut. Mick stepped up and banged his right into the kidneys of one of the Gisberg boys. His face was dead white, and he looked cold. And when he looked cold was the time he was really hot. The Gisberg boy spun round and banged him over the eye, sending him crashing against the wall. But the fool followed up too quickly and was just in time to receive a bottle over the top of his head. Mick jumped clear as the boy went down and kicked the other

Gisberg boy in the stomach. He grunted, straightened up and hit Mick in the jaw. Mick felt his teeth rattle in his head. He shook the Gisberg boy with a left and swung his right hard. He landed on the bridge of the Gisberg boy's nose, and felt the bone splinter under his knuckles. The Gisberg boy's eyes closed and he sagged. Mick brought up a savage knee and finished off the job. He was on fire now, and wanted to keep going. Behind him, Swing was making for the door. Everyone in the place seemed to be yelling at the top of his voice, and there was so much trampling around that Jim got up again. It was safer up than down, the way things were going. As he got up, Swing was just passing him. Jim grabbed him by the shoulder. Swing half-turned, slipped on the squirt of blood by the Gisberg boy on the floor, and stumbled. Jim's right uppercut travelled about twelve inches. Click. It would have been impossible to miss.

Just by the door itself MacRay closed with Mick. He was scared, and wanted to get out of it. Mick was holding him very tightly, and banged an iron-hard head into MacRay's face, four times. It didn't look very pretty after the second time. There were a lot of people fighting now, and the noise was so loud you couldn't hear anything. The Welsh boys were charging about and yelling at the tops of their voices. One of them sent young Benny spinning into a table behind which a man and a woman were hiding. The table went down, and young Benny went with it. Out of the corner of his eye, Jim saw that the woman on the floor had no under-clothes on. The man with her was blubbering with fear and shouting something about the police. He had come up from Epsom to see Life, and didn't like the view.

The noise was worse than the fighting now. More red-capped Welshmen had joined in for the love of the sport. Young Benny got up and threw one of them over the top of the bar and into a corner. The Welshman was very drunk, and didn't seem to feel anything. 'I tell you man, this is grand,' he roared. 'Some fights at home have I seen. But not like this one indeed.'

The barman who had ducked out in the beginning came back again. There were two policemen behind him. The Welshmen got very excited and pitched in harder than ever. You would have thought they were fighting for money.

In the corner farthest from the door, Bill Franks and the larger Gisberg boy were trying to strangle one another. Mick found himself near Jim, just by the door. 'Come on, for God's sake,' Mick shouted. 'Beat it, Jimmy! Beat it!'

Jim put his head down and fought his way through the mob milling in the doorway. Mick was just behind him, and together they raced down the stairs and into the street. Their faces were filthy, their clothes torn, and in their ears was the screech of police whistles.

Up in the Club the room was a shambles. Swing was lying in the middle of the floor, his face bleeding. Near him, draped over a broken stool, was MacRay. He was out cold. In a corner the Williams boy was being sick. His face was a strange colour, and he was looking bad. Johns and one of the Gisberg boys were still conscious, but had lost interest. The Gisberg boy's broken nose seemed to be hurting him a lot. The other boy and Bill Franks were being held apart by the barman and a policeman. Behind the bar itself, the Welshmen were ceasing action with every manifestation of reluctance. It had been fun while it lasted, whatever. But too short, look you!

When the supporting police arrived there was a large crowd on the pavement waiting to see how many pinches there would be. And after a few minutes they found out . . .

The bored policemen took ten men to Tottenham Court Road Police Station, while the crowd jeered and cheered. The policemen remained unmoved. Fights, drunks, jeers, and cheers, what the hell was the difference?

If you were attached to the Tottenham Court Road lot you would appreciate the way they were feeling.

* * * * *

In the magistrate's court on the Monday, no one did very much talking. Swing and his boys were fined ten pounds apiece; the Welshmen got the usual. But Bill Franks had been found carrying a razor, and one of the Welshmen had a cut face. The magistrates knew Bill, the police knew him, and if the authorities at Wormwood Scrubs Prison didn't know him, they were going to have a good chance to do so. Bill Franks received three months.

* * * * *

By the Tuesday morning Jim discovered two important things. He had not very much money, and he was out of work again.

He went down to see Louie, and Louie went to telephone the others. At midday six of them met at Mrs Franks's flat to arrange what to do. Louie and Jim met Benny and young Benny at the corner of the road, and at the entrance to the flats where Bill lived they met Lew. They all went up the stairs together. The door was opened by Mick. He was looking a bit rumpled, and said he was bored with waiting.

Mrs Franks seemed to be in bed. She called out to Louie that she didn't feel well, and would Louie see the boys got all the drinks and things they wanted. Louie looked at Mick. 'Had all *you* want?' he said. Mick just looked at him.

They all sat round a table in the sitting room, trying to figure out what to do. They were all worried – except Benny. They were all Wide Boys, and only Mugs worked and saved money. All the Wide Boys were broke. Bill was inside for a spell, and they looked like being broke until he came out. Life could be a proper bastard sometimes.

'Well, I'm all right, and I dessay I can fix up one or two of you temporary,' Benny said. 'I can do with a tic-tac boy, anyway. Can you do that, Jimmy? That'd be something, wouldn't it? I'll give a few quid a night if you're any good – and what you pick up. You can take it or leave it.'

Jim nodded his head, and felt relieved. 'I'll take it,' he said. 'How long'll it be before I can learn the game?'

'Aw, it's easy,' young Benny said. 'You could pick it up in no time. Any mug can tic-tac . . .'

'Shut your face up, sonny,' Benny said.

The boy looked wild. Hell of a fine old man he had. Talked at you as if you were a bloody kid. 'Yes, dad,' he said.

'You can come along with me tonight, Jimmy,' old Benny said. 'I'll get in a boy who'll put you wise.'

Jim nodded his head again. 'Yes, that's fine,' he said. 'That'll do me fine.'

Louie leaned back in his chair and crossed his plump legs.

'What about you, Mick?' he said. 'What are you going to do?'

Mick looked straight at him. 'I'm taking a holiday,' he said. 'I got some dough saved up. I'll be all right.'

'Going away alone?' Louie said slowly.

Mick just watched him for a second or two. 'Yes,' he said, 'I'm going alone. What are you going to do?'

Louie smirked. 'Oh, me? I've got a friend who'll look after me for a while.' He giggled stupidly.

'You're a schlemihl, Louie,' Lew said. 'Playing around like that. I heard my old man talk about you the other day. He had your old dad in his shop in Berwick Market. You better watch out for yourself. I'm going up to Liverpool for the races next week, so I'll be out of trouble. But you, you better *keep* out of trouble.'

Louie groaned and looked at Jim. 'Gawd! Jimmy,' he said. 'All us Yiddisher boys and our families! Families all the time. Got to do this, got to do that. When you're a kid, when you're an old man – doesn't matter what you are, there's the family behind you, in front of you, spreading out all around you, all ready to start a wail when you give 'em a chance. You're lucky, boy. You've got a casual sort of feeling about your family – but not me. Gawd! I can never get away.'

Benny laughed fatly. 'Your old folks must be wailing most of the time,' he said.

'That's my affair,' Louie said. 'And I'm all right at looking after myself.'

Benny looked thoughtful. 'Werl,' he said slowly. 'I think I – yes, better do it straight away.' He turned to Jim. 'You ain't fixed up any dates for this evening, or this afternoon, have you, Jim?'

'No, not me,' Jim said. 'I'm not doing anything.'

'All right then. You come back with me. I got an idea.'

They all stayed around talking for a bit, and then Louie went off with Mick. Jim, Benny and young Benny went along to the Benny place. It was in a quiet street off Hampstead Road at Camden Town. They walked there.

On the corner of the street a man spoke to Benny.

'Afternoon, Mr Gold,' he said. 'How's it going?'

'Mustn't grumble,' Benny said.

Jim grinned. 'Mr Gold! eh?' Funny, that was. He had always thought of Benny as just Benny. Mr Benny and young Benny. Mr Gold, eh? And young Gold. Ha, that seemed funny.

'What's your name, kid?' he said to young Benny.

'Sid.'

Jim nodded. Sid. Yes, it would be.

They went into a fair-sized house halfway down the street. It was in good repair and well painted. The interior decorating was fairly expensive. Benny Gold had a nice business and salted his winnings. There was a heavy oily smell in the back rooms, and too much furniture.

'Put your hat in this cupboard, Jimmy,' Benny said, and opened the door. Jim hung his hat on a peg. In the corner of the cupboard leaned Benny's stand. The red-and-white painted sign, the boldly lettered satchel, the iron frame and umbrella looked somewhat improbable hiding away in the dark. Jim looked at it all. Caw! wouldn't mind all the money that had been put in that satchel.

'Come on, boy, what the hell're you doing?' Benny said.

In a few minutes Mrs Gold came down. She was a fine, handsome Jewess, with flashing eyes and a figure like the Michelin tyre advertisement. She smiled at Jim and said something about making a cupper tea.

Sid had been sent out.

When they had finished the tea, Jim sitting shy and silent, the Golds talking frenziedly about Mrs Gold's sister's husband, Sid came back. He had a pale, insolent-eyed young ruffian with him, who was introduced as 'Ted'.

'Ted, this is Jim Bankley,' Benny said. 'This is Ted Slode, Jim boy.'

''Lo, Jim.'

''Lo, Ted.'

'How's it goin'?'

'Mustn't grumble.'

Mrs Gold began clearing away the tea things. 'You men will want to be alone,' she said. 'Always leave a man in peace and quiet when he wants to talk business, I always say.' She tittered like a canary.

Jim grinned at her politely. Silly old bitch.

'Werl, Ted,' Benny said. 'Now young Harry's pushed off, I'm thinking of giving Jim here a chance to do his job. Only temporary – see?'

Ted looked Jim over with a cold eye.

'C'n you tic-tac, then?' he said.

Jim shook his head. 'Werl . . .' he began.

'Carm on! Can you – yes or na?'

'Na!' Jim snarled. This chap was a right cowson.

'All right, then. Whyn't yer say so?'

Jim said nothing. He looked at young Benny. He was leaning on the back of Ted's chair, absently picking his nose.

'Werl, you can give Jim the idea, Ted,' Benny said. 'You'll soon fix him up.'

Ted looked annoyed. 'Yerce, but I got to take a bramah to the pitchers 'sevening,' he said.

Benny waved his hands excitedly. 'Oy, oy,' he said. 'Dat's silly! Eight o'clock! You got three hours already. My God, Ted, a smart boy like you – the smartest tic-tac boy I ever got – you don't need that long!'

Ted looked superior. That was right enough. He was a smart boy. He was as smart as a whip, he was.

'All right, guv'nor,' he said. 'You leave it ter me. I'll fix this joker.'

Benny got up and smiled fatly. 'Werl, you get to it, then,' he said. 'Come on, Sid boy. We'll go into the other room. I got some accounts to look at, and Ike'll be here in a minute.'

Ike was Benny's clerk.

When they were left alone in the room, Jim and Ted looked at one another uneasily.

'Werl,' Ted said at last. 'I'll tell you what to do. You ain't any idea at all, I s'pose?'

Jim looked doubtful. 'Werl, I dunno about that. I . . .'

'Aw, shuddup. You better listen. Yerce, you just listen,' Ted said. 'Look, it's like this, see? We're both working for the same guv'nor. Right. Werl, you're in the big ring, and I'm in the 'alf-dollars, see? Geezer comes up to the guv'nor and says what's 'e laying Bright Beauty. Looks at the board. Fours. Right, says the geezer. Four fifties. Guv'nor takes it. Four fifties Bright Beauty. 'E looks at 'is book. 'E's got four fifties down already. The rest of 'is book balances – what 'e's got on the other dogs, see? Whatever wins 'e's made 'is book right so 'e shows a profit, get it? So 'e's in the clear. This geezer's fifty 'e don't want. It's too much. If the dog wins 'e'll be paying out four hundred nicker on the one dog. Na poo, see? 'E don't want the geezer's bet any more than 'e wants a kick in the guts. Right, so 'e signals to you. You signal me. Guv'nor wipes the board clean, see? 'E don't want no more of that one till 'e can cover. In my ring Bright Beauty is maybe showing nine to two – the small ring's sometimes half a jump behind the big money, get it? Right. I get nine to two to fifty nicker.'

'How do you know which dog it is, and that?' Jim said.

'Wait a minute, will yer?' Ted said. 'I get nineter two, and the guv'nor's covered. Race is run, and maybe Bright Beauty wins. So what? Guv'nor loses on 'is book? Na! 'E pays the geezer the two hundred. My bloke in my ring pays me two-twenty-five. Guv'nor wins twenty-five nicker. Dog loses, say. Boss 'olds geezer's fifty. My bloke 'olds my fifty. Boss is covered. I may even 'ave gotter better price and 'e's in a bit, win or lose.'

'Then,' Jim said, and hesitated. 'All the bookies lay 'em off like that, eh?'

'Sure they do.'

'Then no one loses.'

'Don't be a bloody fool, boy. No one loses! It's the first one in, the one wiv the smartest tic-tac man, the one who gets 'is price quick – 'e's the one in the clear. The late ones get stuck wiv it. And that's another thing. You got to let your partner know the prices quick. You got to be first every time.'

'H'm. What's it pay, this job?' Jim said.

'Depends,' Ted said. 'Two, three, four quid a night. Depends 'ow good the boy is, and 'ow good 'is boss is. 'Course, the bookies on the cheap side can't always afford a couple of tac boys – or even one. So some of them drop a couple of og to one bloke who works from the centre of the stand. House Tic-Tac, 'e's called. And a bloody nice job it is.

Pulls in about forty-odd half-dollars and two-og-bits every night. But 'e can't afford no bleeding mistakes, see?'

'Werl, suppose you do make mistakes,' Jim said. 'What happens?'

Ted grinned sourly. 'You'll find out – I 'ope not,' he said.

Jim didn't say anything.

'Right, then,' Ted went on. 'Now 'ere's 'ow we go. You're me for a minute, and I'm you. Boss gives you signal to lay off the bet for the four fifties, see? You wave at me. I wave back at you. Like this, see? Now then. It's four fifties, ain't it?'

'Yerce. Four fifties.'

'Werl. You tap yer right 'and against your left – that's the trap number of the bleeding dog, see? Right 'and on left – One; on left elbow – Two; on shoulder – Three; left 'and on right – Four; on elbow – Five; on shoulder – Six. Got it? All right then. Trap one – right 'and on left – that's right. Four – left on right. Fifties – two fists bang together twice.'

'Two fists,' Jim said.

'Yerce, two . . . oh, I fergot. Fist – twenty-five. Two tap – fifty. Left side of 'ead – fiver; both 'ands – tenner; and so on. I'll give you a list of those later, and you learn 'em. Now then, let's try out some of the or'nary ones. Go on, now. Four fifties . . . go on . . .'

For an hour they worked on it. And at the end of that time Jim had it almost pat. It was only a question of concentrating. It was easy, really, so long as you thought about what you were doing.

When Benny came in again, he found Ted morosely proud of his pupil.

'That's fine, Jimmy,' Benny said. 'I knew young Ted would fix you up. Better make sure of it, though, boy. You'll be on the job ter-morrer.'

'Where is it, ter-morrer?' Ted said.

'Other side of the river – *you* know. And look, Ted, be here at seven sharp. You as well, Jimmy,' Benny said.

* * * * *

The next night Jim turned up early. There was an old and large Daimler outside Benny's house. Whenever you see one of these cars with half a dozen men inside it you can have a bet with yourself that it is going to, or coming from, the races. If you do, you will win.

Ted arrived five minutes later, and when Benny gave the order to start there were six people in the car. Benny, Ike the clerk, Ted, Jim, Sid, and the driver – a remotely hostile man called 'Hey you.'

'Hey you,' Benny called out. 'Go the way you went last time. It was quicker.'

The car rolled along steadily. Jim was sitting with the driver. In the back of the car, the others were arguing about something or other.

In his mind, Jim was going over his orders. Turning them round and round. One, two, three, four, five, six. Seven to two. Nine to two. Six to four. Seven to four. Five to two. Shade of odds on. Fifties. Twenties. Three score. Century. Gawdstrewth!

They arrived early, and Ike unloaded the stand with Sid. A lot of bookies kept their stands at the track, but Benny didn't. His stand was a grand affair in chromium and red paint.

They walked in to the track in a bunch and took up their pitch on the rails. Benny strolled across to another bookie and began some sort of discussion about a man who owed them both money. Sid went to look for a drink, and Ted went with him.

When the stand was ready and the battery working the lights properly, Ike began to get his books out. Jim just hung about. He was getting nervous.

Fifteen minutes before the racing, three men came into the ring. They were big, badly-dressed, and tough. They didn't look too particular. One had a box in his hand, the second carried a small bucket, the third carried the responsibility of looking after the other two.

Ike looked across at them. 'Hell, here they are,' he said, and moved off to get Benny. Jim was left alone.

The three men came up together. 'Chalk,' the first man said. 'Come on. Drop.'

Jim stared at him. 'Chalk? What the hell you mean?'

The man looked bored. 'Aw, carm on. Drop, will you? Chalk, I said.'

Jim looked at the box in the man's hand. There were pieces of chalk in the box. 'You mean – buy it?' he said.

The third man looked annoyed. He was a shade dirtier than the other two, and looked uglier when he spoke. 'Listen, you,' he said quickly. 'What're yer tryin' ter do? Don't waste my bleedin' time. Drop!'

Jim looked at each one of them in turn. 'How much?' he said.

'Half a dollar,' the chalk man said.

Jim hesitated. Then Benny came over. 'Don't argue about it, boy,' he said. 'Hullo, you mugs. Here you are.'

He took a piece of chalk and dropped the man half a crown. The second man stepped up. 'Wet yer sponge?' he said, and grinned at Jim. Jim took no notice. It was that sort of a grin. Benny dipped the sponge in the pail and handed the man half a crown. Jim just stood there staring.

The third man spoke to Jim as he moved on to the next stand. 'Fresh 'ere, aintcher?' he said. 'Werl, that's lucky. You don't want trouble, do yer? Werl then, when yer get the office ter drop – just drop. Yer know now, dontcher?'

Jim said nothing until they had gone. Rotten bastards. He hated even to look at them, yet Benny was talking to Ike as though nothing unusual had happened.

'Benny,' Jim said. 'Who are those mugs?'

Benny looked up. 'Gisberg's boys,' he said.

'Ike Gisberg? The bloke we see at the City?'

'Na. Not him – his brother's lot. Ike's nearly respectable. It's Lew Gisberg's the hot one. Nice gang of boys he's got working for him at that. Eyetalians, Yiddisher boys, slum rats – a bleeding fine collection!'

When Ted came back Jim grabbed him by the arm.

'Listen, Ted,' he said. 'What's this knackers about buying chalk and water from these toughs? I don't get it.'

Ted looked knowing. Nothing pleased him more than giving information. 'Gisberg's boys?' he said. 'Yerce. I'll tell yer. They go abart everywhere, every track – na, not every track, but nearly every track – 'orses, dogs, all the same to them berks. Bookies 'ave to use chalk, 'ave to use sponge and water for their boards. Gisberg's boys sell both, 'alf a dollar a time. Nice business an' all.'

'Werl, why the hell do the bookies cough it up then?'

Ted laughed shortly, and spat. 'Why? 'Cos if they didn't it would be just too bad, that's why. Their stands would get knocked over – kind of accidental, see? And their faces might get trod on – unfortunate, ain't it? And their money would sort of disappear. Na, yer got to drop 'em their whack the way they say.'

Jim felt suddenly angry. 'What!' he said. 'Why don't the bookies go to the perlice?'

'Perlice? Don't make me laugh! What could the perlice do? The Gisberg boys are *selling* chalk, ain't they? What can the perlice do about it? Caw! you always 'ears folks talking about the bookies as if they was in clover. I should cocoa! They pays 'alf a dollar fer their chalk, 'alf a dollar fer their sponge, two og fer their printed cards of the races – the cards of the runners they pin on their boards – *you* know what I mean. All right, it's American gangster stuff. All right – so it is. D'yer think America's the only country where there are blokes like that? Garn, this Gisberg mob 'as been 'anging abart nice fer fifteen years or more. No one can do nuthin' abart it. "Sport er Kings", eh? Dog racin'? Yerce, a bleedin' lot they care about *that*! You got to give 'em their drop or you gets a kick in the belly – or worse.'

Jim began to imagine the worst. 'Yerce, but the public don't know about this, though – or the papers, do they?' he said.

Ted grinned. 'Dunno. Might do. But if anyone finds out 'e keeps 'is mouth shut. Difficult to do anything, reely. And what's the good of buckin' the trouble. See this mark on me forred? That was made by a bleedin' cigar what was aimed for me eye. Na, Jim, you pays yer dollar and yer gets a quiet life. That's the way it goes.'

Jim said nothing. Somehow this sort of thing seemed a lousy trick. It wasn't tough, or smart, it was just dirty. Strewth, what was the matter with people that they could get this way? What was the matter with them? What the *hell* was the matter with them?

That evening he made only one small mistake, and Ted covered it. Benny had a good evening, and they all went home happy.

Mick was still away somewhere, and Louie had temporarily disappeared. And for the next two months, Jim was too busy to worry about either of them. Benny was paying him plenty of money, sometimes £3 a night. He worked four nights a week, and, apart from throwing his weight about in the Clubs, losing a bit on the races, and buying himself clothes and things, he was saving a good deal.

The week before Bill Franks came out of the Scrubs, Jim bought a car, a fourth-hand Chrysler saloon, which cost £35. It made him feel grand, but it was a bum idea because he couldn't get his mind off it. He was Somebody. He was an owner-driver. He was a Wide Boy who had bought a car out of his pickings, by God! He began to get careless, and Benny, at the end of the second expensive evening, told him to clear off. He knew Jim was one of Bill Franks's favourites, and that made him polite about it all. But polite or no, favourite or no favourite, it wasn't good business. Jim Bankley had to go. That was that.

Jim was out of work again.

* * * * *

At four o'clock in the afternoon, six days later, Louie appeared. Jim was in his room, reading a magazine. He was bored, and annoyed with himself. He had met a tart the previous night, and had made a date to take her out in the car for a ride. Somehow he had expected to give her the trip, buy a few drinks, and then get her to give in for nothing. She was a small, bitter-tongued girl, but quick-witted and lively enough. She took the car ride, and seemed to enjoy it, she swallowed the drinks, she was pleasant. She even allowed him to park in a wood and do some reconnoitre work with his hands – but that was all. 'No fear, dearie,' she had said, blast her! 'I got my price. Can't go altering my rules and cheapening myself. You know me. Two quid or nothing. Come on and be a sport now, Jimmy. I got to stick to my rules, dear. Three years ago I might have said yes, but it's no bloody pleasure to me since I . . . since I come out of the Lock.'

He had wanted her too, and would have paid up, but some little corner of him was still with a touch of bourgeois caution. Two quid was a lot for tumbling a judy. And this one, this Doris girl, she was a bit, well, a bit hard-boiled and indifferent. Besides, girls like that, girls who went on the bash every night like she did . . . well, a chap had to look out for himself.

So he spent the afternoon in his room, reading a magazine called *Spicy Yarns*. There was a hell of a fine cover to it. A judy unconscious, sprawled backwards over the arms of a big tough mug. You could see the judy's breasts, and right up her skirt. Caw! it made him feel worse.

Gawd! it was hell having nothing to do when you had no

one to do it with. However he threw a chest at the Clubs, however much he stood blokes drinks, he didn't seem to get friendly with people. He almost envied the bowler-hatted Mugs who went to their homes in the suburbs every night, reading their newspapers, comfortably smug in their conservative opinions. Strewth! they at least had somewhere to go, someone to talk to, someone to sleep with . . .

Louie came in without knocking. He was looking pretty dissipated. His face was white, and there were shadows under his eyes.

'Wotcheer, me old Jim,' he said. 'How's the boy? Been having a right good time, I have. Just got back. Saw old Benny 'smorning, and he said you had scrammed off on your own. How's tricks? Been doing anything good?'

Jim shrugged his shoulders. 'Oh, I'm all right,' he said. Then he brightened up suddenly. 'Seen my car?'

'Yerce,' Louie said. 'Not bad.'

Jim got up from the bed and put on his coat. 'Werl, now you're back,' he said. 'What's the news, eh?'

'News?'

'Yerce. Seen Mick, or . . . or anyone?'

Louie grinned. 'Yerce, I seen Mick,' he said. 'And Bill's back, too.'

Jim turned round. 'He's back? You mean he's out?'

'Yerce. We're going to meet him tonight at his place. You ready?'

Jim felt better. Now things would brighten up again. Good old Bill. What the hell did it matter if he made trouble and started fights and rows? You at least had something to do when he was there. 'Let's get going,' he said.

* * * * *

Bill Franks returned like a giant refreshed. He seemed to bear no ill feeling towards anyone, and inside a week he had picked up all the threads of his complicated and silly existence. All right, he had been in stir. All right – what about it? He had been put away for beating-up the Gisberg boys and that mug Swing. He had trimmed Swing pretty, hadn't he? He and the boys had wiped old Gisberg's eye for him, hadn't they? Well, he had done his three months for it, and it was a bloody good cause. The more a bloke bucked the Gisberg lot, the better for everyone. Around all the Clubs in Soho, Bill was a hero. His luck was right in, too, and on the third night out he took a trip to Wandsworth and 'went through the card'. There was no stopping him.

Jim was in clover. Bill was being very nice to him, and never went anywhere without taking him along. He knew Jim admired him, and that was the reason. The others hung around for what they could get out of it, but Jim was a hero-worshipper, and a tough boy who would do almost anything. The boy was a gambler, too. Give him two tips and he would stack the whole lot off the first winner and put it on the second.

After a few weeks the rush eased off. The White City Derby would be coming along soon, and all the smart money was beginning to come out. Every knowing gambler in Town was laying ante-post bets. They were solid for a dog called War Havoc. War Havoc, they said to you. Gawd! there's a smasher. Watch him doddle home, they said. He had the breeding, he had the speed. It ought to be a lay-down. Bill Franks listened to them. He wasn't sure, and he had to be sure.

He went into a huddle with himself to work it out.

The heats started. War Havoc won the first round by six lengths in 29.80. He won the second round and the quarter finals easily in 29.78 and 29.76. In the semi-final he had a race for it with a fast-breaking dog called Trim Cutlet, catching him on the line to win by a head. Everybody said the favourite was unlucky. The time was 29.84.

More of the Smart Money came out. It was four to one the field, bar one. War Havoc was steady at six to four. Bill Franks listened, and kept quiet. Right up to the day of the race he kept quiet. He was beginning to get an idea.

* * * * *

A narrow door jammed between two shops; a dim passage; worn brown linoleum; two short flights of stairs covered with cheap cord carpet; the wall at the halfway landing badly marked by the passage of innumerable drunks; another door; and then the Club. Three large rooms; in the first, a dozen tables where silent men sat playing cards with their hats on. On the wall beyond them is a green-baize noticeboard. In the middle of this is a printed card about betting slips. The card is dirty, and in one corner of it someone has made an obscene drawing in indelible pencil. The rest of the notice-board holds strips giving the racing results of the afternoon, names and prices, written in board-school copperplate, and pinned up every half-hour by a pimply youth in a skin-tight black suit. The youth's name is Perce, and he looks as if it would be. His face is the colour of a dirty plate, and no one has ever seen him without a half-smoked cigarette drooping from his mouth.

The second room is noisy. There are pin-tables, and a few chairs; a table with some newspapers on it – until they are either stolen or so rumpled as to be unreadable. This room is always full, and it is here the trouble occurs, when it occurs. The man in charge is called Ham. Not Ham anything – just Ham. He is big and fat, squints and has a cauliflower ear. And he smells like acetylene. No one ever remarks on his peculiarities, unless drunk, in which case the remark is only made once. In 1935 Ham did a stretch for throwing two men out of a window.

The third room is larger still, with bare, polished boards

and a piano. This piano, and a saxophone which is played by a talented but consumptive Jewish boy, provides the music for the dancing. Music starts at seven o'clock and goes on, with intervals, until two. There are a few tables and chairs round the walls, and at one end of the room another door leads out to a passage which leads to another door, which opens on to the stairs again. This has great strategic uses. You can follow someone into the Club and think you have him covered, and then find you haven't. The tarts use this door, too, for their unobtrusive entrances and exits.

A few queer young gentlemen come here to dance with one another, or with other young men who are willing to assume the mantle of perversion for the evening and a consideration.

The rest of the mob consists of tarts, touts, ponces, louts, bookies, ex-pugs, petty gangsters, perhaps a stray newspaper reporter trying to feel tough and Metropolitan, and a few fools, like me.

The manager's name is Lew, and he looks like . . . well, he has been there three years and no one has ever got beyond trying to work up the nerve to ask him to cash a cheque.

A mild little overworked waiter called Tony trots in and out with drinks for the boys. He buys these at the restaurant next door – or he says he does. He is there all the time, all day and all night, probably. No one has ever seen him go home. He has a wife and six children, poor little devil, and gets about five pounds a week – losing nearly half of it on the horses, naturally.

If life in this sort of place isn't quite raw, it's pretty underdone, anyway.

There are hundreds of little places like the 'Club' around this part of London, and in every one you seem to be seeing the same people. They are shoddy and garish, wildly extravagant and mean, often dangerous, nearly always unhealthy. They are flush and broke, but they go on just the same. And the Clubs go on just the same, too. They open, the police look in, sometimes they are closed and pop up again in the next street. There is no reason for their existence even, except that they, too, are part of the general joke, and some people manage to have a good time in them. Still, you don't want to go to any, because you wouldn't like it.

* * * * *

Bill Franks led the way in. He had a cigar in his mouth, a good dinner and four whiskies in his stomach, and he felt good. Mick and Jim were following him. They looked, and felt, bored.

As they went into the card room, one of the players nodded and got up from the table. He had just started to deal, and he pulled in the cards and left the pack on the table. He said something to the other players. Then he walked into the next room. He was employed by the house to see nobody took too much money away, and he had not been doing too well. He knew Bill Franks and was glad to see him. Bill was a good hand at picking a dog or a horse, but he was no good at the cards. There was another house player at the table, and things should look a little brighter.

'Well, gents,' Bill said, 'I got an hour to have a little flutter, and then I'm off.'

'Going to the dogs – Derby night, ain't it?' one of the men at the table said.

'Yerce. Sure thing I'm going.'

'Who'll win it, Franks?' the house man said.

Bill shrugged his shoulders. 'Wish I knew,' he said.

The man who had asked, sniffed. He hated Bill, and he clenched his hands underneath the table. You could stand the bastard drinks, let him win at poker, lend him money, do any bleeding thing for him – and he never gave away a sausage in return. 'Wish I knew!' Gawstrewth! He knew all right, the bastard! Or if he didn't, no one did.

They played for half an hour, and Bill lost £10. And while he played, Mick and Jim wandered about the rooms. They fiddled for a time with the pin-tables, talked with some of the boys there. Harry Walcott was there, and he was always interesting to talk to. Harry was a Lad, and he had just come out of the Scrubs and was full of himself. He had done a stretch for rape.

Once Jim danced with one of the girls. She was a tart, and she had the toothache, which made her feel bad-tempered. She was wearing a thickish woollen frock, and smelled of armpits while she was dancing. But Jim got very jovial and knowing with her, and told her a few stories that Benny had told him. He kidded her along all the time, but the girl knew he was with Bill Franks and wouldn't be doing business, so she was not amused. God! it was bad enough to have the bloody toothache, to have to pick up three quid to pay the rent by tomorrow, without having to laugh at a lout like this one – a lout who thought he was funny.

After an hour, and losing £13, Bill decided to go.

When the boys were waiting for him they heard him asking some of the people there to a party he was giving. It was to be in some place in Greek Street which had been hired for the night. A good many of the mob accepted, and Bill threw out his chest, doing his big Popularity Act. He was in fine humour – he never minded losing at cards, anyway – and started shouting and laughing and slapping everyone on the back. Jim didn't hear him mention the address where the party was to be, because he was not paying much attention. He supposed vaguely that Louie would know all about it, anyway.

When they went down into the street, they saw that Louie had brought the Buick along and had parked it behind Jim's car. Louie was asleep, huddled up in the back seat.

Mick drove the Buick, and led the way with Jim just behind him. The traffic was heavy after they reached Hammersmith, and they drove into the car park at the City only ten minutes before the first race. The place was crowded.

* * * * *

Twenty minutes before the Derby came on, Bill led the others outside. Lower down the stand, the Gisberg boys were watching him. They were spread out in a fan, waiting to see what the Franks crowd were going to do.

Bill said something to Benny first. Benny nodded; then he trotted off into the cheap ring. One of Gisberg's boys followed him.

'We'll wait until he's there,' Bill said.

'Which one is it, Bill?' Louie said.

'You'll know,' Bill said.

Louie swore and spread out his hands. 'For Gawsake,' he said. 'Twenty minutes to go and you haven't opened your north and south. I'm sick of this wise-guy stuff of yours, straight I am. All this keeping quiet about everything, and going about with a couple of tame strong-arm men all the time. You're like Al Capone or something!'

Bill flushed a dark red. He turned and took his right hand out of his pocket. Then he hit Louie very hard across the side of the face, knocking his hat off.

Mick nudged Jim and winked. No one said anything.

Bill was taking no more notice of Louie. He was watching the layers' boards down below. His face was still red, and the others knew he was still wild. Louie had pricked his vanity, and that always got him on the raw.

'Gisberg's boys are all over the place, boss,' Mick said.

Bill didn't say anything. He had been strained towards Mick all the evening, hardly speaking to him. He seemed to have something on his mind. And Mick seemed to know what it was, although he said nothing either.

After a few minutes, Bill leaned across to Jim. 'It's all right, now . . . They're pushing out the one I want. Now then. You and Louie go down the far end to Mike Jacobs and Harry Loew, Solly Freed, and the Wandsworth Baby. They're laying threes. Get three fifties Trim Cutlet from all of them.'

Louie pulled his hat on. He seemed to have forgotten about being hit, although his face was red on one side.

'All right. Three fifties. Come on, Jim boy, come on. You take Mike and the Wandsworth Baby. I'll take the other two.'

'What about me?' Mick said.

Bill looked at him. 'You go after them,' he said. 'If the Gisberg boys get funny, you can give 'em some trouble.'

Bill went inside the Club again, and the others went down into the ring.

Jim pushed his way quickly and roughly through the crowd by the layers' stands. Then he waited for Louie's shout. As soon as he heard it, he grabbed hold of the yelling Mike Jacobs, and spun from him to the man on the next stand – a fat, red-faced lout with three chins and a waxed moustache – the Wandsworth Baby. 'Three fifties Trim Cutlet . . . Three fifties Trim Cutlet . . . down to Bill Franks.'

Still yelling their odds, the bookies repeated the bets to the clerks and jabbed thick wet fingers through the prices on their boards. Louie had got his, and the Gisberg mob, crowding in, lost it. All along the line there was the frantic scuffle of a 'Job'. The layers' runners fought clear of the press, shouting like madmen. The tic-tac boys' white gloves worked like high-speed machinery, flashing the message all over the ground, laying off the bets. The price sank out of sight.

Up on the track, the central point, the focus of the

excitement, a 67-pound bunch of muscle and bone, on whom depended a sum of money sufficient to keep several families in comfort for a year, pranced daintily along behind a kennel lad.

In front of the stands this slim-headed Trim Cutlet turned his back on the crowd, and urinated on the grass.

* * * * *

Jim pushed his way up to the top of the concrete steps, dodging Louie and Mick purposely. He wanted to watch the race by himself. He had punted £10 of his own money on the dog.

The six barking animals were in the traps, scuffling at the bars, yelping and restless. On the far side the hare was gathering speed.

The lights over the crowd went out, leaving a huge, restless sea of faces, a huddle of dark-clad bodies, a growing roar of confused noise which died suddenly for an instant or two until the traps shot up. Then uproar from ten thousand throats.

The six dogs broke almost exactly together, their puttering feet tearing at the ground, their bunched muscles heaving and stretching as they flew out on to the brilliant green track. Fifteen yards ahead of them, the hare swerved into the first bend.

Craftily, the dogs, racing now at thirty-five miles an hour, leaned in towards the rails. A brindle in Trap 6 was pushed out wide, slipping and checking to lose three lengths. Trim Cutlet, in Trap 2, squeezed a fawn dog in '1' and bumped through into the lead. He was a big dog with a raking stride. The fawn dog, hardly checked, came up strongly in the back straight and pulled level. Then War Havoc, in the white jacket of Trap 3, got going.

He travelled very fast on the outside with a clear sight of

the hare, bringing the crowd up to the boil, filling the huge stadium with a crash of shouting. At the third bend he moved wide, cannily dodging the bump of the two inside him. Halfway round the bend the three of them were dead level, heads down, their powerful legs flashing, their tails up as they steadied themselves for the run in. The noise of the crowd was like thunder.

Jim kept his eyes glued on the light-blue jacket of Trim Cutlet, saw him squeeze the fawn dog away from the rails as the favourite moved wide. Now they both had a clear sight of the hare, and they went for it. Stride for stride, the light blue and the white jackets flashed in muscular rhythm for the line. They were two lengths clear of the field. Not a foot apart, they raced together, flying past the beam at the finish in a spatter of mud. You couldn't tell which one was in front.

The crowd almost stopped shouting, waiting for the numbers to go up. Jim fixed his eyes on the huge board at the end of the ground. His stomach felt tight and hollow, and his mouth was dry. 'Oh, God!' he prayed silently and urgently. 'Oh, God! make Trim Cutlet the winner. Please, God! I'll do *anything* if you make him win. Oh, let Trim Cutlet win, God! For Christ's sake, Amen.'

Then, to a jubilant roar from the bookies and the violent disapproval of most of the crowd, the result flickered on to the board: '*2. 3. Short Head. Time: 29.71 secs.*'

Jim threw his arms up, yelling at the top of his voice, dancing up and down like a madman. Then he went down to collect. It was the biggest moment in his life.

* * * * *

For the rest of the evening Bill Franks could do no wrong. He had picked the Derby winner, hadn't he? His prize selection had showed the clever boys they were wrong.

Standing in the bar he stood drinks to anyone who spoke to him, and for half an hour that was amusing. After that it became a bore.

Mick nudged Jim with his elbow and moved away. Jim followed him, and they went outside together.

'God! that fat old bastard makes me sick sometimes,' Mick said. 'The way he shows off. Caw!'

'Well, he's done us all a bit of good, hasn't he?' Jim said.

Mick grimaced sourly. Then he looked at his card. 'You doing anything in this one?' he said.

Jim nodded. 'Yerce. I put a couple of nicker on Tenderloin. He's a good lepper at that. Bill said have a go on him.'

Mick gave his short, explosive laugh. '"Good lepper!"' he jeered. 'Got all the jargon, haven't you? "Good lepper!" – strewth!'

Jim flushed up. He had heard one of the press boys use the expression. Blast Mick, anyhow. He tried to crab everything you did.

They watched the parade. There were four dogs this time, because it was a hurdle race.

'Look good, don't they?' Jim said. 'They sort of remind me of people on the stage, the way they go on and do their stuff and then come off again.'

Mick shrugged his heavy shoulders. 'They remind me of something different,' he said.

'Yerce? What?'

'You ever seen people meet for a fox hunt?'

'No. And what's more I . . .'

'Well, I have,' Mick said. 'They come up in their cars – just like these tykes here; trim and well got-up – like these tykes; snooty-looking, and most of them unimaginative, but well bred – like these dogs. They parade up and down, they get started, they fly at the jumps without thinking about it. They race after something they don't really expect to catch. They don't know why the hell they do it, even, except that they and people like them have always done it – like these tykes here. They're silly, laughable, and they're doing nothing except put on a spectacle – like the dogs. And when they're too old to turn out any more they're no use to themselves, and no damned use to anybody else.'

Jim stared at him in amazement.

'Strewth!' he said. 'What's the matter with you, for God's sake? Talking like a book, that's what you're doing!'

Someone standing behind them laughed. It was Louie. He was half-drunk.

'Don't pay any attention to him, Jimmy,' he said. 'He's crazy, old Mick is. And I'll tell you something else. Old Mick's the sort of bastard who'd get into heaven by a trick, or by a special favour at the Gates, and then turn round and tell everyone there that old St Peter had halitosis.'

'Where'd you get all that heavenly-gate stuff, and the old St Peter? You're a Yiddisher boy, Louie, aren't you? Still, it's a good crack, anyway. You must be tight,' Mick said, and laughed.

Louie wagged a podgy finger in front of his eyes. 'Heard a feller say it,' he grinned. 'I don't give a monkey's — about being a Yiddisher or not if I can get a laugh out of a — like you. Boy! that's something!'

Then they watched the race. Skimming round with easy powerful grace, Tenderloin came in by six lengths in 31.33.

* * * * *

The last race is over, and the six dogs, their breath panting loudly, their heads down, walk with the kennel boys to the paddock. The lights go up and the loudspeakers blare out the dance music – negro rhythm watered down and syruped by Jewish commercial enterprise. The last pay-out is done, the last cards torn up. Resignedly, bitterly, miserably, the torn paper floats to the littered ground.

Shouting, whistling, talking, their feet drumming unevenly on the concrete, the crowd flows towards the gates. Louts in puce shirts and gamboge shoes; young toughs with pale faces and loose mouths, losing their quid a week as regular as clockwork; coarse-speaking rascals with whisky voices, raw as onions, owners of cars; three-guinea suits with fifty or sixty nicker in the pockets . . .

* * * * *

By the time they decided to leave, Louie was more than half-drunk. Sulkily contemptuous waiters watched them go, a liftman with the expression of a tranced yogi took them down, and Jim steered the way to the car park.

They found the car easily enough, and Jim propped Louie against the side of it while he took off the radiator muff. Louie was crooning softly.

'Come on, Lou,' Jim said. 'For Gawsake, get in, will you? Come *on!*'

Louie waved an airy hand. 'Jim, you're a lovely boy,' he tittered. 'You're a lovely boy, a bovely loy, a . . . a . . . Jim.' He leaned in through the open window as Jim got behind the wheel, and planted a sticky kiss on his cheek. And Jim, with the whiff of brandy, stale vomit, and cigarette smoke in his nostrils, wiped his face viciously. 'Shut up, that,' he snarled. 'And get in, you boozy sod!'

He was fuddled himself, but he seemed to be holding it, and, apart from an almost unbearable desire to urinate, he felt fine.

He drove out onto the tramlines and accelerated away down the road, but every jolt made the pressure on his bladder worse. And at Shepherd's Bush he stopped the car, darting down the bowels of a convenience like a homing jack-rabbit, finding relief even more blessed in this palace of chromium and tile . . .

Five minutes later the car picked its way through the tangle of Hammersmith and headed on towards town, and, lolling carelessly in the seat, Louie was singing at the top of his voice. But Jim got scared and told him to mucking well keep quiet unless he wanted the cops after them, sniffing their breaths and making trouble.

All the way to Hyde Park Corner Louie alternately argued and sulked, and Jim was as jumpy as a cat. And as they went past the Ritz he turned on Louie savagely. 'A hell of a fine pal you are,' he said bitterly. 'Going to have a cele-bration, eh? All the gang together, eh? We lose Bill and the rest of the boys, and you've lost the address, and you're soused as a herring – so now what?'

Louie sat up straight and pulled his hat on. His face was owlishly serious, but his voice began to whine.

'Ah, come on, Jimmy, don't be peeved over a thing like that. All right, I did lose the address; all right, I did. But anyway . . . look; we've got plenty of money. Let's have some fun by ourselves. We can celebrate without Bill, can't we? Look,' he went on, suddenly louder, 'I know a place. Turn up here. No, not this one – the next. Yes, that's right, the narrow one. It's all right behind . . . That's right.'

Jim swung the car round and drove up the quiet street and stopped when Louie said so. They were opposite a little sandwich bar called Tommy's Place, and it looked harmless and quiet as a vicarage – and it was, or the part you could see was.

Louie went in first. He seemed steadier when he was walking, and almost normal. And he seemed to know his way about, as well. He nodded to the two barmen, and winked.

'Evening, Jock; evening, Bill,' he said. 'Club. Is Mr Howard down there?'

One of the men nodded. 'Yes, sir. He's down there,' he said, and jerked his head towards a door in the corner.

Louie went over and opened it, and he and Jim went unsteadily down the narrow staircase which was on the other side. Louie was in front, and he stopped halfway down and laughed. 'Another stage in your initiation, Jimmy,' he said. 'Another aspect of the human being – or arsepect, I should say. Arsepect – get it? That's funny, isn't it? Well, then, laugh, you schlemihl!'

'Oh, get on,' Jim said. 'Where the hell are we going, anyway?'

At the bottom of the stairs Louie opened a heavy door which led into a basement, and, like the sudden switching on of a gramophone record, a babel of sound came out to meet them. The basement was one long room, and low-ceilinged, and there were too many people there. The combined smells of drink, smoke, and people made the air heavy and stale.

Louie gave a confused shout to someone in the far end of the room, and went ploughing his way through the mob, leaving Jim by himself.

Jim scowled round suspiciously, and someone tapped him on the shoulder from behind. He turned sharply, instantly defensive, and looked into the eyes of a pink-skinned elegant little weed with curly hair and a face like Jessie Matthews.

Just for a second the little man blinked at him, and then squealed with laughter and drew back.

'Oh, my *dear*,' he giggled feebly. 'Too *awful*! You're not Jack at *all*. Really, but you simply must for*give* me! But I *know* you will.' And he moved off, calling out, to nobody in particular: 'My *dear*, so *shaming*! I just stopped a complete stranger, but a *stranger*, my dear, and . . .'

Jim slumped down heavily into a chair which was pulled a little way from a table against the wall. The noise in the room was incredible, with everybody talking, and nobody listening. He looked across the table beside him and saw a girl looking at him. She had sat down almost at the same time as he had.

The girl was quite pale, with a scarlet mouth, and almost black circles round her eyes, and she seemed to have nothing on under a thin silk jumper.

She looked at Jim, and he smiled at her. The drink was getting to work in his head again in the heat of the room, and he felt confident and wide.

'Hello, care to have a drink?' he said.

The girl looked at him carefully. 'Why not?' she said, and called out to a chalk-faced waiter who was pushing through the crowd just behind her. 'Two brandies and sodas,' she said, and the waiter nodded and struggled away.

Neither the girl nor Jim spoke a word until the drinks came, and then Jim woke up. He pulled a big roll of notes out of his pocket – over half of the money he had won was there, nearly twenty-five pounds, and the girl looked at it quickly, flicking her eyes away to see if anyone else in the room had marked it down. The waiter grunted mild thanks at the ten-shilling note Jim peeled off for him, showed no surprise at being told to keep the change, and disappeared.

The girl smiled, leaning forward, her elbows on the table in front of her. With their faces only a few inches away from each other, Jim could see right down inside the gaping neck of her jumper, could smell the mixed perfume of some kind of scent and hot flesh. He smiled slowly, and suddenly found himself talking to her.

He talked big, about how he had had a clean-up on the Derby, about his knowledge of the dogs, about the wideness of himself and his friends. But some innate caution made him keep names out of it, made him fence off awkward questions with generalities.

Their table was in a corner, just by the door that led to the stairs, and as isolated as anything could be in that inferno of noise and fuss. Jim was feeling fine now, everything seemed brighter. This girl, another drink, a place where he could feel he was watching people, and not them watching him, a place out of the way of the stares of these little pansies that talked and giggled at you.

'Where do you live – near here?' he asked.

The girl looked at him. 'Why?' she said.

She could see the way the money was bulging in his breast pocket as he leaned across the table. And she smiled into his eyes. 'Not far from here. Why don't you come up and see me? We could go back there now, if you like, and play the gramophone – or not play the gramophone.'

Jim laughed thickly, and wiped his mouth with his hand. This girl needed some figuring out. He knew she was after it all right, but he couldn't quite place her properly. He had seen tarts, plenty of times, at the Quarter, at the Club, at Greek Joe's, at all the places Bill and his crowd hung around. Loud-mouthed, coarse-swearing bitches raddled up like dummies; lazy bitches who preferred earning a living between the sheets to any other way. But this girl was different. She was well-spoken, her hair grew nicely, and was really blonde, and her hands were the sort of hands you didn't often see on tarts.

He stared back at her closely as he smiled, looking at the bright eyes, the small firm breasts that were pressed together as she leaned forward, and the blood ran quickly in his veins.

'All right,' he said, 'let's go.'

The girl picked up her coat and led the way to the door. They went up the stairs together, and out into the street, and Jim went towards the car at the kerb.

The girl started a little. 'No,' she said quickly, 'not the car. Let's take a taxi. It isn't far, and it would be – better.'

Jim laughed, and waved his arm at a cab that was rumbling past them, heading for Piccadilly.

Before she got in, the girl spoke to the driver, and as the

cab rolled away from the kerb she leaned back in the cushions. And Jim pulled her close to him, kissing her slackly-open lips desperately, his clumsy hands all over her, under her clothes. She laughed softly, holding him tightly, foraging shamelessly for herself . . . But the lights from the shop windows near the Circus flickered in through the windows, the traffic thickened, and the cab slowed down to a crawl, a mere unit now in a tangle of vehicles.

'Please; not now, please,' the girl said shakily, and drew away, straightening her hair. Then, in a moment, she had the door open, and had darted through onto the pavement. Without pausing a second, she ran quickly into the gloom of Swallow Street and disappeared.

For five stunned seconds Jim just gaped after her. Getting out and chasing her was hopeless now, quickly he felt his pockets. Blast her! She had got away with one roll – nearly twenty-five quid; blast her for a crafty bitch! Caw! she'd worked it properly, hadn't she, the cow! Played him for a mug – *him*! Played *him* for a mug, blast her!

Now the driver was shouting at him, asking what the hell was going on. So Jim opened the window and leaned out.

'Where did that girl tell you to go?' he said.

The driver looked round. 'YMCA, Tottenham Court Road,' he grunted.

Jim swore viciously. YMCA – Caw! The bitch had never intended . . . 'Go back where we came from, will you?' he snarled, and flopped back in the cushions, buttoning himself up, cursing bitterly.

Ten minutes later he reeled down the stairs into the basement at Tommy's Place, followed by the protesting squeals of the upstairs barmen. He pushed savagely into the crowd in the basement room, shoving between the tables, elbowing his way through the mob of people, looking for Louie. And over in a corner, his arm round the waist of a pale, fair-haired young man, Louie called out to him.

'Jimbo! Jim!' he shouted. 'C'mere. Here's a frenomine. Here's Tony, good ol' Tony. He's going to take us to a party. We don' have to think about ol' Bill any more. Ol' Bill an' his party is out – *out*! Ol' Tony . . .'

Jim scowled. 'You're drunk, you sod,' he said, 'and I'm sick of this. I'm going back to sleep, I tell you. And if you're coming, you better buck up and come now.'

The fair young man with Louie looked up. 'My *dear*,' he cooed. 'How *pagan*! How *savage*! Louie, you've got to tell me who he *is*! My dear, his *eyes – ter*rifying!'

Someone came over with some drinks, and Jim found himself taking one. He was still blazing angry, and the drink seemed to make him more sober. He swallowed it and took another, and sat down. The fair young man was delighted and very polite, and in five minutes Jim was agreeing to go to the party Louie kept talking about.

'I'll drive the car,' Louie said. 'I'll show you how I can drive – drunk or sober – sunk or drober – shrunk . . . I'll show you!'

'You won't,' Jim said. 'You can't see ten feet. You're too mucking tight to walk, even – and so am I,' he finished up sulkily.

'I'll drive then,' Tony said. 'My dears, this will be such *fun*!' He looked at Jim, pinching his arm almost savagely. 'I'm glad you're coming. I'm simply *longing* to show you off, you *quarrelsome* person!'

'You pinch me again like that, and I'll kick you in the belly,' Jim snarled.

Tony shrilled with laughter. 'My *dear*!' he said. 'Too *Nazi*!'

They went across the room and upstairs by degrees, every step of the way heavy going. Louie was almost paralytic, and Jim bundled him across the pavement and into the back of the car while Tony took the wheel.

They went slowly westward, Jim wrestling with Louie at the back, Tony driving dreamily in front.

Halfway down a wide road off Westbourne Grove they stopped. On both sides the stern houses frowned down with bitter Victorian disapproval. The street lamps too, lit the scene discreetly, as if reluctant to expose the departed gentility.

'Well, here it is,' Tony said. 'Come on.'

He opened the door and helped Jim pull Louie out, and close together the three of them climbed the steps of the house and went inside.

'It's the third floor,' Tony said. 'And for God's *sake* be quiet. There's a fearsome man on this floor – but *fearsome*!'

Louie planted his feet on the staircase and giggled. ''Snescolator,' he said. 'Moves, too.'

Jim scowled and pushed Louie sideways, catching him, as he fell, under the knees and shoulders. Staggering, he carried the inert drunk up the three flights of stairs, dropping him at the top, propping him against the wall. Then he leaned back against the doorpost, panting hard. His heart seemed to be breaking through his ribs, and he felt very hot. Beside him, Tony gave an admiring squeeze. 'But, my *dear*, you must be *terribly* strong,' he said, and laughed.

For a moment none of them spoke, and then Louie gave a quiet laugh and said almost soberly: 'Take your time, Tony. Don't rush him.'

Tony took no notice, and just smiled at Jim again. Then he opened the door with his key. 'Enter, my dears,' he said, 'and be prepared. There will be a lot of queer people here, my Jimmy, but you mustn't mind that. I share the flat with a friend, who is *quite* sweet, but *so* odd.'

The door opened into a short, wide hall, beyond which stretched a corridor with five rooms running off it. Every door was open, and there was a considerable noise going on.

Louie gave a triumphant cry and went straight over to a table in the hall itself, a table with a tray of drinks on it.

Jim just stood still and stared around.

'Like it?' Tony said quietly, and smiled again.

Jim nodded. 'Yes, it's fine,' he said. 'Damn fine.' He had never hoped to see anything like it in real life. It was like a flat in a William Powell film, spare and rich.

Tony was watching Louie out of the corner of his eye, and he held Jim by the elbow. 'Let's go and meet people,' he said.

Together they crossed the hall and went into one of the rooms. There were a lot of people in it, and a large supply of sandwiches and bottles on a sideboard. It was like diving into the sea, and immediately they were swamped.

Everyone knew Tony, and everyone shouted something at him before immediately resuming the monologue where it had left off. And a white-faced girl in a black satin frock and shoes and nothing else, began a bitter speech to Tony, something about a young man of hers. She talked quickly, the words almost strung together, and backed Tony into a corner, where he writhed and bleated pathetically.

There were more men than girls in the room, though everyone was of the same sex, and they all talked and no one listened.

Absently, Jim shouldered his way between a young man in a ragged coat and sandals and another man with black hair nearly a foot long and fingernails to match, bounced off a young exquisite in a blue suit who smelled strongly of lavender water, and picked up a couple of sandwiches. The feeling of strangeness, of being ill at ease, had worn off now. He just felt one more, another interloper into magnificence. He stood thoughtfully, on the fringes of three chattering groups, occasional sentences entering and chasing round inside his head, meaningless and confused.

'My dear, she's no good at all, Myra says her tone values

. . . It's the best thing I ever did . . . smacked his bottom with a strap . . . my new novel is about that, you know . . . it's his Œdipus complex, my dear, sticks out a mile . . . well, Humphrey told me it was Douglas *Fairbanks* that came in . . . have you read *Confessions Of A Pimp*? . . . my dear, I said, who wants to *draw*, anyone can *draw* . . . but his intuitive sense of mass always is obvious, don't you think . . . this chap is a pimp in Marseilles, it's marvellous . . . his mother told me something *disgusting* – it seems that . . . but *everybody* simply *adores* Charley – or don't they? . . . well, it seems that pimps have the most *marvellous* fun . . . and, my dear, when I saw him with *Hugh* I thought I'd *die* with jealousy . . . of course, the real joke was on the wedding night . . . but, my dear, he said the *rudest* thing . . . according to this chap I'm telling you about, Turks have terrific . . . Hugh said "Good God! The man's entirely Freudulent" – *Immortalising* that sort of remark, don't you think . . . my dear, I nearly *died* – but *died* . . . Ronald says that when he got there they were measuring with a ruler – with a *ruler* . . . try one of those sandwiches in the corner. No, not those, they've put too much Marmite on them – *too* awful . . . with Hugh's racing-driver boyfriend – did ninety-two in third gear – *simply* terrifying. And so *draughty*. My dear, my *hair* . . . just Van Gogh and a couple of others, and you don't need any more . . . Marseilles must be . . . of course, Hugh's driver was *quite* handsome, but *smelly*, my dear . . . too much to drink before they came here . . . really, Tony's *nostalgie de la boue* is *too* grotesque . . . rather like that *divine* Helpmann . . . but, I mean, such *toughs* . . . my dear, anyone would think I *wanted* to be representational . . .'

Jim sighed and moved gradually towards the door. As he drifted into the hall, Tony came up behind him. He was looking rather cross and embarrassed, and was red in the face. 'That *awful* girl, Jimmy,' he said. '*Too* embarrassing. And such a *fuss*! My dear, I'm *quite* exhausted, and I haven't had even a *drink*. Come with me to my own room, will you?

We'll shut out those *awful* people and have a quiet talk. My dear, I don't know why we *know* such people. I mean, one gets little pleasure out of it – and it isn't *cheap*. This way, Jimmy. I'm dying to hear *all* about you. That absurd Louie Franks told me simply *nothing*.'

'How long've you known Louie?' Jim said.

'Oh, *ages*. My dear, he's rather . . . well, *you* know. But he knows the divinest *places*.'

Jim laughed and said nothing. He walked slowly beside Tony until they reached the last door at the end of the passage.

'Here we are,' Tony said. 'Come in, and I'll show you *all* the treasures of my boyish home.'

Inside the room there was one light burning, in a pale gold shade on the bookcase which ran all along one wall. The walls were light, the carpet thick, and dark brown. Two queerly formless and colourful pictures, a small reproduction of Marie Laurencin at her most chocolate-boxy, a wide, low divan draped with brown silk . . . it was even more Metro-Goldwyn than the rest of the flat, and just as slightly improbable.

Jim hardly listened while Tony showed him round, invited him to look at the pictures, asked him to punch the divan bed and see how softly firm it was, chattered and asked an opinion about everything.

'You don't go in for girls much, do you, Jimmy?' Tony said suddenly.

'Don't I?' Jim said. He spoke slurringly. His eyes seemed to be floating slightly above the top of his head, and there was pleasant humming in his ears all the time. He sat down heavily on the bed and belched.

From the open doorway the sound of a girl's voice, eager and quarrelsome, rang out as she passed along the corridor. 'I tell you the new medium of glyptic expression offers the most amazing possibilities for abstractionism. Duodinko's

'Choreographic Head' in copper wire and glass has a pure intuition behind it that . . .'

Tony swore softly, and closed the door, and the room seemed quiet, detached almost.

Jim sat slackly still. The phantasmagoria of the evening's happenings flickered across his mind. He could see the lights on the grass, the movement, the black stirring of the crowd, the excitement of everything . . . the car . . . the girl in the taxi . . . the faces here at the party . . . pale, flaccid faces, bright eyes . . . the smell of perfume and drink . . . and now the quiet order of this room . . . cigarette smoke curling bluely from the ashtray . . . London seemed far away . . . like death . . . a car down below in the street changed gear to go round a corner – a Chantrey-Six . . . he could see the works, the long line of cars always moving, always moving . . . men working . . . it all seemed like part, another part, of a dream . . .

Suddenly he felt very tired.

Tony came across the room and sat beside him. 'I'm glad we're alone, Jimmy,' he said thickly, and smiled. He was breathing very quickly.

Jim hardly heard him, hardly noticed him until he started pawing about.

'Jimmy,' Tony said, 'why do you think I wanted to know you? Why do you think I asked that drunken Louie to come and . . .'

Jim's head cleared quickly, as if he had been douched with cold water. Tony was stroking him on the knees and whispering, whispering something that made him sweat.

He stood up quickly, and Tony stood up too.

'You take your hands off me! What the hell d'you think I am?' Jim said fiercely. 'A bloody pansie?'

Tony narrowed his eyes and laughed. 'You don't want to get rough, Jimmy, do you?' he said, 'or – do you want it that way? *Too* caveman, and *too* exhausting!'

He reached out his hand slowly, and Jim made up his mind.

He hooked upwards with his right fist, all the weight of powerful shoulders behind it, and Tony took it in the stomach. He coughed retchingly, and, as he doubled forward, Jim smashed him in the face with a vicious knee, dropping on the writhing figure as it fell. Quickly he struck downwards, socking hard and scientifically on the unprotected jawbone, once . . . twice . . .

Tony gave one groan, and twitched over onto his side before he lay still. Jim got up quickly and went to the door, listening with every nerve, a sickening feeling in the pit of his stomach – but there was nothing. Only talk and noise outside. Nothing.

He turned the key in the lock, and stood thoughtfully pulling at his lower lip. He was breathing very quickly, and sweating with the reaction.

Crossing the room he turned back the bed coverlet and hoisted Tony into it. Quickly he ran through the pockets of Tony's clothes, glancing at the wallet and putting it aside as he pocketed the small change. There was a lot of money in the wallet, and he took it all except three pounds. This would even things up a bit, thank God. Even things up from the mess that tart had made.

He went over to the door, unlocked it, and took out the key. There was nothing for it now but to take a chance, so he went boldly out into the corridor. Some people, two men and a girl, were going towards the hall, just ahead of him. He shut the door quickly behind him, locked it, and pocketed the key. From somewhere he could hear Louie's husky voice raised in song, and, in another room, a gramophone was playing 'Chinatown'. Louie was winning.

Jim wandered into the rooms, trying to locate the singer, cursing as he drew blank.

> *'Ratatattat – three times she shot*
> *Right through the hardwood door.*
> *Into her man – 'cos he'd done her wrong . . .'*

Blast! Have to find Louie and get out of here before the trouble started. And trouble there was going to be . . .

> *'Roll me over easy, roll me over slow,*
> *Roll me over on the left side,*
> *'Cos your bullets hurt me so . . .'*

He went into room after room, trying not to hurry, trying not to panic, looking quickly round with drink-blurred eyes, laughing once at something a girl said to him, not hearing. But when he found Louie he saw it was no good. In another shot the little fool would pass out cold. There was a small, shocked, but admiring crowd round him, listening to an obscene version of the song he was blurring out in a hoarse voice. A small, attentive audience doing some intellectual slumming.

Jim shrugged his shoulders and went out. Louie would have to take his own chance, that was all.

Outside in the corridor, a fat young man in a grey suit and blue suède shoes stopped him with a soft hand.

'My *dear*. This flat! So *eye*-opening, and too *spacious*. Too *spacious*!'

But Jim shook him off. Soft, damp bloody awful hands – like some fat old woman. Too spacious, my backside! Fat fool! What the hell was the matter with him to have to talk like that? Good heavens, what was the matter with any of these blokes? Too much money, or soft living, or something. Good heavens! Made you sick. Just made you sick.

He found his hat on a peg just inside the door, and looked quickly over his shoulder, expecting comment. But no one seemed to notice him as he went out of the place and shut the door after him.

He ran down the stairs like a cat, dodged round the car outside and climbed behind the wheel, praying that the engine would start . . .

By the time someone came running down after him, he was gone.

* * * * *

He drove home carefully. The drink inside his head made every nerve in his body seem on edge, and sharpened his eye-sight even as it distorted. His head seemed weightless, and every now and again the road sliding evenly towards him would lurch and blacken out. Street islands would lean in towards him as he passed, shadows become knots of people preparing to run across the road.

He left the car in the mews, too tired to back it into the garage, and walked unsteadily along the street towards Number 22.

The hall was in darkness, and he fell over the mat as he went inside, cursing savagely.

He took the stairs gently, fighting against the feeling that he was on an escalator, and made the second landing still going well. But outside his own door he stopped, searching for his key. He went through his pockets doggedly and repeatedly. Muck the thing! It was gone. So now what?

Dejectedly he sat on the top stair, leaning his hot face against the wall. A deep feeling of gloom flooded his whole being. He was alone, alone and deserted. No friends, no one to go to, no one to trust. He was all by himself. Drunk – yes. Miserable – yes. All alone. Quietly he began to moan in an orgy of self-pity, his eyes tight-shut, his black hair tousled as he ran his hands through it every few seconds.

Behind him a door opened, and light flooded out. Jim felt his muscles stiffen. A thought came into his mind and stayed there. But he didn't move, and crouched there sobbing.

'Oh, hullo. It's you, is it?'

Good, it was the girl all right, and she was talking very quietly. From the corner of his eye he saw the bottom of her dressing gown, the fringe of a silk nightdress, and mules. She was undressed. Good. Better.

'What's the matter?' the girl said.

Jim stood up, startled. 'I – oh! I'm sorry,' he muttered. 'I've lost my key. And . . . and . . .' he tottered against the wall, 'I'm not feeling very well.'

'You're drunk,' the girl said.

'I'm not. I'm not drunk at all. That's typical of this place,' Jim said bitterly, 'I hate it! I hate everybody. They're all selfish and hard, and no one cares or has any decent feelings left.'

The girl looked closely at him, staring at the pale face and blue eyes, the thick black hair. He was good-looking, wasn't he?

'Well, come into my room a minute or two, and have another look for the key,' she said. 'I'll make some tea. But,' and she hesitated, 'no rough stuff, mind.'

Jim followed her and sat on the edge of the bed, searching his pockets again while she put a kettle on the gas ring. Just for ten seconds the gas burned, and then went out with a pop!

'Damn! No gas,' the girl said.

Jim fumbled in his pocket, pulled out a handkerchief, a roll of bank notes, and a few pieces of silver. 'I've got a shilling,' he said, and watched to see the girl's eyes flicker from it to the notes in his other hand. It was funny, though, but she didn't seem interested at all.

'Thanks,' she said.

He stared curiously around the room, admiring the way

she had made it look comfortable. Decent clean curtains, two good chairs, a table for magazines, a shelf for a few books, gramophone, a hanging cupboard for clothes, screened by a curtain. It was all tidy, and looked pretty good after his own room.

He looked at the girl as she bent over the teapot. Caw! she looked all right, too. Keeping his eye on her, he began to talk quietly and earnestly about himself.

He told her about Swing's, the long hours he had done there, the boredom, the awful people. He described his home, his father, the works. He enlarged on his boredom, the disappointment and loneliness he had found in London, the selfishness of everybody he had met, his almost complete friendlessness, except for the coarse Louie Franks downstairs, a man he *had* to keep in with.

They sat talking for half an hour, and the girl listened sympathetically, even if she talked little herself. She was sitting forward in an armchair, facing the bed, watching Jim all the time. And suddenly he looked her in the eyes and smiled. 'You're fine,' he said. 'It's damned fine to be able to talk to you like this. I never met anyone like you before. I never had a mother, or – or anyone like that. It's all new, being . . .' he stopped, burying his head in his hands.

For a time neither of them moved, and Jim sensed the right moment to act. He slid down on to the floor, putting his head in her lap, his shoulders shaking. He could feel the warm flesh through the thin wrap she had on, and he put his arms gently round her knees. His heart bumped hard as he felt her head go down towards him, her arms round his shoulders.

For long minutes neither of them moved, and all the time Jim's brain was working fast. God, he thought, I'll get cramp if this goes on much longer. The girl was stroking his head, and he could feel her breasts rising and falling as she breathed. He moved back on to his heels and knelt upright in front of her, staring at her with shining eyes. Both of them could feel the tension, and suddenly Jim broke it. He reached out for her, pulling her close against him, kissing her mouth, her face, her throat, and shoulders, just gently enough, just fiercely enough.

Together, on a common impulse, they stood up and strained against one another. Seen close to, as he kissed her, the girl's eyes looked enormous, and he kissed her mouth hard and greedily, his right hand pressing her body to him, stroking the warm flesh . . .

Shakily, breathing hard, he released her and reached to turn out the light. And still neither of them spoke.

The girl made no resistance when Jim forced her backwards onto the bed . . .

Half an hour later he woke and sat up, leaning over her as she lay in the crook of his arm. He stared eagerly at the faint sheen of white flesh in the darkness. Cautiously he shifted his weight, and the girl wakened, her eyes staring up at him as she lay there.

'What's the matter?' she said.

Jim smiled, and kissed her. 'What's your name?' he said.

They both laughed and sat up. 'Anti-climax,' the girl said, and laughed again as Jim looked puzzled.

'Can I put the light on?' Jim asked presently.

'Yes, all right.'

He got up, pulling his clothes straight, doing himself up, wishing he had had the sense to take his coat off. Then he switched on the light. The girl was under the bed-clothes when he turned round, straightening her fair hair, half-hiding her face.

'Well?' Jim said.

'Audrey Thomas,' the girl said. 'That's my name.'

'I knew it was Thomas,' Jim said. 'My . . .'

'Yes, your name's Jim Bankley. I knew that.'

Jim laughed awkwardly, and the girl sat up and hugged her knees. And Jim saw she wasn't very young any more. Now her hair was mussed, and the powder rubbed from her face, she looked different. She was a slashing tart all right, but older than he was – much older.

He strolled slowly across the room, smoothing down his hair in front of the mirror. There was a red crease in his cheek where he had been lying on a fold in the sheet. His clothes were rumpled proper, too. Caw! all those books that described fellers going to bed with girls! They talked about it up to the point where they got going, and then went on after it was over and they had no clothes on. No perishing book he'd seen yet had described the bloody fumbling about with stiff buttons, and the struggling out of a coat. And just look at those bags – for Gawsake!

At the far end of the mantelpiece was a picture of a man. And as Jim stared at it the sound of Audrey's voice in his ears became a meaningless burble. The eyes of the man in the photograph stared back coldly at him. He could feel his stomach contract. He was dead sober now. The man in the photo was Mick.

'. . . if you knew how bored I've been,' Audrey said. 'God! I've sat here some damned nights, wishing I was dead!'

Jim turned round on her. 'Who's this in the picture – this feller?' he said.

The girl smiled bitterly. 'Him? Proper swine – used to be a friend of mine.'

'How d'you mean, "used to be"?'

'Just that. "Used to be". He was a terrible boy.'

'How d'you mean, "terrible"?'

'My God, proper Mister Question-Asker, aren't you? "How d'you mean this?" – "How d'you mean that?" I told you – he was terrible. Fair wore me out. Never saw such a chap. He was generous, though, and a good spender. I always

had a good time out with him. But when he got me home –
well, I had to pay for it all right. He was – sort of . . . vicious.
If you know what I mean.'

Jim nodded, although he didn't know. Then he sat on the
edge of the bed. 'I expect I do,' he said.

The girl looked surprised. 'You don't know Micky, do
you?' she said.

'I – met him,' Jim said. 'He scares me sometimes.'

'Me too. Though in a way I – missed him. I s'pose I missed
what he . . . It was funny you coming along just tonight. You
struck lucky. You were just what I needed – although I didn't
expect it to end this way.'

'End?' Jim said. 'Why should it end? We could have a lot
of fun together, you and me.'

Audrey laughed. 'Have to see about that,' she said. 'My
old sugar might find out.'

'Your old . . . What d'you mean?'

'My God! There you go again. My old sugar – my old
boyfriend, that's who I mean. Though he's not so old, I
s'pose. He used to come to the City Tea Room where I
worked. He "took me out of all that". His wife didn't "understand" him, no kids, the usual stuff. Not a bad old geezer,
though. He's a widower, didn't I tell you?'

'What was this tearoom place then, that he fished you
out of it?' Jim said.

'Oh, just one of those places. It was near the Stock
Exchange. There's any amount of the blasted places in the
Courts around there. They're all chintzy, with armchairs
and sofas, and not too much light. They charge about a bob
for an apple and one-and-six for a cup of coffee, and you get
it served by a pretty girl who isn't a very hard hand-slapper
– God! they get plenty of customers! Stock Exchange men
mostly, they are; dirty old swine who paw the girls about
because they don't get enough from their wives at home.
They all think they impress the girls with their high and

mighty talk, and they're all just slimy, dirty-minded old bastards. God! there's a few wives in damn big houses in the suburbs who would get a shock or two if they had a word with me about the City! Still, it was never hard work – and that was something!'

Jim shook his head impatiently. 'But this old bastard – the one you talked about,' he said.

'Oh, him. Yes, he used to come in sometimes. And he was kind of simple, so I told him how unhappy I was and that. He got me out of it in no time, and found me the room here. Comes to see me every now and then. Proper sexy old boy he is, too, sometimes. He's still soft about me, but still I got to be careful, you know. No good just spoiling things, Jimmy, my dear.'

'How long you been here, then?' Jim said.

'Two months – no, three – no . . . well, I don't know. But what's the difference. All these places are the same. And I'm damned sick of the lot of them. Shopping at delicatessens; making tea on the gas ring; eternal egg-and-bacon breakfasts. Oh, the whole damned thing gets me down sometimes. I'm trying to get my old boy to ditch his scruples and marry me – but he won't – so far. I wish to God there was some way to get away from all this.'

Jim looked unhappy. 'D'you think he *will* marry you, this old boy?' he said.

'If I play the right game he will. That's why I've got to be careful. I lead him up to a point, and leave him there. If you make it a dead line at six inches above the knees they always want to come on. I've had him on the run quite a bit lately.'

'Yerce, but how'd you like being married to an old berk like that, though?'

Audrey laughed. 'What do you think?' she said. 'I can play the game all right. He won't have to grumble, either, because he'll be getting what he wants. And I'll have some spare time, I s'pose.'

Jim laughed. She was tough all right, this girl. You had to admire her for it.

'You and me can step out sometimes, I s'pose, can't we?' he said.

Audrey laughed. 'Be safer if you stepped in once in a while – but not the way you did tonight, see? Tonight was an exception, young man.'

'Yes, but you . . .'

'But I nothing! You were lucky, that's all. You got something for nothing – and that's not too common in this damned town! No, my dear, I've got to watch my step – and people in this house Talk. And anyway, I'm always scared of seeing Micky again. I don't want him up here causing trouble and spoiling everything. I've got to be careful.'

'Well, maybe you're right,' Jim said bitterly. 'I got something for nothing, eh? You're right. It's the first time ever in this bleeding town. Why don't you change your mind and give this old berk the go-bye. I've got plenty of cash.'

The girl laughed, and rumpled his hair. 'Change my mind to what?' said little Audrey – and she laughed and laughed and laughed!

Half an hour later they heard a taxi drive up. There was a lot of blurred argument and swearing out in the street. Then the sounds of Louie stumbling upstairs.

Jim went to the door and opened it, listening carefully. Good, Louie was alone.

He turned and smiled at Audrey. 'Well, that's Franks – my friend. I better get a kip in his room. It'll save a lot of fuss, won't it?'

Audrey sat up and got out of bed. 'Yes, you'd better buzz off,' she said. 'Go on. Good night. No, don't be silly, you don't want to kiss me again. You buzz off. Go on. We'll have another talk later on.'

'Tomorrow night?' Jim said.

'Don't know. Perhaps. But go *on*! You'll be locked out again if you don't hurry.'

Jim grinned at her and went out. He tiptoed down the stairs in time to see Louie fumbling with the door, and he laughed.

Louie jumped round. 'Strewth! You! Where the hell have you been? Proper ol' shemozzle at the party after you went. You . . . my God! I'm going to be sick again . . .' he pushed open the door and stumbled across the room to the wash-basin in the corner; leaned over it, puking his heart out.

Then he went over and sat on the bed. 'God, I feel lousy,' he muttered. 'I can't take it like I could at one time, Jimmy. Grrrrk! Brrrarrp!' And he belched shatteringly as he stooped to unlace his shoes. 'Hell of an uproar when you went, boy. Tony knocked cuckoo in his room and everything. They said you did it, said you pinched his dough, too. I said I didn't know who you were, never saw you before this evening.'

Jim said nothing. He just sat still, watching Louie's face, despising the bleary eyes, the unshaven chin, the stench of stale vomit that filled the room.

'You'll have to watch out, Jimmy,' Louie went on. 'It's all right to go knocking people around, but you don't want to make a habit of robbery with violence. You get the cat for that, boy. The mucking old cat, boy.'

Jim watched him undress and struggle into bed. He curled himself up in the armchair and closed his eyes as soon as Louie turned out the light.

'Mind if I kip here, Louie?' he said. 'Lost my key.'

Louie grunted and flopped into the bed. ''Sall right, I don't care. Good night, boy. God! I feel terrible. Oh God! Graarrarrpp!'

* * * * *

Jim stirred. There seemed to be lights spinning in front of his eyes, spinning round and round, faster, faster, faster, changing colour, swerving in and out. And then voices shouting. He was inside the traps at the White City, and Tony was there and Louie and Mick, and a lot of the people from the party, and the girl who had robbed him. He kept trying to push through the others to get to the girl, to tell her what he thought about her, but the crowd outside was making a terrific noise, and kept distracting him. Inside the trap they were all squashed and cramped together, but the fat young man with the damp hands kept laughing and saying, '*Too* spacious, *too* spacious, *too* spacious,' until Louie pulled out a revolver and shot him. Everybody was talking at once, and the fat young man, with a large hole in the side of his head, began to sing very loudly . . . 'Roll me over easy, roll me over slow . . .' Then Tony started whispering, 'Tell me *all* about yourself,' he murmured, over and over again. 'You don't have to get rough . . .'

Over in the far corner, Louie was being sick again, and beside him, the fat young man was still singing . . . ''Cos your bullets hurt me so . . .' Then Audrey came up and opened the door and said: 'What's the matter? You're drunk, aren't you?' And they all raced past her out onto the track. Jim was in front, and keeping just ahead of Mick, who was racing hard at his elbow. The hare went straight on and dived down into the crowd instead of taking the bend. Mick gave Jim a push, and he fell over, bringing down Tony and Louie as well. 'Too *brutal*!' Tony shrieked. And Louie laughed and said: 'Jimbo, you're a bovely loy, a bovely loy, a bovely loy! Barrarrarrp!' and he belched like a bugle . . . But the hare had swerved off again and was racing away down the tramlines towards Shepherd's Bush. So Jim dodged into the car park and climbed into the car. And Audrey was there in the front seat, in a nightdress, and all the time he drove she was kissing him, pulling him down so that he couldn't see where he was going. The lampposts leaned over and swished at them as they went past, trying to hit the car, trying to wreck them . . . and Jim knew that soon they would get him, knew it, knew it, knew it . . . and then one did and he was lying in the road, dizzy but not hurt badly, although his head was aching. And Mrs Phillips was shaking him by the shoulders and shouting, 'Breakfast extra! Breakfast extra!' into his ear. And all around him were people shouting and pointing at him. Bill, Mick, Benny, Louie, Tony, Swing . . . they all pointed at him, jeering. He looked away from their staring eyes and saw that he had run some people down, two of them. He must have hit them when he crashed the car, and now they were lying very still in the roadway, very still and twisted. And that scared him badly, and he got up and tried to run away. But the others hemmed him in, shouting at him, jeering . . . jeering . . . jeering . . .

Sweating and frightened, he woke up.

Louie was snoring loudly. It was six o'clock, and fairly light. Turning over uneasily, Jim went to sleep again. He was feeling fairly sick.

* * * * *

Late in the morning Benny came up to see them. Mrs Phillips let him in, and he came upstairs by himself. Jim was just coming out of the bathroom, and met Benny on the stairs. They went into Louie's room together. Louie was still asleep.

Benny sat down and spread himself. His round fat face was shining fresh from the razor, and he was smoking a cigar. He didn't say anything at all while Jim was waking Louie.

'C'mon, Lou,' Jim said, banging the little man on the

shoulder. 'Here's Benny wants something. Caw! aren't you ever going to wake up?'

Louie grumbled bitterly. He looked as bad as he felt as he sat up in the bed. His thick hair was tousled and there was a blue stubble on his chin. When he got out of bed and began to pull on some clothes he kept blinking his eyes and belching. He went downstairs to the bathroom without speaking to either Jim or Benny. But when he came back washed and shaved he had perked up a little. His face was pale, with black shadows under the eyes. He came in and put on his shirt and coat, and drank a cup of coffee Jim handed him. Then he faced Benny.

'Hullo, Ben,' he said. 'What's up? What you here about, eh?'

Benny smiled fatly and looked at Jim. Louie said nothing, so Benny said: 'Bill sent me to tell you two mugs to go along to the Greek's place this evening. Five o'clock.'

'What for?' Louie said. 'I got a date for this evening.'

'Cut it then,' Benny said. 'This is business.'

'All this sending people about, all this talk,' Jim said sourly. 'Bill's going to too many gangster pictures. He's crazy.'

'Shall I tell him that?' Benny said softly.

Jim got up and walked to the window. He didn't answer. Benny made him sick.

Louie got up and began looking at himself in the mirror over the mantelpiece.

'Well, you better be there,' Benny said. 'I think there's going to be some fun.'

'What sort of fun?' Jim asked, and looked at Louie. Louie was squeezing out a spot on his chin, his dark eyes narrowed as he watched it in the glass.

Benny got up and flicked the ash from his cigar into one of the saucers on the table. 'It's about Mick,' he said.

Jim looked at him quickly. 'Mick? You say Mick?'

'Yerce, Mick,' Benny said. 'He's been fooling around with old Bill's missus. She says he just made suggestions to her – but nuts to that! I bet they had the old Sir Berkerley all right, and then she got scared. Old Bill's sore as hell about it.'

Louie laughed. 'Well then, Mick won't be such a fool as to show up, then,' he said.

'He'll show up, all right. He don't know Bill knows,' Benny said, and laughed. 'Hope the schmock gets it good and strong.'

Jim didn't say anything. He remembered the way Mick had told him he was fed up with Bill and the piddling little swindles he worked off. He remembered the way Mick had smiled and said that one day he would show Bill where he got off, and no mistake. A lot of the boys were scared of Mick, but they thought he was Wide all right. If it came to a showdown between him and Bill – well, what? No one would bet on which way things would go. And Bill's missus in it, too? Caw, that was a hot one. He had seen her a couple of times. A real hot-looking bramah, a fine flash judy with something to get hold of. Jim licked his lips. Caw! if he ever had a bride to tumble that was like Becky Franks he'd kill any son of a bitch who barged in on her.

Benny went over to the door. 'Well, so long,' he said. 'Five o'clock – and bleeding sharp, see? Thought I'd tell you instead of ringing up. And don't you be late, see?'

Louie nodded his head. 'Right, Benny boy. We'll be there,' he said.

When Benny had gone, Jim sat down on the bed and scratched his head. 'Looks like trouble,' he said.

Louie grunted. 'Trouble? Yerce, you said it. Caw, I hate all this fuss. Mick's a bloody fool to start anything, if you ask me,' he said, and belched resonantly. 'Pardon me,' he said.

* * * * *

As they walked along towards the Greek's place later in the afternoon, neither of them spoke much. Louie was surly, anyway. He was still feeling top-heavy, and his head sang. He thought walking would do him good, so he walked. He knew talking would do him no good, so he kept quiet.

Jim was thinking. And he had plenty to think about. Apart from a few fumbling, clumsy exploits in the park back home, sprawling about with wenches as nervous as himself, last night had been his first conquest. It was the first time he had tumbled a girl in a bed, anyway. And that needed thinking over carefully. Maybe he hadn't been quite tough and casual enough, blast it. Audrey was a slashing tart, and hard-boiled and experienced, too. There wouldn't be any of that worrying he had gone through back home once or twice. Not much chance of ringing the bell there, thank God. No fear, she was no chicken, and she could look after herself. Looked good, too; seemed like a good person to know. And even if Mick . . . yes, Mick . . . mustn't let him find out . . . bound to be trouble. Must get the idea of Audrey marrying that old geezer of hers out of her head, too. Ought to be easy enough to make her see sense if a bit of money was splashed around her.

They turned into Oxford Street. The little black and chromium-fronted shops looked shoddy and impermanent in the sunshine; the large stores pretentious and absurd. At every corner, placards for the Sunday newspapers glared vulgarly back at them. Most of the statements on the placards were of unbelievable stupidity, some macabre, some even menacing. The streets were dusty and not over-clean from Saturday night's hangover. There is no street in London quite like Oxford Street on a Sunday afternoon. It looks third-rate and vulgar, and disgracefully indifferent about both. If the rest of the West End shopping district is fighting hard against the increasing tawdriness of Smart Aleck salesmanship, fighting hard to be elegant even in defeat, Oxford Street just sits square on its behind and cocks a snook with coarse indifference.

They went along slowly, Jim kicking at stray pieces of paper with a careless foot. He wasn't looking forward to this meeting with Mick and Bill. If there was going to be a row there would be a split about it, probably. Bill Franks he didn't like much, but realised just how important he was. And anyway, the boys were mostly afraid of Bill as well as Mick. Thinking it over, trying to work out the best line to take, Jim realised he was going to have a job in keeping up his air of callous toughness. Kicking people in the belly when they started in on you, using your dukes in a fight – all that was easy. Anyone could do that. But this cold-blooded beating-up the Franks mob were capable of, well, God! that was different.

'What's going to happen about this, Lou?' he said.

Louie grunted. 'What? Oh yerce. To Mick, you mean? Bill'll just face Mick out and then tell him to go to hell. He only wants the boys there in case Mick turns nasty. He's a funny-tempered little schmock, and old Bill's had it in for him a long time. I reckon he wants us all to see him tick Mick off, too. There won't be any trouble.'

They went up through Charlotte Street, past the grubby little shops and houses whose continental atmosphere still managed to withstand the ordinary London back-street touch.

In a few minutes they got to the Greek's place. The Club didn't open until eight o'clock, but Louie knocked and rang at the door. After a second or two, a snotty-nosed little urchin dressed in a flannel shirt and trousers opened it and let them in. The passage smelled of onions and unmade beds, and the stairs creaked badly under worn linoleum.

Bill, Benny, and two other toughs Jim didn't know, but had seen before, were upstairs already. Benny and the two toughs were playing solo at a table in the corner. But Bill was sitting slackly on a chair by the window. He looked as surly as a bull.

When Jim and Louie came in, he looked up quickly for a second, and then down again. Louie nudged Jim and led him over to watch the card game. No one said anything.

Five minutes later Mick came up.

He stood in the doorway for a moment or two, looking round the room. Then he closed the door behind him. He was dressed in a light-grey suit, a dark blue shirt and tie. He had no hat. As he looked round the room, a half-smile on his face, Jim thought how tough he looked.

'Hullo, Bill; want me?'

As soon as Mick spoke the card players stopped playing and looked up. Everybody was watching Bill.

Bill lumbered to his feet and stared at Mick. His face was a dull red. 'Yerce, I want you,' he said slowly. Suddenly he began to shout, 'You dirty ponce, I looked after you, didn't I? Picked you up when you were out of the Scrubs, when no one else would look at you! And what do you do, you rotten cowson? Eh, what do you do? You go messing around my wife, that's what. Thought I wouldn't find out, did you? Well, I did, see? Don't you go opening your dirty mouth to start denying it! Caw, I could . . . I could . . .' He stopped, breathing hard, his big face white now, like paper.

Mick said nothing. He just stood leaning against the door, watching Bill's face.

'Well?' Bill roared out. 'What about it?'

'You're barmy,' Mick said. 'I haven't been messing about with your missus. I've only seen her a few times.'

'You had a headache last night, didn't you?' Bill roared. 'Went home early from the party, eh? Knew I wouldn't be home till late and thought you'd take along a bit of sympathy to my missus for being alone, eh? Well, Mr Bleeding Smart Aleck, someone saw you going in – and someone saw you come out – and not for the first time, either. Caw! I ought to . . .'

'Someone's talking a lot of tripe,' Mick said, 'or else you're just trying to start a row.'

Bill moved forward quickly and grabbed Mick by the tie, pulling him upwards until their two faces were only a few inches apart. 'You're right, I want a row,' he shouted. 'You're too cocky, that's what. You're too cocky by half, you little twirp! You haven't been with my missus! You dirty ponce, I *know* you have!'

Mick said nothing. He just went on glaring into Bill's face. So Bill said: 'All right then. Now the boys are going to see what happens to a geezer I employ when he tries on any funny business. You're in a tough spot, Mick, and you're going to take a beating. And then you're going *out*. And you're staying out – see? You can go back to your thieving and your petty con-tricks! You can go to hell for all I care . . .' Suddenly he stopped speaking. He was almost insane with rage, and he threw Mick heavily backwards against the door and banged a terrific punch into his stomach.

Jim felt sick, and expected to see Mick collapse. But Mick just gasped for a second, and then straightened out. He darted forward, slid a little to the left, and banged his right fist hard into Bill's face. The blood spurted out like hitting a sponge; and before Bill could recover, Mick rushed him right across the room, slashing and kicking at him until he fell. Benny, shouting hoarsely, jumped at Mick's legs and took a kick on the ear for his trouble. And then Benny's friends started to move. One of them tripped Mick from behind, bringing him to his knees. The other bashed him in the face with a vicious right. But Jim, hardly knowing what he was doing, pushed in front of Mick, giving him time to get up again, backing with him to the door. Bill was up again now as well, and beside him the other three began to close in. Jim backed against the wall. From being an

167

onlooker, he found himself lined up with Mick – the two of them against four. His stomach felt cold and drawn up, and the sweat was running down his face with funk. Then Mick acted again.

Quickly he jumped at Louie, who was half-behind the table keeping out of danger. He threw an arm across his face, pulling him backwards. There was something shining in Mick's hand now – a razor.

The others stopped short, and Jim, his eyes on Louie's terrified face, heard Mick's voice as if it were a long way away.

'Now, then,' Mick said, panting hard, 'the first that moves – I cut Louie's face open. The first move – that's all!'

'Bill! Bill! Benny!' Louie gasped out. 'Get away! Get back! For Gawsake, get back! Don't let him touch me with that thing. Don't let him! Don't let him! Bill! For Gawsake get away!' his face was working, his eyes staring. He looked like an animal.

Nobody moved for a quarter of a minute. Then Mick said: 'All right. Jim! Open the door, and put the key on the outside.'

Jim looked from him to Bill, from Bill to the others. There was no sound in the room except the quick breathing of them all. Outside in the street the voice of a little girl floated up. 'Mar-eee! Mar-eee! Coming aht ter plaaay?' Jim hesitated. The others were leaning forward, tense as cats, waiting for Mick to give them a chance. Louie was blubbering like a kid.

For an instant Jim met Bill's eye, and nodded. He moved behind Mick to get to the door. Then he crashed his foot into Mick's kidneys, hurling him forward. Mick cried out sharply as he fell, and Louie twisted clear, knocking the razor right across the room. In a moment the others had piled on top of both of them. Still standing at the door, Jim watched Bill, white-faced and sweating, looking for an open-ing. Mick, his arms pinned behind him, twisted half-clear, rolling over on to his side. Bill gave a short shout and bashed his foot into the unprotected face. Once . . . twice . . . Mick gave a choked scream, and there was a spurt of blood.

In a few seconds it was all over.

The others got up and began dusting their clothes. Louie was slouched in one of the chairs, mopping his face and swearing to himself. 'Oh God!' he kept saying. 'Oh, my God! Razors! Caw! Razors! Oh, my God!'

Mick stayed crouched on the floor, his suit torn and spattered with blood. One of his teeth was lying just beside his hand. They could hear his quick gasping breathing, but otherwise he made no sound.

Bill stepped back and straightened his thin hair. He looked a bit uneasy. 'Well, come on, you blokes,' he said. 'We'll leave this dirty schmock here to think it out.' He turned to Mick again. 'And you – Mick – you're through! Get it? We don't want to see you hanging around any more. And don't you forget it, see?'

Mick raised his head. His face was appalling. His lips were so swollen he could hardly speak. He looked at Bill, and his pale eyes were like murder. 'No,' he croaked out, 'I won't forget it.'

Bill smiled sideways. Well, he'd cooled off the Hot Boy all right. He'd showed these other bastards who was the boss. By God! he knew how to handle Mugs like Mick! Let 'em all come. He didn't give a monkey's — for any Tough Guy in the town. He looked across at Jim.

'Smart work, Jimmy boy,' he said. 'You're all right.'

Jim said nothing. He was looking out of the window. He was remembering the way they had handled Mick, remembering that last kick in the face. Underneath the crust he had hardened about himself, underneath the armour of the Tough Guy – he was scared sick.

* * * * *

Louie had gone, and Jim went back alone. He walked slowly, hands deep in pockets, shoulders hunched.

There were a lot of people about now. Tottenham Court Road at the Corner House End had its usual crowd of loafers, eyeing one another, staring hotly after every girl who passed. The girls walked mincingly, mostly in pairs, sometimes in threes, never alone. They had their Sunday best on. They talked to each other about nothing, without listening. Every now and again they gave a peacock-shrill laugh, half excitement, half self-consciousness.

Two girls said something about Jim as he passed them. He knew he looked pretty good in his new suit and his snappy hat, but although he looked back at them he was not really interested. All those judies wanted was a bob's worth in the pictures and a hold-hand. They weren't worth a minute of a Wide Boy's time. He scowled, and walked on. He was feeling pretty low. Poor old Mick, eh? Caw! he was a right bastard all right. But still . . . Gawstrewth! . . .

'There's a Mister Bad Temper for you!' one of the girls said. The other gave the high-pitched, screaming laugh. Silly bitches.

He turned away from Oxford Street because of the crowd. Charing Cross Road was worse – but what the hell? The people there seemed to be terrible. Tiny little Jew boys with even tinier girls; coarse, spodgy tarts who looked as though they slept in their clothes; poxy-looking old men with leery eyes. Caw! what was the matter with everybody? What was the matter with the whole world? He turned aside and looked into the window of a rubber shop. Strewth! did people really need all those things? Seemed to make tumbling a bride look the hell of a complicated business. And that thing . . . and that . . . and that . . . for Gawd's sake! . . . Those books at the back looked hot stuff. Caw! look at that one with the . . . and *that*. Wonder what they charge for them? He turned away thoughtfully. Mick had said something once about books. 'Why not read something decent if you're going to read anything,' he had said, the bastard. Well, books cost money, didn't they? Poor old Mick. Caw! the way Bill . . . Caw! his face. That had been a right bashing they had given him. Wonder what he would do now. What could *anyone* do?

He stopped and looked into Foyle's window. There were some high-toned looking books in there all right. Seven-and-six, ten-and-six, twelve . . . that was a bastard of a price to pay for reading. And what did people want so many books for, anyway? Probably only the mugs who write could tell the answer to that one.

Shaftesbury Avenue was full of people, so he cut through Wardour Street to Coventry Street. In Lisle Street there were a lot of tarts about. The usual sort. Frowsy old bags, most of them, or girls with harsh voices and hair like chromium plate.

He felt low and depressed. A taxi trundled past him and he stopped it. Might as well spend a few bob on going home as having a few drinks he didn't really want.

Leaning back in the cushions, half-sleepy, he stared at the lights, the colours in the shop windows, wondering what to do. He was still scared, and felt very lonely.

'When I get back I'll write to Dad and Ernie,' he said aloud. And funnily enough that made him feel better.

* * * * *

Old Bankley looked round as he reached the gates and called out to the porter. 'Seen my boy Ernie go out, Frank?' he said.

'Yerce. Went out a minute ago.'

Old Bankley nodded. He stood out of the stream of men and waited at the side of the gates, filling his pipe. Ernie seemed to be avoiding him nowadays. And what with

Jim . . . Maybe when you had seen the kids grow up and that you didn't realise they changed all the time. He sighed and lit his pipe, ramming the loosely-packed tobacco down with blackened fingers. Then he walked on with the crowd.

At Number 6 the tea was set and Ernie was reading the paper. There was a letter on old Bankley's plate.

'Letter,' Ernie said, without looking up.

Old Bankley sat down and put his reading glasses on. He slit the envelope with a knife and pulled the letter out. As he read it his lips moved slowly, his eyes narrowing with concentration. He looked across at Ernie. 'It's from Jim,' he said.

Ernie put down the piece of cheese he was about to put into his mouth. This was just as well, because his mouth was full anyway. 'Wasshay?' he grunted. 'Leffum Jim? Bow tibe, too.'

Old Bankley nodded and poured himself a cup of tea. 'Yerce. He says he'll be coming here for a weekend. Next Sat'dy and all. Says he's doing well, the young devil.'

Ernie swallowed violently. 'Huh? *Says* he is. That don't mean anything,' he jeered.

Old Bankley opened the letter again. There was a five-pound note pinned to the first page. He didn't know it, but that gesture had cost Jim plenty of thought.

Ernie looked at the note like a rabbit looking at a weasel. 'Caw!' he said. 'Caw! A fiver!'

He said nothing more all through tea. When he had finished he stood up and went to the door. Then he looked round. 'He's coming *this* weekend,' he said.

His father went on eating. He was reading the letter again. 'Yerce,' he said absently. 'Friday night, or Sat'dy morning. He's coming in a car he's bought,' he said, and laughed. God! this was going to be something to tell his mates down at the Goat tonight. His Jim with a car, and giving away fivers and all. Jim was a hot one, all right. A proper young tough, too, but you had to hand it to him. The old man chuckled, shaking his head.

Ernie went upstairs and shut the door of his room. He sat slackly on the bed, leaning his head on his hands. He was worried. He had seen Betty Wilson at five-twenty, just as she was leaving. And it was no good. Oh hell, hell, hell! Bloody hell! Old Reg had said that stuff would fix her up, and all. Oh God! That made it four months. God! Four months. Too late to do anything. Life was a mess for some chaps. Just when you looked like getting a rise you had to have this crop up. All this for a couple of minutes' fun. Oh God! why hadn't he looked out for himself? Why the hell hadn't he? Another thought flicked into his mind. Perhaps Betty hadn't taken the stuff. Perhaps she thought she had hooked him and it didn't matter! Perhaps she had led him on that night when . . . no, no, that was silly. He remembered the way she had cried and carried on about it afterwards. Proper scared and all, she had been. Wild thoughts of packing his bag and beating off, the way Jim had done, entered his head. If Jim could do well in London, then perhaps . . . no, that was daft too. Oh, hell, hell, hell! Now Dad would make a fuss – and old Ma and Pa Wilson. Caw! What a mess. What a bleeding mess everything was in. Well, they would have to do what Betty said and get married, that was all. Make a small splash, or no splash at all. Half the mugs in the town counted up the months after every wedding. He was going to look a proper fool all right.

Ernie got up and slouched to the window. He had better clean himself up and go along and see old man Wilson. Maybe it wouldn't be so bad being married, anyway. She was a nice kid, Betty. She had been nice, too, that time when she let . . . that time when . . .

Ernie sighed heavily and took off his coat.

Old Bankley shifted his feet restlessly. 'Wish he'd buck up, Ernie,' he muttered.

Ernie sniffed. He was wearing his best suit, and his hair and face shone with cleanliness and attention to detail. If Jim had done well for himself, well so had he. If Jim arrived all dolled up, well so would he be all dolled up. Ernie looked at the well-brushed serge sleeve of his coat, and smiled complacently.

Old Bankley got up and started wandering about the small room. He and Ernie had been waiting half an hour. They were in the front parlour, keeping a look-out onto the street. Stopping by the bay window, old Bankley peered out. Jim's arrival had been heralded. There were several window curtains a-twitch. Old Ma Rhys, the nosey old bag, was in her upstairs front room, peering between the lace curtains and the wall. At Number 20, old Barney was poking his long, dew-dropped nose into someone else's business, as usual. Caw! could you beat it?

Old Bankley sighed. On the piano top a studio portrait of Mrs Bankley stared bleakly back at him. Poor old girl, she would have liked the fuss of all this, wouldn't she? She had always said that Jim was a One. He sighed, and pulled out his pipe. A subconscious twinge of guilt made him look at the photograph again. Mrs Bankley's face seemed even bleaker. He flushed, and put the pipe away again.

From the corner of the street there was the sound of a slick gear-change, and Ernie stood up. That would be Jim; you could tell by the way he changed gear without using the clutch.

With a slight jerk, the Chrysler, well-polished, spotless and shining, pulled up at the kerb.

Ernie went into the passage.

'Wait a minute, Ernie,' old Bankley said quickly. 'Stay

here. Let him come inside. We don't want a reunion in front of the neighbours.'

Ernie scowled and held back. They both waited while Jim got out of the car and stretched himself. He was wearing the grey-striped suit, with a dark-blue shirt and light tie. The hat on his head was small-brimmed, and pulled down over one eye. It was called the 'Ronald Colman Hat', and had been bought in Charing Cross Road. Jim was extremely proud of it, although he failed rather badly to resemble Ronald Colman in any way at all.

Under a battery of curtained eyes, he swaggered up to the front door and went inside the house.

Old Bankley grabbed him by the arm excitedly. 'H'lo, Jim,' he said. 'Thought you were never coming. How's everything going, eh? Come on in, boy.'

Jim came on in. ''Lo, Dad. 'Lo, Ernie.'

Ernie grinned. ''Lo.' He was feeling awkward. He was impressed by Jim's magnificence and easy manner. Old Jim was a proper Boy now, nothing like the lout he had been before.

'Well, how's tricks, Ernie?' Jim said. 'Still at the Works?'

Ernie nodded dumbly. Somehow he felt ashamed of being still at the Works. The grandness of the drawing office seemed futile against London clothes and Chrysler motorcars.

They all went into the back room to have lunch.

'It's only a snack, Jim,' old Bankley said. 'We got to go to tea at old Wilson's 'safternoon. Proper spread-out, I 'spect. It's Ernie's idea, see?'

Jim looked at the table. He was as hungry as hell, and the sausages and mashed potatoes his father brought out of the oven looked pretty good.

They sat down and ate steadily. Jim did all the talking. Wealth and glamour flowed from his lips. He had been everywhere, he had seen everyone. Ernie fed him with questions, believing every word of the answers. But, after the first ten minutes, old Bankley sat silent, just watching. He could see through Jim quite easily. All these explanations of gambling coups, of tic-tac, of booze-ups, of race gangs! It was crazy. Maybe these things did really happen; but if they did, and you came into contact with them, how could you take them as normal? How could you think them unremarkable, and not be shocked and angry into trying to stamp them out? It was all wrong. Men handling huge sums of money as if it were so much paper; boys like Jim, with twenty or thirty pounds in their pockets – money unearned, money picked up and spent with equal casualness. It was all bloody wrong, that's what. Jim was turning, or had already turned, into a Smart Aleck, a Wide Boy, a despiser of the Mugs who worked. If Ernie was impressed with it, well, then, Ernie was a fool. A chap who worked a precision machine, a chap who used his hands to make things, a chap who earned his four quid a week in the shops – he was worth ten of these crooks, these loud-mouthed swine who put their fifty or a hundred quid on some rotten dog or horse, better than any of these crafty little swine that just ponced on society. Why, strewth! It just made you want to spit. Jim was a fool, and one day he would find it out. 'Damn *you*, Jack – *I'm* all right!' There was a fine motto for you! Strewth! the world was like a madhouse if rotten blackguards could sit pretty while a chap who used his hands and his brains for productive work could only hope for a few quid a week as a reward for it. All these gamblers; all these tricksters who hung about the places Jim described so much; all these bastards with their jewelled-up bitches – they were all ponces, that's what. They were ponces, and nothing else.

'. . . nine times out of ten it's in the bag,' Jim said to Ernie, and laughed. He looked at his father. 'You're not saying much, Dad,' he said.

Old Bankley smiled. 'No, I'm just listening to you, boy,' he said.

An hour later they all went out. Jim drove the car round and about the town. At four o'clock he pulled up outside the Wilsons' place. The house was almost exactly like Number 6 Lark Street.

They went in through the gate in single file. Old Bankley did not go visiting much, and was awkward because he was on new ground. Ernie was in agony, because he knew what to expect. Jim felt that the tea party would cramp his style a little, and was annoyed.

They rang the doorbell three times, without getting an answer. Frowning, old Bankley opened the door himself, and put his head inside. He could hear old man Wilson saying something in the back room. 'Those damned Bankleys will be here in a minute, Maggie,' old Wilson said. 'Buck up, for Gawd's sake.'

Old Bankley shut the door softly. Then he knocked. He turned towards the boys. 'Bell's not working,' he said, and grinned.

Betty Wilson let them in and led them into the parlour. There was a good deal of 'no-after-you' and 'no-you-sit-there' before everyone was settled on chairs and sofa. Betty was in charge. She was looking flushed, and wearing a loose smock. Her manner was rather shrill and jumpy, and she avoided looking at, or talking to, Ernie altogether.

Jim lolled back in an armchair and stared tolerantly round the room. He was wishing he didn't feel so much at home. He looked from Betty to Ernie, and narrowed his eyes. So this tea party was Ernie's idea, was it? Looked as if something was up. Looked as if old Ernie had been letting himself go.

Old Ma Wilson, a round, black-clad woman with a puce complexion and grey hair, was ominously silent. Pa Wilson was sweating a good deal. He was talking in rapid undertones to old Bankley the whole time. He talked about the Works. Nothing else interested him. The Works was his whole existence.

Jim felt that if the party was to be saved, then he must save it. He cleared his throat, covering his mouth with a classy lift of his hand. He started to speak at the exact moment that Betty Wilson started.

'Er – if you . . .'

'Do you . . .'

'Sorry,' Jim said. 'Go ahead.'

'Sorry,' Betty said. 'I wasn't going to say anything.'

Jim looked silly. 'No, nor was I. I was just . . .'

'Well, go on,' Betty said.

Ma Wilson sneered. 'There's some that talks and then regrets it after,' she said with sinister slowness.

Betty flushed a deep red, and Ernie looked unhappy.

Jim laughed lightly, and coughed again. He caught Ma Wilson's eye.

'You've dribbled on your tie, young man,' she said.

Tea dragged on. Nobody felt like eating anything. Hardly anybody talked. There was an atmosphere of tension. Jim wished he had not come; old Bankley wished he had the nerve to ask if he could smoke; Ernie wished he was dead.

Betty handed round the plate of sandwiches. They were of bloater paste, and the hard butter had flaked the bread. Ma Wilson's heavily-pressing hand had flattened them out a bit, but they were still rebellious.

Old Bankley, Ernie, and Pa Wilson took one each. Jim, rather absently, took two. He glanced quickly at the others, flushed, and tried to put one back again. His hand jerked the edge of the plate, sending the whole lot to the floor.

'Caw! I'm sorry,' he said abjectly.

Ma Wilson folded in her lips. Clumsy lout, and greedy as a pig. Fat lot of good it was brushing carpets for fools to come chucking bread all over the shop. 'That's quite all right,' she said. 'No offence taken where none intended.'

Jim and Betty picked up the sandwiches. Jim glad of the chance to hide his crimson face.

'Here, less'ave a look at 'em,' Pa Wilson said. He picked one up and blew a piece of fluff from it. Then he met his wife's outraged eye and subsided. He sat back in his chair, holding the sandwich in his hand as if it were something dead. There was an awkward silence.

'Any more . . .'

'Have you . . .'

Ernie and Betty spoke together, and stopped. The others pretended nothing had happened. Old Wilson began praying that someone would talk, because he wanted to drink his tea. No one talked. He raised the cup. Well, here goes. The tea swept through the paltry barrier of his moustache and burst against the sluice gates of his teeth. Checked only for an instant, it rolled on down his throat like water running out of a bath. Ma Wilson and Betty shuddered. Old Bankley felt sorry, and began talking – talking gossip. Had Mrs Wilson heard that the works manager's daughter had left her husband? Did she know that the Rhys down his road had twins? That Tom Richards was going pretty good with the garage over at Natefield? . . .

Betty Wilson sighed. Oh God, this was awful. She had hoped everything would be sort of jolly, and then when she and Ernie made their announcement there would be some friendly remarks and jokes, sort of. It had been a mistake to have told Mother about it first. Oh dear, everything was mistakes. She glanced across at Ernie. Poor Ernie, he looked miserable and unhappy. He must be feeling the strain as well. Poor Ernie.

Poor Ernie, he *was* miserable. The second cup of tea, on top of a few beers, had made him wish he had paid a visit before he had arrived. And what was the proper thing to do? You couldn't get up and just stroll out. You couldn't say: 'Excuse me a minute.' Someone, probably that old fool Wilson, would say: 'Where are you going, boy?' Hell! It was five-fifteen. They would be another half-hour yet – strewth!

Didn't you die, or something like that, if you held yourself in? Your bladder turned to stones, didn't it? Or was it juric acid? Thirty minutes, eighteen hundred seconds. One, two, three, four, five, six . . . oh God! Still, it was lucky the others were talking now, and taking no notice of him. He sat up straight, pressing his knees tightly together.

'How are you gettin' on, Ernie?' old Wilson said.

Ernie jumped. 'Fine,' he said.

Old Bankley looked from Betty to Ernie, and smiled. Poor silly kids. Proper mess they were in, and all. He met Betty's eye, and suddenly made up his mind. He cleared his throat, and waited for a lull in the talk.

'Well,' he said, 'I was pretty glad, Mrs Wilson, when my Ernie told me he wanted to marry your Betty.'

Ma Wilson flushed red. This wasn't right. What was the man doing?

'Yerce,' old Bankley went on. 'I always felt very fond of Betty, and she'll make a good wife, too, I'll bet.'

'Na doubt about that,' old Wilson said. 'Takes after her mother, see?' He grinned ingratiatingly at his wife. He had a lot of leeway to make up, and knew it.

'Not in *all* ways, thank goodness,' Ma Wilson said darkly.

Old Bankley hurried on. 'Well, when Ernie told me about it,' he said, and glared Ernie into a scared silence, 'I thought that was pretty good news, see? And so did Jim here – because Jim made a very nice offer.'

'*I* did?' Jim said. Caw! Dad was going barmy. 'Suggestions!' Strewth! what was he talking about? What was *anyone* talking about?

'Oh? What?' Betty said. She felt she wanted to laugh, or cry. Old Bankley had made it all easy now. Everything was going to be all right after all.

'Werl, you see now Jim's in London, ther's only Ernie and me in Number 6. Plenty of room for us – specially as I go out evenings, see? Werl, *ther's* your home – only tempory of course – but why put it off? And Jim's offered to give you a weddin' present so's you c'n be buying a few new things fer the place – see?'

Jim opened his mouth, met his father's eye, and closed it again.

Mrs Wilson and Betty smiled. Well, that was ever so nice. Mr Bankley was a real gentleman, and *ever* so tactful.

There was a lot of talk, a lot of handshaking. Old Wilson pumped Ernie's hand, patting him on the back. Ernie went white. He was near enough the limit, without being pummelled. Oh God, don't let me make a fool of myself. He clenched his teeth, praying with all his might. Make me hold out, oh God. For heaven's sake, Amen.

Jim sat back, watching them all contemptuously. Pretty flat, all this stuff about marriage. And old Ern was hooked proper, too. Rung the bell already, he had, the mug. Could you beat it? Caw!

He watched his father and the two old Wilsons talking placidly together; Ernie and Betty sitting on the sofa together; Ernie very stiff. Jim swore. He was out of it. The Wide Boy, with his smart clothes, and his money; he was out of it. Well, he was superior, that was why. He was up-to-date and sophiscated – was it sophis – or sophistic? Anyway, these people, *his* people, were just small townees; pathetic, really. He tried to convince himself of it, and couldn't.

Betty looked happy, as if she were getting what she wanted, and the others were pleased because they were relieved; relieved because old Bankley had saved them at the taboo barriers at the last moment. He had saved them from mentioning the unmentionable.

Jim scowled, and lit a cigarette. He was out of it. He glared across at Ernie. Thought he was a wise man, didn't he? Well, anyway, the fool had certainly bagged all the publicity at this party. And what with old Dad tricking a wedding present for the fool, well, blast him!

Ernie gave a strangled sigh. Oh God, just another few minutes, that's all. Just another few minutes. Caw! what wouldn't he give to change places with Jim. Look at him sitting there, easy and comfortable. Look at Dad, old Wilson, Betty . . . oh God . . . he caught Mrs Wilson's eye, and smiled feebly.

'Whatsa matter, Ernie?' Mrs Wilson said.

Ernie flushed red, stood up quickly, and, with his hands clutched into his stomach, stumbled out of the room.

* * * * *

Jim drove back on the Sunday night. He was out of humour, bored, somehow discontented – and the poorer by five pounds.

He drove fast the whole way, his mind turning and turning on the same point. He tried to think about Bill and the others, tried not to feel a silly jealousy of Ernie. What was Ernie, anyway? A four-quid-a-weeker, who was going to marry a girl already in the family way! And yet he was happy about it, and seemed to be looking forward to it, even. Jim scowled. He had heard them talking about it, a lot of silly, sloppy rot. Caw! compare young Betty with a slashing tart like Audrey! Audrey with her wideness, her snappy way of dressing – and undressing – her style, her . . . why, God Almighty! young Betty wasn't in it. And yet she was a nice kid, at that, quiet and nice to talk to if you liked that sort of thing. No, it was all silly. A girl like that just made you into an ordinary bloke, a working stiff, a wage-packet-bringer-homer. No, it was all wet, and no good thinking about. He was going to be a Wide Boy, see? The hell with the lot of 'em!

He pushed the throttle wider open. The lights stabbed ahead, whitening the trees and the grass at the roadside. And the road itself, uncurling blackly, rolling smoothly, raced beneath him. He glanced at the clock on the dashboard. Good. In about another half-hour he ought to be in.

* * * * *

At ten o'clock the Club was full. There was nothing doing anyway, and nothing to do. Jim left the rest of them and went home. The talk, the noise everyone made, was jarring on him. He wanted to get away from the whole lot, from the stink, the silly bloody jokes. He wanted to be alone.

He let himself into Number 22. Mrs Phillips was in the hall. She was reading some postcards, taking them down from the letter rack and replacing them when she had finished. Mrs Phillips took an interest in other people. She liked to know what went on. It added colour to her life. And you would do the same if you lived in one room in a beetle-stinking basement of a rooming house, doing housework for fifteen people or more, dragging yourself through life on twenty-five shillings a week and your bed. Good God Almighty! you would do worse than that, I can tell you.

She brushed the hank of hair from her eyes.

'Evenin', Mr B,' she said. 'Nice evenin' for a change, though it ain't been so bad reely this last few days. Have a nice weekend? Been to see your dad, haven't you? I always say a young feller orter see his family soften as he can, because they sorter worry, and anyway it makes a nice change, doesn't it?'

'Yes,' Jim said. Funny old geezer. Talked like water running out of a tap.

'You're an early bird tonight, Mr B, aren't you? Well, I always say a young feller needs to slow up every so often, or he'll regret it later on when he . . .'

Jim grinned absently, and went upstairs while she was still talking. As he reached the second landing he could see there was a light in Audrey's room. Without pausing, he knocked on the door.

From inside there was whispering and scuffling about. He knocked a second time.

'Who's that?' It was Audrey's voice.

Jim didn't answer. He knocked again.

'Better see who it is,' someone said, and Audrey came over and opened the door. She was wearing a new frock of dark blue, and had mules on her feet. Her hair was slightly mussed. When she saw Jim she went red with anger.

Jim looked past her. So that was the old geezer, eh? He looked at the man who stood awkwardly by the fireplace. He was a shortish, thick-set man, with a pale face and a small moustache. His clothes were good, and he looked as if he fed well.

'Go away,' Audrey said. She turned to the man behind her. 'This is a young man who lives in the house,' she said. 'He . . .'

Jim pushed past her and came inside the room. He had that tight feeling in his stomach. He knew he was behaving like a fool, knew there was no excuse for it, and knew he would have to go on.

'Hullo, darling,' he said. 'Who's this?'

The man by the fireplace coloured up. 'What the devil do you want?' he said. 'Who are you, anyway?'

Jim walked over to him. 'You leaving soon?' he said.

'Jim,' Audrey said. 'You mind your own damned business.'

The man looked surprised. He glanced. '"Jim," is it?' he said. 'I see. Yes. I see. Lives in the house, eh? What are you trying to do, Audrey? Come on, what are you trying to do?'

Audrey sat down on the edge of the bed. What was the use of arguing. He would work it out for himself now. She looked up at him. He looked angry – and jealous. God! yes, jealous. Maybe this was not such a bad line to play, after all. Good God, yes. The man was jealous of Jim.

'Well,' Jim said. 'I'll be seeing you – I hope not.'

'You're not threatening me, are you?' the man blustered. He was scared, and thought he didn't show it.

'Yes,' Jim said slowly. This old boy was nothing.

'Listen, Mr Carden,' Audrey said.

'Listen nothing, Mr Carden,' Jim said. 'Just goodbye.'

Carden looked at Audrey, and picked up his hat.

'I think you're being very silly, my dear,' he said. 'After all ... well ... I ... you know where to find me, when you realise your mistake.' He looked at Jim. 'When you're through with young bullies who won't do you any good,' he said.

'Do you want to be chucked downstairs?' Jim said.

'Do you want me to fetch the police?' Carden said.

Jim laughed. 'Police? Yerce, bloody likely you'll call the police! Look good in the papers, wouldn't it? "Mister Carden, who was in the habit of havin' the old Sir Berkerley with Miss Thomas . . ."'

'Jim!' Audrey said quickly.

'Shut up!' Jim snarled at her. He went on: '". . . with Miss Thomas, said to the magistrates: 'This young feller assaulted me . . .'" . . . Go on, you ain't got a chance!'

Carden swallowed hard. Damned young scoundrel. Like to bang his head against the wall . . . like to . . . like to . . .

'Good night,' he said, going out. He slammed the door after him, without looking round.

Audrey dropped her head into her hands and began to cry. Jim strolled across to the window and looked down into the street. He waited until he could see Carden walking angrily away. Then he laughed. He felt fine.

'You swine!' Audrey said in a muffled voice. 'Why the hell did you have to come messing into my affairs? What right have you got to interfere with me?'

Jim sat beside her. He pushed her backwards until she was lying full length on the bed. 'You're *my* girl,' he said. 'I'll bash any son of a bitch that comes fiddling around you. That old cowson and all the others you met in the Tea and

Tickle place – they're all *out* now, see?' He watched her. By God, this was the line to take, all right. He had got her taped properly.

She looked up at him, glaring into his eyes. He was very strong, and wild, too. It was nice to have a boy like him feeling this way about you. Why didn't the fool follow up his advantage. 'You let me go,' she said.

Jim grinned, and leaned over her. She smacked his face hard, and he laughed at her. She struggled, and he pulled her closer to him, kissing her face, her neck, wrestling with her until she stopped fighting him . . .

Then he got up, and straightened his clothes. 'Werl?' he said.

She scowled. 'You've torn my frock, you lout.'

He laughed. 'Buy another. Buy two,' he said, and threw some notes onto the bed.

She lay back and laughed at him suddenly. 'You win, Jimmy,' she said. 'I never thought you had the guts.' She watched him straightening his tie in front of the mirror. He was a fine clean boy, and as tough as they came. With his money, and his looks, well . . . old Carden could wait – and *would* wait.

Jim came over towards her as she stood up. He put his arms around her shoulders. 'Well, satisfied?' he said. 'I told you once before we would have some fun, you and me. And we're going to – see? Get it?'

'Why don't you?' Audrey said, and looked at him.

'Why don't I what?'

She laughed softly. 'Come and get it?' she said.

* * * * *

During the next few weeks, although Audrey did not get on with or think much of the Franks crowd, Jim felt better. It had been different before, being on his guard all the time, being with boys wider and tougher than himself. It had given him no chance to boast. With Audrey it was different. She didn't like the boys, and kept away from them. Jim was the only link between the Wide world and herself. He could throw out a front, strike an attitude for the first time since he had been in London. Louie he hardly saw, and a good job too. Louie had been bitter about Audrey, but then he was bitter about any girl, the silly idiot. And within a few days of Jim's return from the north, Audrey had said she wanted to move camp.

They found a large double room in a house in Paddington. Most of the other people in the house seemed to be members of that army which exists apparently without money, hanging on to the outer fringe of the theatrical, dance-band world. They were among London's biggest mysteries to Jim. Always 'broke', they were inevitably well-dressed, and had cigarettes and the price of a drink on them. You could see them in dozens wandering about Leicester Square, haunting the Agents, always neat, always hard up. It was a bloody knockout how they lived.

Jim himself was still in funds, for when Bill was operating well, his boys lived well. Audrey was given four or five pounds a week to spend. She lay in bed every day until eleven. Then she had lunch, and went to the cinema. Sometimes she went shopping, sometimes she lounged about. In the evenings she went to the cinema again, or occasionally to the theatre. Jim was on duty four nights a week, and then was not home until about two in the morning. So Audrey found life very pleasant. No work, plenty of time, money to spend, a wild, tough boy to sleep with. Good God, this was something like it. And Jim was easy to handle, too. Just let him talk big, tell you what a smart guy he was; just let him think himself the perfect he-man lover, and it was in the bag.

The third week after they moved into the new room, a young man downstairs discovered that four days a week

Jim was not about the place until the small hours. He was a sensual-mouthed young man who played the guitar in a dance band, when he could find a band to play with. He discovered Audrey's presence by accident, her accessibility by Audrey's design.

A good time was had by all.

* * * * *

But after a time Bill began working the horses. The close season was on for dog racing, and he had to find something else to do. The horses were all right in one way. If you got the smell of a job, the odds were something to look at. But as the smell was something to look *for*, that made it a mixed blessing anyway. New pals had to be made; more difficulties about keeping clear of the Gisberg boys arose; life, often a bastard, became a complicated bastard. Bill cut down expenses. Jim and the boys felt the draught.

Sometimes Bill did nothing for weeks on end, and except for an occasional touch, and what he could pick up at solo, Jim was bringing in no money at all. The car began to be an expense, Audrey began to be an expense, and he realised that he would have to do something about it.

Instead of going along with Bill, doing what he was told, and being paid off, he tried to operate on his own initiative. After all, betting was only a question of being smart and using your head, wasn't it? Full of confidence, and with six pounds in his pockets, he went to Hurst Park.

Fortunately, he bought a return ticket.

* * * * *

Up one week, down the next two, that was the way it went. After a time he had sold the car, told Audrey it was to be laid up for the quarter, and flashed the money he had got for it, pretending he had made a kill on the horses. He didn't know it, but already he had put one foot on the toboggan.

But even with things going badly there was plenty of fun. And all the time he was meeting people whom he before had never imagined possible. There was the Bishop, a middle-aged con man, who looked more respectable than any man had a right to look, and who had done ten years in Parkhurst, in three stretches. There was the Eel, who made a living out of phoney passports. There was Mr Rix, who owned thirteen spielers and was a passionate Baptist.

One evening Louie took Jim along to a cocktail bar in Regent Street. It was a small place, and full. Near to them, as they sat against the wall with their drinks on a table in front of them, a bland, polite-looking man was sipping at a Martini. He was beautifully dressed. His hair was smooth and black, his moustache thick and Guardee. He wore an Old Etonian tie.

Jim watched him, envying his confidence, his poise. Caw! say what you like, it took three generations of being gentlemen to look like that.

The man met Louie's eye and came over. He sat down on the next sofa. 'Hullo, Louie,' he said quietly. 'How's tricks? Doing any good?'

''Lo, Mory,' Louie said. 'Mustn't grumble. How you doing?'

'Okay.'

Louie jerked his head sideways at Jim. 'There is Jim Bankley, Mory. He's with Bill and me. Jim, this is Mory.'

'Mory what?' Jim said.

'Just Mory,' the man said. 'How do, Jim Bankley.'

Jim grinned at him. 'How do,' he said.

Louie began talking in a quiet voice. The dark man listened, but sat stiffly upright, keeping his eyes moving round the room.

A tall, white-haired man dressed in thick tweeds came

into the bar. He saw Mory, and glanced from him to Louie, frowning slightly.

Mory raised his voice slightly. 'Ryahly,' he said, 'I'm afraid I am not able to give any information on that point at all. I am expecting a friend. You . . .' He looked up and met the white-haired man's eye. 'Oh, Major,' he said, 'there you are. Thought I'd come to the wrong place. Afraid I'm not quite up to date with this part of town.' He stood up, and shook hands.

Together, the two of them walked out of the doorway. Jim could hear Mory say: 'Didn't like the look of that feller who was talking to me in there. Lot of funny people about these days. Glad when you came along . . .'

'Who the hell's that?' Jim said.

Louie laughed. 'Him? Name's Mory Levine, or he says it is – sometimes. Other times it's Gerald Mansion, or Arthur Raingeld, or anything you like.'

'Well, what's his line?'

'Share pushing.'

'What d'you mean. What's that? What's he do?'

'Werl, depends, see? Mostly he works this way. He hires a Rolls or a Daimler, and goes down to a place like Marlborough, or Eton, or Oxford – anywhere where ther's a big school, or college, see? He stays in the hotel there when ther's a "do" on at the school. Gets talking to a parent or two in the bar at night. Swell talker he is, too. Talk about any-thing. Get's proper chatty, old Mory does – and then talks politics, or something like that. Says: "Well, I'm glad I've got my little bit in a good thing, the way things are shaping nowadays . . ." All that stuff. Flashes cigars worth a dollar, talks about his car. Plays on the mugs' love of getting some-thing for nothing. Godstrewth, Jimmy, he's unloaded that sort of bloke you saw just now a hundred times. He never misses, boy.'

'Caw! sounds easy,' Jim said.

'So it is – if you've got the bloody nerve, and the looks to go with it. Old Mory *looks* a gentleman, see? But he's got to have guts, too.'

'Guts?' Jim said. 'I don't see what . . .'

'You don't see a lot, boy,' Louie said. 'If he gets pinched selling those phoneys, he gets seven years – and no argument, see?'

'Seven years?'

'Yerce. Seven years. That's the cop. That's why he's getting blokes to work for him on commission. He's got his family and his kids to think about, and he's getting on, see? Of course, the managers of the big hotels he stays at when he's working a job always tip him off if the bogeys have been sniffing around asking questions – Mory makes it worth their while. And sometimes the bogeys themselves have to be paid to lay off. Still, it's worry for a man.'

Jim thought about the smooth, polished Mory. He imagined the big house, his expensive wife, his kids at good schools. Local Boy makes bad. Wide Boy makes good. Strewth, could you beat it? He laughed out loud. What a scream.

* * * * *

Living always on the edge, staying up late, drinking, smoking, it all began to hit back. Jim was of good stock, and the hard work and fresh air he had had at Chantreys had built up his constitution. But as the winter months went past he could feel himself softening. His skin was getting bad, and his wind was short. That the other boys were like that didn't matter. He had grown up enjoying his strength, his vitality, and it annoyed him that it was going back on him. So, to the disgust of Louie, the bewildered surprise of the others, he began to cut out the drink. Several afternoons a week he would go with Sid Benny to a gymnasium and punch the bag, spar, and go through light training with some of the boys old Benny managed. At first it just made him stiff, but as his muscles became supple and his wind mended, he liked it. Sid, bored and half-wishing he was back in the game, took trouble with Jim because he liked him. He taught him all the tricks, good and bad; showed him how to fight like a fighter, and quit boxing like an amateur; showed him the heel-of-the-glove trick, the head trick, the off-balance clinch trick, the elbow trick – and Jim lapped it up.

Sometimes, when he lay in bed at night, he would feel the hardness of his stomach, the powerful weight of his arms, and smile. By God! he was in good shape now. Bill, Gisberg, any of the bastards, had better watch out if they tried anything. If only the money was coming in, everything would be fine.

Playing cards, punting on the horses, punting on the fights at the small halls on Sundays, he was making nothing. His capital was going, his nerve was going. And Bill Franks did nothing. The weeks passed slowly, Audrey spent and spent. Jim began to borrow. And Bill Franks did nothing.

Jim would watch him sometimes, watch him playing poker at the Clubs; watch him lose.

All right then, there was only one thing that could be done, and that's what he would do.

* * * * *

There were a lot of people in the upper card room, but little talk. In one corner six men were at the big table. His back to the wall, Bill Franks faced Jim, who was nearest the door. Jim was winning. The two House men had dropped out, and one was watching Jim closely. The other two players were scared about the way the betting was going, and were just paddling along. Bill was losing badly and not liking it much. He had lost £7 to Jim the previous night, and it made him look silly. In the middle of the table there was a large pile of money.

'Raise ten,' Bill said slowly.

Jim looked at him. 'Me too,' he said.

For a moment no one spoke. The sweat was rolling down Bill's face. He sighed heavily, and put his cards on the table. 'Let's see you, boy. You're crazy. I got a Flush,' he said.

Jim drew a deep breath. 'Full House,' he said.

The man beside him stood up quickly and grabbed Jim by the arms. 'He's a piker, Bill,' he said, 'he's cheating.' He pulled two cards out of Jim's pocket. 'Look.'

Jim's face was dead white. He could feel the blood pulsing in his head, and a small nerve twitching under his eye. He looked at Bill. There didn't seem to be anything to say.

'You . . . you better get out,' Bill said, and suddenly raised his voice, swearing. This dirty cheating little son of a bitch had tried to make a Mug out of him. All right, then. He called over to the doorway. 'Someone go and tell Ham I want him,' he said.

Louie Franks and someone else appeared in the doorway. Jim felt them almost before he saw them, and acted quickly. Pushing back his chair, he heaved the table upwards, crashing it against Bill. He jumped back, hitting the House man in the mouth, and, before the two in the doorway could move, had darted between them. On the next floor he saw Ham waiting for him. He hit Ham in the jaw. Ham grunted, and hit back. The jar of it shook Jim's teeth in his head. He spun backwards and fell against the wall. His mouth tasted salt and sticky. Ham picked him up by the collar and threw him down the stairs to the street door.

Jim crawled to his knees and stood up. His head was singing, and his mouth was swelling up. There was a tear in the sleeve of his coat. Mechanically, he smoothed down his hair. Ham was shouting something at him, and someone laughed, but Jim said nothing. He went out into the street moving as if he were drunk. Caw! what a fool! What a fool . . . what a fool . . .

He stopped a taxi, and opened the door. 'Elmbury Street, Paddington,' he said dully.

The driver looked at him. 'What you bin doin'?' he said.

Jim glared. 'You get going,' he said, 'and mind your own business.'

'Got 'ny money, mate?'

Jim pulled out a handful of silver. 'Yerce. Now get going,' he snarled.

He sat back in the corner of the seat, hiding his face with his hands. He couldn't think clearly, couldn't think . . . think . . . think . . . His head was throbbing, his jaw aching where Ham had hit him. Oh God! what a fool. He'd botched up the whole works now. No one would look at him . . . He was through. Oh God! Oh God! Putting his head on his knees, he began to sob.

He straightened out as the taxi stopped outside the house, and paid up without saying a word. He went in slowly, and climbed the stairs. There was a light in his room, so Audrey would be home.

He opened the door, and went in.

Audrey was lying on the bed. She had a loose wrap on, and nothing else. There was a young man with long hair with her. He was lying half-across her, kissing her shoulders. He jumped from the bed like a cat as he heard the door close, and backed up against the wall, looking scared.

Audrey instinctively pulled the wrap across her, hiding the whiteness of her body. She looked at Jim, staring at his bruised face, the hot anger in his eyes, and was frightened.

'Listen, will you,' the man against the wall said. 'I can . . .'

Jim went towards him slowly. He was breathing in gasps. This dirty swine. This dirty swine. Slinking in . . .

He hit upwards with his left fist, and as the man fell, uppercut him with a right. He went to the door, and opened it. 'Get out,' he said. The man said nothing. He was holding his face with both hands. He wasn't badly hurt, but had the sense not to show it.

When the door was shut again, Jim turned to Audrey. 'You can get out, too,' he said dully. He went across and sat on the bed. There was no one now. No one, and nothing. He was finished.

Audrey came over and put her arms round his shoulders. 'Jimmy,' she said, 'I don't know what made me do it. I don't, I tell you. Oh, Jimmy . . .' Blast him! What a piece of rotten luck, getting caught like that. Lucky he hadn't come in five minutes later. My God!

Jim shook her off, glaring into her face. 'I told you, didn't I?' he said bitterly. 'Get out!'

'Oh, Jimmy,' Audrey said. 'I tell you I . . .'

Jim swore, and hit her across the face. She fell backwards, rolling from the bed to the floor, her face hidden, crying. The wrap fell open, showing the whiteness of her back, her long slim legs, as she lay there. Jim glared at her, the blood beating up in his head. Then he turned away.

What the hell did it matter? What did anything matter? He was finished. He was through, and he had to have somebody. Oh God! what could he do?

He rolled over onto the bed, burying his head in the clothes. He heard Audrey get up from the floor, felt her come over to him. She lay beside him, pillowing his head in her arms. He hated the dirty little bitch for fooling him, but he had to have her. He had to have someone, because he was alone. His face pressed into the warm softness of her breasts, he lay quite still.

She was stroking his head, smiling. Poor old Jimmy. He was such a fool. Such a simple silly fool.

She listened to him as he told her what had happened, and said the right things to him. Her brain was working quickly now. All this business had been fun while it lasted, but now it would soon be over. In a few weeks Jim would be in a mess. The Wide World motto was the only sensible lead: 'Damn *you*, Jack – *I'm* all right.' Every man for himself – it was what Jim himself would have said.

'Poor darling,' she said, 'you mustn't worry about it. You mustn't, Jimmy. Everything will be all right in the end. Poor darling. Poor darling . . .'

* * * * *

In the morning, Jim went out alone. It didn't matter now about Audrey. That other bastard didn't matter either. Nothing mattered any more.

He walked the streets slowly, hands in pockets. It was Sunday, and there were plenty of people about. It was midday when he reached the park.

The crowds round the speakers at Marble Arch were bigger than usual, because all the Stars were out. Bonar Thompson's cynical witticisms; the thunder of the Anti-Communist League; the roaring of the Socialist; the earnest arguments of the man who believes Matter to be Concentrated Thought – they all had a following.

Jim listened to them for a time, and passed on. Down at the end, a little man was just leaving his stand to go home, his audience dispersing. He touched Jim's arm as he passed.

'Hullo, son,' the man said. 'How are you getting on?'

Jim stared at him. 'Who the hell are you?' he said suspiciously.

'Still know what you want, do you?' the man said, looking at him. 'That's what you said in a train, some months ago. "I know what I want," you said. Remember?'

Jim grimaced slightly. 'I remember,' he said. 'I'm doing all right.'

The man smiled. 'Yes,' he said, 'you're doing just about what I expected.'

Jim shook off the detaining hand, and turned away. Silly

bastard, thought he was clever, didn't he? Another minute, and there would have been another sermon let loose. Gab, gab, gab. That was all some blokes ever did.

He walked on along the path. There was a young man sitting on a seat just in front of him. Jim looked at him, meeting his eyes. It was Mick.

Mick stood up as Jim passed, and walked beside him. For a moment neither of them spoke. Then Jim said: ''Lo, Mick. Where you been?'

Mick shrugged his shoulders. 'Scratching about.'

'Doing any good?'

'Sure. I'm fine. You?'

'Me? Yerce. I'm doing fine.'

Mick laughed shortly. 'Go on, Jimmy. Don't let's talk silly. I know you're in the cart, and I'm in too.'

Jim flushed. 'You are, eh? Caw! Everything's proper messed up, isn't it?'

'You're telling me. I heard about you and the boys at the Barn last night.'

'You did, eh? It was a frame-up, Mick, I tell you. I wasn't cheating!'

Mick looked at him out of the corner of his eyes. 'No. Sure you weren't. I know Bill, don't I? He framed me, too. I wasn't sleeping with his missus.'

Jim flushed again. He knew Mick was lying. Mick knew he was. There was nothing to say.

They walked and talked for an hour. At two o'clock they went into a Lyons shop and ate lunch. They were friendly, and felt optimistic now they were together again. The two ex-Wide Boys. All right, then, the other mugs had better look out, because things were going to happen.

In the evening Jim took Mick back home with him. Better play square now, and let him see Audrey. Show him there was nothing to hide.

Mick was amused; Audrey embarrassed; but in a week

the three of them were on easy terms again. Audrey was a little constrained at times when she and Jim were alone, and she would never be in a room alone with Mick at all. Sometimes she went out nearly all day, and was vague about where she had been. Jim hardly cared now, and asked very few questions. He had other things to worry about.

Together, pooling their small capital, he and Mick went to the races. Week after week. The sources from which the jobs leaked out were closed to them. The places where the boys went, they had to avoid. Winning, or getting money, was hard; borrowing it, almost impossible.

After a short time, Jim took another room, a small one in a grubby street. He and Audrey skipped late one night, when their landlady was out. They owed her six pounds, and were lucky to get away with it. Landladies are becoming more and more wary, more and more skilled as time goes on. And small wonder that they are.

Going racing was a habit now, and nothing else. They hardly expected to win any more. Some days they picked up a little, but watching, sweating, and shouting, knowing the damned things had *got* to win . . . got to . . . got to . . . got to . . . made them hate it.

The weeks dragged on. Jim never thought about the future now. He still swaggered, boasted, lied, and spent whatever he had. But he knew he was being licked, and he was afraid.

Once a week he wrote home to his father. Once a week he had to make up lies. He was glad his address still read 'West'. Yes, thank God for that, anyway. 'West' to old Dad still meant West End. Gawdstrewth, that was a laugh!

Nothing was going right now, nothing. Even Audrey was beginning to kick. She kept complaining about giving Jim money; about pawning the valuables he had given her; and avoiding Mick. She was bad-tempered and bitter, and one morning Jim had a shouting match with her which lasted nearly half an hour. He stormed out when it was over, and stayed out all day.

The rotten bitch. He would show her. By God! he would show her, all right.

He went to an early cinema show, and sat chewing his knuckles all through the performance, hardly seeing or hearing it. By God! he would go back and tell that girl where she got off. It would do her good.

He went back late, and let himself in quietly. But in the hallway, the old cow who ran the place made another bawl about the back rent. Silly old fool. 'Pay tomorrow, or get out,' was it? All right, then. All right. That was fine. Let them knock you down! Let them kick you in the face. It was all the same – and – everybody! – the whole world! . . .

He opened the door of his room, and went in. Everything was exactly as he had seen it in the morning – except for one detail. Audrey had gone.

He stood looking stupidly round the room. There was a note for him on the mantelpiece.

* * * * *

Jim read the note slowly. Caw! it wasn't . . . it couldn't be the finish. No judy could run out like this. Not when a bloke was flat . . . oh God! what could anyone do when . . . oh God!

He sat down on the edge of the bed and let the note drop through his fingers. It spun round as it fell, and landed just by his left foot. He could still read it. He looked round the small room. Well, they were going to sling him out at the end of this week, anyway. He stared round at the things in the room, as if they were his own things. The bed was unmade, and rumpled. There was still the water in the hand basin, the water he had used to shave in that morning. There were small clots of congealed soap and whisker floating on the surface of the grey water, just as he had scraped them off the razor blade. The water was dusty, too. Just by his feet he could see a stocking of Audrey's. It had a large hole in the toe. Audrey. Gawd! Audrey! She had run out on him . . . run out. Werl, poor kid, maybe she couldn't stand it any longer. It had been too tough, maybe – and hopeless, too.

He stood up and ran his fingers through his thick curly hair. He felt suddenly deserted and cheated. 'Poor kid' me foot! The rotten bitch! Hadn't he given her everything he'd got – when he'd got it? Hadn't he taken her around, bought her all the things she had wanted? No! God Almighty! She was like all the other bitches in this rotten town. She had just run out on him.

He jammed his hands into his pockets and began striding up and down the room. All right, then, let her run out – all right, let her! Let them all run out. Bill Franks, Louie – blast him! Audrey – what was the difference, anyway? They were none of them any good. Even Mick. No . . . no. Steady on. Mick was different. Mick was going to stick. Mick was all right.

He stopped short and looked down at the narrow street below him. He would have to get some money, have to get away from all this. He turned away heavily and flopped onto the bed. On the pillow nearer the wall he could still smell the scented stuff Audrey had put on her head to set the hair in waves. Audrey. Fancy that old runt of a suburban mug coming round after her. Fancy him being such a goddamned fool!

Jim rolled over onto his back, staring sulkily at the cracks on the ceiling. Someone knocked on the door.

'Carm in,' he shouted. Then he jumped up. 'No! wait a minute, will you?'

He went over to the door and opened it slightly, looking to see who was there. It was Mick.

Mick came in. He just flicked his eyes round the room,

and seemed to take everything in. But he made no remark about it.

Jim sighed and sat on the bed again. 'H'lo, Micky,' he said dully. 'Anything good?'

Mick began walking up and down the room. 'Listen, Jim,' he said, 'I been thinking things out, see? You're flat – and I'm flat. We've got to do something. I've tried every bloody thing I can think of. I even went to see Bill Franks – he nearly went for me again, him and his two new boys.'

Jim looked up. 'We were mugs to have mucked about and lost that job, you know, Mick,' he said slowly.

Mick scowled. 'What's the good of taking that line of stuff, eh? We might have been mugs – and we might not! Who the hell's Bill Franks, anyway?'

'He was the bloke with the payroll, anyway,' Jim said.

Mick stopped prowling, and stood squarely in front of Jim. 'Jim boy,' he said, 'I found out *something*. And it's good.'

'Werl, what?' Jim grunted.

Mick sat down. 'Well, listen, Lew came after me when I left Bill. You know Lew – long-nosed bastard, worked for Benny once.'

'Yerce, I know Lew,' Jim said.

'Well, then. Lew told me he had a job on day after tomorrow. Bill and all the boys are pulling one off at Haydock Park, see? Proper carve-up and all, it is, Jim. They're all going down at eleven o'clock. Lew wouldn't spill anything much – he couldn't, anyway. You know what old Bill is for keeping the boys guessing until the last minute. Still, seems to me if you and I can be on the spot we might get in on the tail end of it. All we want is enough dough to get down there, get in the same enclosure the boys will be in – and then step in.'

'How'd you know Lew wasn't kidding? He doesn't owe us anything, so why should he talk?' Jim said.

Mick smiled. 'No, he doesn't owe us anything, Jim. But he's scared. All Bill's lot are scared. Gisberg is pulling one tomorrow, and he'll have his boys there on the job. Bill's idea is in the same race, and that's going to be unhealthy for someone. I guess Lew thought that if he tipped you and me off about this thing we would help him out if any rough stuff was tried down there.'

Jim frowned. 'Eh?' he said. 'Is old Gisberg in it? Are we going to have all that trouble again? I don't care a damn what Lew wants, or what anyone wants. I ain't getting mixed up with that murdering gang Gisberg totes about with him. All right, then, we win a few quid – so what? We get into a roughhouse with them and we maybe get cut open. Naw, I'm out.'

Mick jumped up. His face was white with anger. 'You make me sick,' he said. 'God Almighty! are you so well off you can pass up a hundred-to-six job? Or are you just plain scared of trouble? Listen, Jim. You're on the mat – we're on the mat – how the hell are you going to get up again? You come in on this, and we can pick up plenty. We'll be on Easy Street again, Jimmy. We can get going and wipe the eyes of Bill and his lot! Just think of it, Jimmy. Come on, and don't be a sucker!'

Jim shook his head and looked obstinate. Well, maybe Mick was right, but he wasn't so sure about it. Those Gisbergs were right cowsons, you couldn't argue about them. They would do anything if their job was balled up.

Mick looked at him, at the worried blue eyes, the sulky mouth. It wasn't any good without Jim. He was tough and he *had* to win. It was only a question of getting him started.

'Oh well, then,' Mick said, and shrugged his shoulders. 'If you're too scared – well, you can pass it up, that's all. But I don't mind telling you that I think you're a fool not to see your opportunity when it comes.' He wheeled round and put his hands on Jim's shoulders. 'Ah, come on, Jimmy.

Where's all the old stuff? What do you care about Bill or the Gisbergs? You and I have licked a few of them before, haven't we? Come on, boy, it'll be fun!'

Jim grinned sheepishly. 'Oh well . . . if . . . well, there's nothing else for it, I suppose. We're on the mat, same as you said. Yerce, all right, I'll do it. I don't care any more what happens.'

Mick laughed and smacked him on the back. 'Fine! That's the bloody way to talk,' he said. 'Now listen. You cough up two quid for expenses – 'fraid I've only got a few bob myself. We can work the platform-ticket dodge on the railway, and then have some dough to spread on the bet.'

'Two quid?' Jim said. 'How d'you mean?'

Mick stopped laughing. 'I mean two quid,' he said. 'You've got two quid, haven't you?'

Jim shook his head. 'No. I *had* a few quid – or that cow Audrey had, anyway – but now I haven't. The bitch ran out on me. Just now.' He stood up, pushing his fists deep into his trousers pockets. 'Dirty little cheat!' he shouted. 'I tell you I gave that damn girl everything I had. And then she has to go slinking off with her rotten old cowson, with his pathetic spiel and his house in some suburb! God! I could . . . I could . . . the bitch! No. I haven't got any two quid. I'm cleaned . . . *cleaned* . . . CLEANED! See?'

Mick watched Jim in silence. Silly bastard, Jimmy. Always showed over everybody what was the matter with him. He could no more keep a poker face about his troubles than fly. Well, he was a fool, that's all.

Jim walked up and down the room, trying to calm down. 'Well, so what are we going to do, eh?' he said.

Mick scratched his head and swore. 'Yes, what the hell *are* we going to do?' he said.

'Pity you didn't try a touch with Lew,' Jim said.

'Don't be a sap. I owe Lew plenty already. I owe everybody plenty. I've hocked everything. I'm cleaned.'

Jim said nothing. He could have said exactly the same as Mick.

'Well, what's going to happen then?' he said.

Mick buttoned up his coat. 'I'll tell you what's going to happen. I'm going to make a touch. Dunno where, or from whom. But I'm going to make a touch *some*where. This is the only chance we got to get in the clear. We've got to have a few quid by tomorrow, Jimmy.' He went to the door and opened it. 'I'll see you later. And don't you go away from here. You've got to stick here until I get back, see?'

Jim nodded, and stared. He went on staring long after Mick had gone. It was eight o'clock. All right, he would wait until midnight. Maybe Mick could do something after all. He knew that Mick was the only chance, that he himself could do nothing. It was funny the way people were. You could be a crook, you could do a stretch for rape, like Harry Walcott, you could be a razor boy, like Slim Benotti who worked for Gisberg – but you couldn't be caught cheating in a bloody silly card game. It was daft, but you couldn't do it. Oh God! he had been a fool, the biggest, bloodiest fool in the world. Just that one damn silly mistake, and now everything was bust. Strewth, life was a bastard for some chaps, and all.

If he had the money now he would go up West for a drink, and go to a cinema. By himself. It would be a change, sort of. Like the old days.

He swore bitterly and lay on the bed. Well, he was broke, so he would just have to wait.

At half-past ten Mick came back. He looked tired. Jim opened the door as soon as he knocked. Mick came in and flopped down onto the bed. 'Oooh, Gawd! I'm shagged. Been all over the place, boy. All the Clubs I'm not too well known at. All the pubs. All the old pals! Then I went down to see Benny – and that did it.'

Jim looked quickly at him. 'Benny?' he said. 'Thought he was in Manchester.'

'H'm. Well, so he was. He got back last week. He didn't like to see me. Didn't show any signs of enthusiasm at all, the bastard. Still got a bellyful of the old Bill Franks stuff on his mind, I expect. Still he came across – somewhat.'

'You mean he parted up with some dough?' Jim said.

Mick swore. 'No. No, he wouldn't part up. But he had an idea.'

'What idea? Eh? Carm on, for God's sake! Don't lie there spouting like a fool. WHAT IDEA?'

Mick sat up. 'All right. Steady on, Jimmy. I'll tell you. You know he still manages some boys in the fight game? Well, then. He knows all the promoters, all the wise men. So he had an idea. He said he wouldn't give either me or you any money, not without us working for it, see?'

'Well, come on, come on! Get to the bloody point, can't you?' Jim said.

'All right, then, here it is. Benny says he can fix you a fight. He can get you a try-out at the Cornwall Club – six two-minute-round stuff. Get a quid for it. He'll tell the boss there that you're a boy he wants to try out, see? You go in and knock some punch-drunk son-of-a-bitch to glory – and then we collect. Get it?'

Jim stared. 'What! Me? Me go and fight in the ring? Me? For a *quid*! Talk sense! Why don't *you* do it, if you think it's so easy, eh?'

Mick glared at him. 'Me? So I would – if my damned nose wasn't still in pieces. If you haven't the guts to help yourself . . . why, s'whelp me, I'm damned if I *don't* have a go, nose or no nose. You dirty yellow cowson, I'll show you up for the louse you are!'

Jim went red. Maybe Mick was right, maybe he was a louse. Still, fighting in a bloody hall for six rounds – for a quid . . . werl . . . a *quid*, mind you. He could do it, though. He had been some sort of a fighter at the Boys' Club back home. Knocked all the others cuckoo, at that. Still, that was different. And yet Sid Benny had . . .

'No,' Jim said. 'You can say what you like. I'm not going to do it. You can think up something else, see?'

Mick stood up slowly. He looked pretty sore.

'All right, Jim Bankley. Have it your own way,' he said evenly. 'I'll give you till midday tomorrow. You can ring me at Vicky's. If you don't – well, you can go and — yourself, that's all. If you're so yellow . . .' He went to the door without looking round at Jim. 'Good night,' he said, and went out.

Jim said nothing. He stood quite still, listening to Mick going down the stairs, listening for the front door to slam, listening to the footsteps going down the street. He was alone.

He undressed slowly and climbed into the tousled bed. Life was lousy when you were alone. There was no one now, no one at all. First the Franks, then Audrey, now Mick. He couldn't go home, either. They still thought he was on top of the world, blast it. They still thought he was making good, that he was a Wide Boy – oh God! A Wide Boy! Oh God! That was a joke, that *was* a joke – a hell of a joke.

He rolled over, burying his face in the grubby folds of the sheets.

In ten minutes he was asleep.

* * * * *

Night again, and the town is still alive.

The lights flicker and race in the Circus, pimpling the building fronts like fungus on dead trees. Isn't it grand, and all? Motorcars and taxis, theatres and restaurants, pavements black with people. Look at all the money! Caw! look at it.

Over in Bethnal Green and Stepney cockroaches and

bugs seep out through the cracks in damp plaster. In small rooms, the children sleep, their paper-white faces too old for their bodies. And who cares about that, anyway? That's not your business. It's that fellow's over there – or isn't it? . . .

In back rooms off Lisle Street ageing tarts who are past it wish the hell they could just go to bed alone and sleep and sleep and sleep . . .

Down in Fleet Street, the Presses roar. Ten million sheets of schmooge, pouring from the machines like vomit.

Houses, buildings, straggling suburbs, new-brick factories. Miles after miles of them. Narrow, twisting alleys in the City – nightmares to turn old Wren over in his sleep. Tall, wide dignity near the Parks . . .

Wotcheer, London! How's the girl?

'. . . the heart of Empire . . . our noble city . . .' And old Ma London, darting out from behind the phoney Junoesque image created for her, shows herself as a boozy old trot. A jolly, dirty old bag in grubby black clothes. She capers around, dancing on shaky legs, ginny tears rolling down her old cheeks as she laughs. She's old and dirty and crazy, and doesn't care a damn – bless her.

Wotcheer, London! How's the girl? Why the hell don't you go to sleep?

* * * * *

It was nine-thirty when he woke. He rubbed his eyes and sat up in bed. Just because he owed the rent that old cow downstairs wouldn't bring up any hot water. The room looked worse, somehow, shabby, sordid, and flat, like yesterday's cold tea.

He climbed out of bed and looked at the rumpled sheets. 'Yerce,' he said aloud. 'That's it. That's like me, like my bloomin' life down here. Untidy. Like a bed that isn't made.'

He looked out of the window at the clock across the street. Well, that left two hours and a half before he had to make up his mind and ring Mick. If only there was some other way of raising a couple of quid. Everything was pawned. All the possible blokes were owed money already. Everyone hated his guts, and Mick's guts, too. If they could only get down to Haydock Park and horn in on Bill's job there . . . It oughtn't to be hard. Tomorrow, though. Pity it wasn't next week. A day was too short a time to raise the wind.

He started to shave, in cold water, swearing at the scrape of the razor, his mind busy. Just six two-minute rounds against a punk. Benny could fix it that the other chap would be a punk, maybe. Yet old Benny didn't love Mick, or him either.

Jim wiped his face and looked at himself in the glass. Laying off the drink, and sleeping a lot, being on his feet when he was out, instead of using the car, had bucked him up. He ran his hands over powerful muscular shoulders, patted his hard stomach, and grinned. He was in pretty fair shape.

He dressed slowly, and looked through his pockets. There was two shillings and fourpence left.

He picked up his hat and went to the door, opening it softly, listening. Mustn't meet the old cow going out. He ran down the stairs lightly, and went into the street.

As he shut the door behind him someone came up the steps. It was his father.

The two of them just stared at one another.

''Lo, Jim.'

'Caw! Hullo, Dad. Wotchew doing here?'

'Came to see you, boy.'

'Oh?'

Old Bankley looked round. 'Not much of a place this, is it?' he said.

'No. I'm only here temporary.'

'Yes?'

'Yerce.'

'Where you going now, Jim?'

'Breakfast.'

'All right, I'll come along with you. I can do with another cupper tea myself.'

Jim swore silently. Blast him! What the hell was *he* doing down here? Who could have tipped him off?

They walked slowly along, side-by-side. As they reached the teashop at the end of the street, Jim suddenly had an idea.

They found a table in the corner. The shop was almost empty, except for a man reading a midday *Standard*, and a tired-looking girl.

While Jim ate his poached egg and toast, old Bankley sat looking at him, noticing the grubby shirt and collar, the not-so-new suit. It was a summer suit. The boy must be cold without a coat or anything over it.

'Things ain't going so good now, Jim, eh?' old Bankley said.

Jim flushed. 'Eh? Oh, not so bad,' he said.

'Don't be a fool, son. I got eyes in me head. Why don't you pack up and come home? Ernie's gone off now – gone to Derby, aero engines works there – I'm on me ownsome. Why don't you come back, eh? There's a few jobs going now at the works for a feller that has any brains.'

Jim kept his eyes on his plate. 'What do I want with a job? I'm doing fine,' he said. 'Only mugs work.'

Old Bankley scowled. 'You've learned that off like a parrot,' he said. 'I been working for thirty-eight years, boy. I know what work is. It's you that's the mug – you and your pals, Jim.'

'My pals get along all right – you can bet on that,' Jim said.

'I can bet on that, can I? Well, maybe they are getting along all right – but what about *you*? Still the gambler, eh, Jim? Shoving your ten bob, your five bob, your half a crown on the dogs, eh? Standing watching the last race with your fists clenched tight and sweat on your face, knowing the dog's *got* to win this time, *got* to – or you don't eat. It's licked you, Jim. You're on the floor, boy – why not admit it?'

Jim dropped his knife and fork, glaring across the table.

'You — off!' he said. 'You keep your nose out of my bleeding affairs, see? I'm doing all right. I've cut down me expenses and that because I'm working things on me own now. I'm getting along fine. I don't want no job. I don't want to go back to that stinking town – I want to be left alone, see?'

'You can't do any . . .'

'Ah, shurrup, will you? I'm working a big coup tomorrow. I got plenty of plans, so you can — off, Dad, and leave me to it.'

Old Bankley sighed. Jim went on eating. His hands were trembling.

'I saw your pal Louie Franks last night,' old Bankley said. 'He told me how to find out where you were, though he wasn't too friendly about it. I went to a feller called Gold, a bookie, and he told me where you were. He told me you were in a tough spot, too, Jim boy.'

Jim pushed forward his empty plate and stood up, leaning forward across the table. 'You saw Louie Franks, did you? And you listened to his lies, I suppose? Well, now listen to something else. I know what I'm doing and I've only just started, see? After tomorrow I'm going to wipe the eyes of that Franks crowd. I only want a bit of capital to do it, and tomorrow's when I get some. You *see*, that's all! They're all scared of the Gisberg boys – all the Franks mob are scared of them. Well, they're soon going to be scared of Mick and me.'

'Don't be a damned fool, Jim. "Capital!" You had "Capital", and you lost the lot. You had a lot of things – and you got cleaned out. Why can't you see your level, boy? Why do you have to be such a fool?'

Jim's face was red with anger, his heavy mouth twitching. 'You can clear out, that's all,' he said fiercely. 'You can go to hell for all I care!'

Over by the pay desk the shiny-frocked Manageress was looking like a harassed bishop. Perhaps the best thing to do would be to get a policeman – still . . .

The man reading the *Standard* was looking on with interest. Trouble, eh? That was fine. That was a stiff-looking kid, all right, and he looked proper wild.

The tired girl watched listlessly. Nice blue eyes that boy had got. Ever so nice . . . ever so nice . . .

Old Bankley sneered. 'You're licked, and you haven't the guts or the sense to admit it, Jim,' he said. 'I took the time off, and all the trouble to find you and make you a decent offer – and you behave like a fool. You're no good, Jim. You're just a wash out, a lazy, good-for-nothing wash out. A Wide Boy, eh? And Wide Boys never work!'

Jim said nothing at first. His face was crimson.

He took a deep breath. 'Werl, are you going – or am I?' he said jerkily.

His father stood up. 'I'll go. Maybe you're just wild now, and you'll come to your senses a bit later on. I'll see you once more before I go back. So long.'

Jim smiled bitterly. 'I dunno where, then,' he said, 'because I shan't be anywhere you know about.'

'You never can tell,' old Bankley said, and walked past the outraged Manageress and out of the shop.

Jim sat down again. Blast! he'd been a fool. If he had kept his head he might have persuaded the old ass to lend him a couple of nicker. Hell! Hell! Hell! A damn good idea gone bust. Caw! this was a proper hell of a fix, all right.

He looked up. The Manageress and the waitress were standing at the table.

'Young man, I think you had better leave at once,' the Manageress said. 'Here is your bill. We do not want any disturbances in this place, *if* you don't mind.'

Jim stood up and picked up his hat. Fat old bitch. Looked like a pantomime dame only not so funny. Snotty old cow, too.

'Yes, all right. I'm going,' he said, and went to the cash desk. 'Give me coppers in change, will you, miss? I gotter make a phone call. Thanks.'

He went out into the street. Mick's number was 1083, wasn't it? Well, it seemed there was only one thing to do.

* * * * *

Benny took off the receiver and dialled a number.

'. . . yerce, Joe. I know all about that . . . yerce . . . yerce. Now look. I told him to go along tonight. He's a real flash boy, cocky as hell. Give him a tough boy you know about, and put 'em up for a six-round prelim, see? This kid is in goodish shape. He knows how to use his dukes, and he's tough, Joe, boy . . . yerce . . . that's the idea . . . that's what I want . . . sure, might be a bit late, but I'll be there . . . yerce? Well, suppose he does? What do you lose? What does anyone lose . . . ?'

Although it was cold, and raining hard, there were already a good many people there when Jim and Mick arrived.

It was a long, high building with a gallery. The ring was at one end, and the ropes were festooned with posters for coming fights. Most of the red-plush seats downstairs were full, and the gallery was more than full. Except for a few women sprinkled around the ringside, the crowd was entirely male – and not only male, but masculine.

The promoter, a bland wary-eyed man, paraded the aisle downstairs slowly and continually. He was smoking a cigar, and showing three others in the outside breast pocket of his jacket. He was tall, and wore a blue hat. He had a nice little business at the Cornwall Club, and liked it run nice. He didn't want no trouble, see?

Jim followed Mick right through the hall, and Mick introduced him to the promoter. 'This is the boy, Mr Gilder,' Mick said. 'Jim Bankley, the one you were told about.'

Mr Gilder ran a practised eye over Jim's powerful shoulders and arms. 'Yeh?' he said. 'Well, if Mr Benny Gold says he's all right for a trial – well, I'll take it. Two of my boys let me down tonight, anyway.' He tapped Jim on the chest. 'Know what to do, kid?' he said.

Jim nodded. His knees felt a bit shaky, and he found speech difficult. He glanced up at the ring. Caw! it was bloody small. About twelve feet square by the look of it. Not much chance of keeping away in that. Like fighting in a bloody shed.

'I'm handling him, Mr Gilder,' Mick said.

'All right, son. There's a regular second, you know.'

Mick nodded. 'Yes, but I'll go up, too. And Mr Gold'll be here soon. He said he would come along. Told me to tell you he would, see?'

The promoter smiled placidly. 'Okay,' he said. 'You go and get your boy changed. He'll be on second, and he ain't got a lot of time, see? He's fighting a kid called Dai Rees. Can he make eleven stone four, your boy?' He talked as if Jim weren't a person at all, as if he were just something Mick had brought along.

'Yes, he can do that all right,' Mick said.

The promoter moved away and Jim followed Mick into the dressing room. Most of the crowd at the ring end of the hall were older men, ex-fighters, managers, trainers. They came to talk, to fix things up, to pass the time, all more than to watch the fights. There was Jim Bullock who had once gone fifteen rounds with Jimmy Wilde; and Johnny Sharp. When Johnny had been a featherweight he had licked Kid Lewis. Now he was chubby and ruddy as a Toby mug, smiling all over his face. He weighed about twelve stone and a half, and the featherweight days were just a memory.

He spoke to Mick as he passed. 'This the boy who's fighting Dai Rees?' he said. 'Dai's a boy I'm interested in.'

Mick nodded. 'Yes. Jim Bankley. He's the boy.'

Johnny Sharp grinned. 'Right.' He looked at Jim. 'Good luck, kid,' he said. 'Keep your chin up.'

Jim flushed and grinned. This bloke made him feel better.

He followed Mick into the dressing room. There were four other boys there. It was a smallish room, fairly dark, but clean. As Jim took off his coat one of the other boys looked up at him. He had fair hair, and the face of an old man on the body of a child.

'Who're you, mate?' he said.

Jim scowled. 'Jim Bankley,' he said.

'Noo aintcher? Who're fightin'?'

Jim nodded and took off his collar. This chap was a stiff-looking little bloke. 'Dai Rees,' he said.

A thin-faced boy in the corner turned round. 'That's me,' he said. 'It's me you're fighting, man.'

He was dressed only in a grubby pair of underpants. Jim looked him over carefully. He was thin, but a tough egg all the same. His narrow, peaky face was pale, with brown eyes and a small mouth. But his wiry body was all muscle. He had almost no weight in his legs at all.

'Hullo,' Jim said warily. Caw! this chap looked easy. Proper skinny, wasn't he?

Mick kept on talking to Jim all the time he was undressing. Two of the smaller boys in the room went out for the first fight. There was some applause, and a good deal of whistling.

Jim laced up the boxing shoes he had borrowed from young Sid Benny. They were a bit tight. When he had fixed on the jockstrap and his shorts he felt pretty good. He looked at himself in the rusty mirror which hung on the wall. Caw! and he looked all right. If that Welsh bloke was tough, well, so was he – and a damn sight tougher.

Mick winked at him. 'Feel all right?' he said.

Jim smiled. 'Fine,' he said, but still felt a bit funny inside. He was trying to remember some of the tricks young Sid had taught him.

'I'm betting a quid on you, Jim boy,' Mick said. He spoke casually, but his eye was on Jim as he spoke. 'Benny said he could get it on for us.'

Jim stared. 'Whose quid?' he said.

Mick looked uneasy. 'Your prize money. You get a quid for this, if you win it,' he said.

Jim sat down. His stomach had gone cold and hollow. 'You – you mean you're betting . . . God, Micky, you're barmy!' he said.

Mick stood close to him, talking quickly. 'Listen,' he said. 'We got to take a chance, Jim. You're a gambler, aren't you? Bill Franks always said you were, anyway. This is a good thing, boy. We'll have enough to get in a good crack tomorrow after this fight. See?'

'If I win it.'

'If you win it! Don't be a mug. You can lick this Welsh mug! Looks punch-drunk to me. If you win it! Why, you can lick *any* Welsh berk, Jimmy. Take a look at yourself, man. Don't be a mug. And, anyway, *one* quid's not much use. We got to take the chance, see?'

Jim pulled a towel around his shoulders. His mind was spinning. He couldn't think clearly at all. Betting the whole quid before it was his, eh? And why should Benny offer to take it. Something funny was going on; must be going on. Yet maybe Mick was right. Hell! yes, maybe he *was* right.

This Welsh bloke didn't look much, anyway. And Bill Franks had been right, too – about the gambling. Yes, damn sure he had been right. Jim Bankley had always been a gambler, and he would be one up to the last. Win or bust. Win or bust – what the hell was there to it, otherwise? Win or bust. Fine.

After a few minutes the noise outside told them the first fight was over. It seemed to be an unpopular decision. After a few minutes the two boys, flyweights they were, came back into the dressing room.

Dai Rees spoke to one of them, the fair-haired one.

'How'd you go, Nobby?' he said.

'Won in the forf.'

'Kayo, man?'

'Na. Smiffy stopped it.'

'Nice work, man.'

The other boy had his manager with him. He was in pretty bad shape, and had a cut eye.

Johnny Sharp came in and started to talk to Dai Rees. Jim wandered to the doorway. Now he was ready for it he felt confident. He knew he could knock this Welsh bloke cuckoo, all right.

There was a fat man with a red face and a collar like a hangman's noose in the ring. He was reading out and commenting on the forthcoming attractions. As he spoke he held the posters at arm's length, and when he had read one he tossed it untidily down out of the ring. He had a fine unctuous delivery, and the crowd loved him. All the boys upstairs were pulling his leg, and he knew it.

'Ge—entlemen,' he roared. 'Next Frideee – Ten rounds special attraction. Ten rounds excitin' boxin', gentlemen, between Sailor Cowan and Young Doug Mays – Doug Mays, gents, 'oo larst week out-pointed Tiny Hume!'

He looked round impressively. The boys upstairs took a deep breath and whistled all together. 'Phe-e-e-e-w!'

The announcer sneered. '*And* gentlemen,' he roared,

'special supportin' baht. Ten rounds excitin' boxin' at nine stone seven. Boy Mullins – and Len Thomas – both of Camden Town.'

The boys upstairs let it go again: 'Phe-e-e-e-e-w!' It would have broken the heart of the film trailer people, it would have damped a trick orator. The announcer sneered.

'Finally, gentlemen,' he roared again, 'a sooper special attraction. A heavyweight fight over six rounds between Solly Humphreys of King's Cross, and Mike Shaun, Ireland!'

'Phe-e-e-e-e-w!'

The announcer threw the last poster away and prepared to leave. 'Finally, gentlemen,' he said.

'Oi!' one of the boys shouted down. 'We've 'ad *one* "final".'

The announcer waved his arms contemptuously. 'I say "finally", gentlemen, and that means you too, sir. I say don't apply for no more of the ten-guinea seats!' He paused, leering. ''Cause they're ALL SOLD!'

Loud and derisive applause flooded the house.

Mick nudged Jim on the shoulder. The promoter had come up. 'Come on, you two,' the promoter said. He looked hard at Jim. 'And you give me some action, kid,' he said. 'Mr Gold wants to show me what you can do.'

Jim nodded, and followed Mick. He climbed up into the ring. The noise of the crowd was swelling and receding in his ears. The gallery boys looked very close, the lights overhead very bright. The canvas floor and the ropes were dirty, and in one corner there was a small bloodstain. The air was full of tobacco smoke, like a fog.

Jim sat down on the stool. In the front row ringside there was a Jewess watching him. She was smoking a cigarette, and staring at him with the steady impersonality of one looking at an animal in a cage.

Jim swallowed uneasily while the announcer climbed up

and introduced him to the crowd. Nobody seemed very interested. Dai Rees was the usual boy for these Trial Horses, and they all knew him. This kid Bankley had a bloody nice pair of shoulders on him, and looked a tough handful and all, but he looked a bit green, too.

Mick and the regular second, a fair-haired man with a spread nose and a potbelly, lolled against the ropes, waiting. Mick was looking confident. He had seen Jim in a rough-house, and knew what he could do when he was mad.

The door of the hall opened and closed with a bang. Two or three more people came in. Jim looked round absently, and watched them sit down about ten rows from the ring. One of them was his father.

For a second or two Jim just stared open-mouthed. Then he felt savage. Interfering old fool! Coming to stick his nose into everything again. All right then, the old fool would see. He would see this Dai Rees get a bloody good hiding. 'You're a wash out, Jim' – that was what he had said, wasn't it? Well, all right then. He would see.

He fidgeted with the black leather gloves on his hands and wished the hell it would start. He looked across at the Welsh boy and saw he was looking bored – the bastard.

The bell clanged stridently, and Jim got up. He walked in stiffly, still angry, and touched gloves. Someone in the gallery shouted something that made the others laugh. The ring seemed very small, and Jim, stepping back from a left lead, cannoned off the ropes he had thought to be some way behind him. As he came off, the Welsh boy hooked him in the mouth. Jim charged and landed two on the body. The Welsh boy backed off, Jim after him. Caw! this chap was nothing. Boxing was nothing. You only had to be able to hit, that's all. He circled warily, feinting with his left. The Welsh boy looked bored, and upstairs someone shouted: 'Won't yew 'ave the nixt dawnce wiv me, dearie?' and everybody laughed.

Jim sweated, and looked angry. Rotten bastards. Thought they were funny, didn't they? He glared at the Welsh boy and rushed, swinging up his left. The Welsh boy slipped him. Jim turned and swung his right wildly. The Welsh boy swayed out of distance and then clipped him on the jaw. Jim ducked and ran into an uppercut which made his eyes water. The Welsh boy danced in and hooked his left to the stomach. Jim grunted and doubled forward. The Welsh boy uppercut again, straightened him up, and threw over his right. It landed on Jim's jaw, and Jim went down.

He scrambled up at once, the laughter of the crowd in his ears. He could see the Welsh boy as if through a red haze, and he rushed. He pushed his left out and the Welsh boy side-stepped him. Jim clinched. The Welsh boy wagged his head savagely, nearly breaking Jim's front teeth. Jim tried to break and found his left glove caught up. As he twisted free, the Welsh boy hooked him in the mouth, jerking his head back. Jim could feel his teeth rattling in his head. As his guard dropped, the Welsh boy hit him in the stomach again. Jim said, 'Ouuff!' and the bell went.

He went to his corner, and Mick pushed him onto the stool, talking fiercely. 'Go in and sock him, Jim,' Mick said. 'Don't play about. Give him one good sock and it'll be all over. He's nothing, this Welsh sod. Take your time and pin him, that's all you got to do.'

Jim said nothing. He looked across at the other corner. He noticed the Welsh boy's long, lean arms, his thin face. The bastard must be all bone to weigh eleven stone odd. He hadn't any flesh at all. Well, all right, next round would be different. He would show all these cocky swine here that . . . Clang!

Jim stood up and closed his gloves. As he rushed at the Welsh boy, his foot slipped. He collided in mid-ring with the Welsh boy's left. The crowd roared with laughter. Upstairs someone shouted: 'Steady, boy, you're busting 'is 'ands ter pieces wiv yer fice!' Jim set his teeth and swung wildly again. The Welsh boy ducked. Jim followed up, landed a right, but took two lefts in the face. He covered up against the ropes, and the Welsh boy came after him. Jim tried to clinch, but the Welsh boy chopped him off, hitting with both hands, hooking solidly. The crowd was shouting very loudly now, and calling for a knockout.

Jim swung again with his left, missed, and fell to his knees. He stayed there, staring blindly round him. He heard a voice shout: 'Say your prayers, son, you'll need it!' and people laughing again.

The Welsh boy stepped back and let Jim get up. Then he ran in and swung a right to the jaw. Jim sprawled across the ring and fell onto his face. He was just opposite the referee, a toughly-built, spectacled young man with frizzy hair. Jim shook his head wearily and panted. His nose was full of blood, running down into his mouth. He stared into the bland face of the referee, and swallowed hard. God! he would have to get up somehow. God! he was getting licked – *licked*. He could hear Mick yelling at him, the crowd laughing.

The referee climbed into the ring, and pushed the Welsh boy into his corner, raising his arm.

'All right, that's enough,' he shouted. 'Rees is the winner!'

The crowd laughed and booed. Down in the ringside, Benny Gold leaned across to Mr Gilder. 'Thanks, Joe,' he said, 'that was fine . . .'

Jim crawled to the ropes and pulled himself up. He felt nearly sick, and ashamed. He looked quickly at Mick. Mick was very pale, his mouth twisted as if he were hurt.

'Come on,' Mick said. 'Let's get out of here.'

They climbed down out of the ring to ironical applause, and went through to the dressing room.

Jim dressed miserably, saying nothing. His face felt as if it had been rubbed against a grindstone. Mick just sat slackly against the lockers, picking at his nails with a bus ticket. When Jim was dressed, the promoter came in and gave Mick a ten-shilling note. Benny Gold was with him, and behind the two of them was old Bankley.

Jim looked at Benny and grinned sheepishly. 'Sorry, Benny,' he said. 'I guess I wasn't much good.'

'He didn't have any luck, that's all,' Mick said quickly. 'He got rattled, Benny.'

Jim flushed. 'Look, Benny, you just . . .' he said.

Benny shook his head. 'Na, Jim. Ferget it, kid. It was just an idea I had, that's all. But you're not cut out for it, boy,' he said. 'Don't be a mug.'

Jim just stared at him, his mouth working. He had just got the idea. Then old Bankley stepped forward and held him by the arm. 'Come on, Jim,' he said. 'You be a sensible lad, and come with me. Come on, son.'

Jim looked from Benny to Mick, but Mick gave no sign. Jim thought about all he had done, all the fun, all the excitement, the money, his car, Bill, Louie, Audrey, Swing, Tony Howard, the lights, the dogs – tonight . . . He watched Mick's white face, his thick, powerful body, his pale eyes. And Mick just stared back at him. His face looked almost dead.

Old Bankley moved towards the door. 'Well, good night, gents,' he said, and looked at his son. 'You coming, Jim?'

Jim drew in a deep breath. Oh God! Oh God! He knew he would have to make up his mind now, and quickly. They had got him in a corner now, and he had to get out, he had to do something. He rubbed his hand slowly across his bruised face. None of the others moved. They were all staring curiously at him.

Jim dropped his hand. 'Yes, I'm coming,' he said. He put down the bag he had been holding, and moved to the door. 'Goodbye, Mick,' he mumbled. Mick didn't move, or say anything.

The two Bankleys pushed out through the crowd and walked to the main door. Together, they went down the steps into the street.

It had stopped raining, and there were stars in the sky.

* * * * *

NOW THEN: I am tempted, literally, to leave Jim here, trying to kid you that he has learned his lesson; that he will be a good boy from now on. But it won't do. Because what will happen to him is inevitable, hopelessly inevitable. Can't you see it?

Jim will go home chastened. He will go back to work, until the bitterness has worn off. But he has tasted blood, and he won't find it easy to forget. The dog track will get him again. Starting slowly, but still confident that his London Wideness puts him one jump ahead of the others, he will start to gamble again. And he'll win and he'll lose, and he'll win and he'll lose again. He will be slack and bitter, and will stop working at the first opportunity he gets. He has got the itch, and the itch has got him.

What can you do with boys like this? It isn't just environment, because you get Jim Bankleys everywhere, up and down the social scale. It is easy to say: 'Oh, he's a pathological case; he is hopeless,' and leave it at that. But you can't get away with it so easily, because it is all Wrong. Someone has to keep the boy, whether it is his family, or Society. He's there, a parasite, hanging on with dead weight. So what are you going to do about it?

He is finished now, and beaten. He hasn't quite the twist of the criminal, but he's no good, to himself – or to anyone.

When the grey-drab queues file slowly through the Labour Exchanges, he will stand among them. There with the decent men, the hard and disillusioned men, he will wait. He will be with them, and not of them. So look at him:

with half-smoked 'dimp' hanging from his upper lip, with his mouth sideways in the Wide Boy's leer, he stands in line; hands in pockets, slackly, and he doesn't give a damn.

Goodbye, Jim Bankley. The Wide World has done with you.

Goodbye, kid – and God help you.

AFTERWORD

Judging from the author's note that Robert Westerby decided to add to the second-edition, Methuen printing of *Wide Boys Never Work* in 1942, and which is reprinted here, the novel appears to have generated some media flak and possibly some direct, uncompromising feedback from the general public. He seems genuinely concerned that he may face recriminations of some sort and counters charges that his characters are exaggerated, reproducing a passage from a leading barrister's entreaties to a jury where he describes the lowlife backdrop to the West End to prove his point that such things can happen in London.

The fact he had to rely on a King's Counsel's naturally biased representations says much about how the underbelly and criminal world of London was still a largely unknown phenomenon in the late 1930s. Even though gangster families such as the Sabinis were active and a young Billy Hill was cutting his teeth – and much else – on the racecourses of the south, their notoriety was mainly restricted to the police and criminal classes. Hill's autobiography *King Of The Underworld*, generally acknowledged as the first London gangster memoir, was not published until 1955, but by then the popular press had long been shining their sensationalist torches into the seedier side of London and beyond.

The 1948 edition of *Wide Boys Never Work*, published by John Lehmann, also includes an Author's Note, but things seem to have quietened down and Westerby deals more in comparisons, while maintaining the humour of 1942. Perhaps in the aftermath of the Second World War, during which it would have been important to present a face of national unity, and with a new generation of tearaways making themselves felt on the streets of a peacetime capital, his novel was less controversial and, in retrospect, more obviously daring.

AUTHOR'S NOTE (1942)

In attempting to draw a picture of the underside of London life – or a section of it – and the effect that sort of environment has on a boy like Jim Bankley, I have tried to refrain from two temptations. The first of these is over-dramatisation of everyday occurrences. In a good many of the Soho Clubs, fights and argumentative disturbances are nothing out of the ordinary; the razor-carrying boy a common-place. The second temptation is exaggeration. Now, it seems to me nothing is more fantastic and bizarre than the way people actually behave, and therefore exaggeration is easy to slip into unawares – yet also unnecessary.

It might seem hard to believe that such things happen in England, and if I only gave you my word that they do, you would be justified in refusing to believe me. So, having been raised in a large family, and consequently having had a surfeit of argument, I will just quote Sir Holman Gregory, KC, who in February last year said: 'Those horrible and vile places that exist in the West End of London under the title of Clubs . . . It is my unfortunate fate to listen to many cases in this court. These places (the Clubs) exist and do untold harm in the community, and I expect, having heard the evidence in this case, you will agree with me that they ought to be stopped. Young men are still being corrupted here, and fights are taking place.'

As for the section dealing with a second-hand car dealer's business, I must confess that my experience is more particular than general. Nowadays, thanks to I don't know what, there are a great number of honest and decent traders in this business. But there still remains an unfortunately large number of Graham Swings, as the dealer you bought your car from will tell you. There are more things in heaven and earth, Horatio 'tumty-tumty-tum philosophy'.

That swindling, racketeering, crooked gambling and terrorism make up a small part of life in a great city is regrettable – and also inevitable.

And if I irritate you, my dear reader, bear comfort from the fact that if a few of the sort of people I have hinted at in the narrative, a few originals from whom I have made sketches, chance to read the book and think I have opened my mouth too wide – they will be pleased to give me a beating on your behalf.

If they should get angry, I only hope I can persuade them to be satisfied with wrecking my publisher's office, and leave me alone. *RW*

AUTHOR'S NOTE (1948)

Wide Boys Never Work was first published in September 1937. The situation then was very different from the situation today. There was widespread unemployment, a *laisser-faire* political philosophy, whole industries idle. There was more excuse for the Wide Boy then. Life offered a restless young man less than it does today. He found it difficult to find a job, more difficult to find scope for his energies. A different cause has the same effect today. The Wide Boy is called 'A Spiv', and Spiv covers a multitude of meanings where originally it meant merely a racecourse character, a rough-house money-getter. But the 'Clubs' described in *Wide Boys* are the same today, just as seedy, and the real Wide Boy has a real existence of his own; too often the 'Spiv' is self-conscious. Another point which was very real in 1938, but outdated now, is the organ-ised intimidation of bookmakers at the dog tracks.

As to the section dealing with a second-hand car dealer's busi-ness, I have to confess that my experience was more particular than general. And it is, of course, dated. The prices quoted show that only too clearly!

Here and there I have edited the original narrative, because the events discussed are out-of-date – but the people dealt with in the story are still with us, undated. Crime marches on. *Robert Westerby*

London Classics

A START IN LIFE

ALAN SILLITOE

Alan Sillitoe's first novel, *Saturday Night And Sunday Morning*, was published in 1958, *The Loneliness Of The Long-Distance Runner* arriving the following year. Both were hits and led to high-profile films, which is turn cemented his reputation. Tagged an 'Angry Young Man' by the media, Sillitoe's ability to record and interpret the lives of ordinary people was nothing short of revolutionary. He has been prolific ever since and remains one of England's greatest contemporary authors.

A Start In Life tells the story of Michael Cullen, who abandons his pregnant girlfriend and heads 'to the lollipop-metropolis of London in the 1960s'. Cullen is, in theory, leaving his problems behind, but he is 'the Devil on two sticks' and becomes involved in a smuggling ring with Moggerhanger, a man who believes 'that you must get anything you want no matter what cost to others'. Cullen is an optimist, with an eye for the ladies, but his new swinging lifestyle is soon under threat.

Includes an introduction by DJ Taylor

London Books
£11.99 hardback
ISBN 978-0-9551851-1-3
www.london-books.co.uk

LONDON BOOKS

FLYING THE FLAG FOR
FREE-THINKING LITERATURE

www.london-books.co.uk

PLEASE VISIT OUR WEBSITE FOR

- Current and forthcoming books
  - Author and title profiles
- A lively, interactive message board
  - Events and news
  - Secure on-line bookshop
  - Recommendations and links
- An alternative view of London literature

ON SALE NOW
All titles hardback / £11.99

THE GILT KID – JAMES CURTIS
Introduction by Paul Willetts
ISBN 978-0-9551851-2-0

NIGHT AND THE CITY – GERALD KERSH
Introduction by John King
ISBN 978-0-9551851-3-7

A START IN LIFE – ALAN SILLITOE
Introduction by DJ Taylor
ISBN 978-0-9551851-1-3

THEY DRIVE BY NIGHT – JAMES CURTIS
Introduction by Jonathan Meades
ISBN 978-0-9551851-4-4

WIDE BOYS NEVER WORK – ROBERT WESTERBY
Introduction by Iain Sinclair
ISBN 978-0-9551851-5-1

read more 🐧

IAIN SINCLAIR

HACKNEY, THAT ROSE-RED EMPIRE

Once an Arcadian suburb of grand houses, orchards and conservatories, Hackney declined into a zone of asylums, hospitals and dirty industry. Persistently revived, reinvented, betrayed, it has become a symbol of inner-city chaos, crime and poverty. Now, the Olympics, a final attempt to clamp down on a renegade spirit, seeks to complete the process: erasure disguised as 'progress'.

In this 'documentary fiction', Sinclair meets a cast of the dispossessed, including writers, photographers, bomb-makers and market traders. Legends of tunnels, Hollow Earth theories and the notorious Mole Man are unearthed. He uncovers traces of those who passed through Hackney: Lenin and Stalin, novelists Joseph Conrad and Samuel Richardson, film-makers Orson Welles and Jean-Luc Godard, Tony Blair beginning his political career, even a Baader-Meinhof urban guerrilla on the run. And he tells his own story: of forty years in one house in Hackney, of marriage, children, strange encounters and deaths.

Praise for Iain Sinclair:

'Sentence for sentence, there is no more interesting writer at work in English' *Daily Telegraph*

'He is incapable of writing a dull paragraph' *Scotland on Sunday*

'Sinclair is a genius' *GQ*

read more 🐧

IAIN SINCLAIR

WHITE CHAPPELL, SCARLET TRACINGS

Following the fading fortunes of a predatory clutch of ragged book dealers scavenging for wealth and meaning amongst the city's hidden tomes, *White Chappell, Scarlet Tracings* reveals a present-day London rooted in a dark and resonant past. The chance discovery of a dust-torn classic is hailed as a triumph, but within its battered covers lie uneasy clues to the century-old riddle of the Whitechapel murders.

Part biography, part mystery, part exorcism, *White Chappell, Scarlet Tracings* explores the occult relationship between fiction and history and examines how their bloody collision has given birth to the London of today.

'A sane, darkly brilliant report from the back streets of knowledge and power' *New Statesman*

'Extraordinary . . . ruined and ruthless dandies appear and disappear through a phantasmagoria interspersed with occult conjurings and reflections on the nature of fiction and history' *Guardian*

'A Gothickly entitled guidebook to the abyss . . . burns with radioactive energy' *London Review of Books*

The journey begins anywhere, detours, doubles back on itself, returns to a place that is no longer there. I had no idea, until John King mentioned it, a titbit of literary gossip, that Robert Westerby was born in Hackney. Fixed bearings implode. Document becomes fiction. The familiar walk converts life into a form of corrupted cinema: that misremembered film is no longer the simple narrative of events it once appeared. Not in a London where identity is never resolved and polarities of geography and cultural affect shift by the hour. The drift out of one territory into the next, one political allegiance to a worse, is registered by skid-marks in fogged celluloid. In charity shop VHS ribbons that shudder on exposure. In fluctuating sound levels. Memories are not accessed in cavernous, smoke-filled buildings, the picture palaces of Tooting and Streatham; not any more. Viewings are private. You meditate on a favoured scene, a misheard line of dialogue: the way a man crosses a road, a woman flicks her hair. What was once a seamless progression, the dream an actor was having on your behalf, is now dirty evidence; the CCTV footage of pain and loss.

Coded sequences, sanctioned by film historians and explainers, transport you to another era. Old gangsters love that corny TV/movie shorthand: midnight tremors, involuntary flashbacks held in suspension with whisky and pain-killers. The Kray corpse-handler Tony Lambrianou – fifteen years in prison, a carcinogenic afterlife on the wrong side of the river – couldn't stop banging on about the gaudy neverland of Carol Reed's London: Petticoat Lane with the implausible backdrop of St Paul's. The heart-on-sleeve pieties of Wolf Mankowitz's Whitechapel fable, *A Kid For Two Farthings*, miraculously legitimatized all that ugly stuff with bread knives, rolled carpets and Ford Cortinas in the Blackwall

Tunnel. Lambrianou had another riff, knuckling moist eyes, about Jimmy Cagney going to the chair, playing yellow, for the sake of a straight priest and a troop of dead-end kids.

I came to Dalston for the first time in 1961, to track down a poorly-released feature by exiled Hollywood leftist Joseph Losey. My own exile, from industrial South Wales, had taken me to a film school in Electric Avenue, Brixton. I relished the anonymity of pollarded avenues, corrugated-tin chapels of exotic allegiance, street markets peddling pulp paperbacks. Navigation of the city depended on finding the places where films were shown. *A Touch Of Evil* as the ballast in a double-bill at the Paris Pullman, South Kensington. (An intimidating reef of inherited wealth in tall white houses. Mansion flats with covered entry-tunnels and uniformed porters. A zone of migrant London that Polanski identified as the correct setting for the token exteriors in *Repulsion*: Italian restaurants with garlic chains and straw-nested Chianti bottle, hairdressers soliciting endorsement.) *Breathless* at the Academy in Oxford Street. *L'avventura* loitering on the King's Road and looking so bleached blonde, so painfully composed, even then. Remorseless Bergman, thumb-prints of the absence of God, at the top of a long hill: the Everyman, Hampstead. *Rio Bravo*, a casual pick-up, walking home through Stockwell. Choreographed mayhem that would, in years to come, leak back into local topography. John Wayne and Dean Martin permeating a covert political execution at the tube station. A moonlighting electrician from Brazil finds himself caught up in the gunfight at the OK Corral. Two, three films a day. Mostly achieved by way of the Northern Line. Connections between cinemas taking years to confirm. The stories of those journeys, the walks, are more convincing than the films that provoked them. Such is the process of ageing with a city. Failing eyes, fading memories.

Darkest Dalston was *The Criminal* by Joseph Losey. Type-casting, even then. My original Hackney excursion involved the suspension of everything I thought I knew about London. The disorientation, crossing under the river, a bus from Liverpool

Street, coloured my initial impression of the Losey film. It became a screen through which I witnessed a city of malign shadows. The Swiss-American photographer Robert Frank used the privileged viewpoint of upper-deck bus travel to provide himself with necessary difficulty. My nocturnal view through a wet and greasy window raised one question: *what are they frightened of?* The extended parenthesis of Kingsland Road became the trailer to Losey's film, the reason for that not-unwelcome retreat to the monastery of the prison system. Under strict discipline, life takes care of itself. Our Routemaster stop-started past hospitals and unredeemed pubs – such as The Fox, where, it is alleged, the Brink's-Mat robbery was plotted. My fellow punters, appreciating that a night out was no guarantee of a good time, were soon to decamp for Loughton, Ongar and the Epping Forest fringe. Film, I understood, becomes part of the occasion of its viewing. Part of the place where it is viewed. Evidence of what is left from one small argument between money-brokers and broken artists, the vanities and insecurities of performers and manipulators: memory traces of the vanishing world in which those events happened. Voyeurs and exhibitionists rub each other up the wrong way. Novelists resent the fee they bank for allowing their work to be mistranslated. If they get lucky, like Robert Westerby, they might even be allowed to hack out screenplays: while their out-of-print fictions acquire a patina of mystery and desirability.

Stanley Baker, who starred in *The Criminal*, played Johnny Bannion, a Welsh-Irish-Cockney hardman. He had got away from the Rhondda to attack the potentialities of the metropolis with a physical hunger that critics called 'American': brooding, in-your-face, finding the right gesture. Losey, before he used Baker for the first time, in *Blind Date* (1959), said that he'd been aware of the beetle-browed Welshman, glowering on the scene, for years. But had resisted the pitch, leaving this insistently working-class actor to another blacklisted Hollywood escapee, Cy Endfield. *Hell*

Drivers (1957), a caravan of overambitious egos and time-serving journeymen – Patrick McGoohan, Herbert Lom, William Hartnell, Alfie Bass, Gordon Jackson, Sean Connery – was shot on 'bad' roads within a mile or two of Pinewood. Dr Who meets James Bond meets the Prisoner: a poverty row audition for the next twenty years of television. *Hell Drivers* is a budget Xerox of *On The Waterfront*. Closet Marxist labour wars cartooned as Baker's no-frills Brando substitute and McGoohan's cod-Irish Iago lock antlers in a Berkshire gravel pit. Home Counties noir at its ripest. The Baker eyebrows, in their full arch, recall Nye Bevan.

Endfield, who named names before commie-hunting committees, couldn't promote himself, in his English exile, as another Kazan or Budd Schulberg. Nobody cared, his apostasy was forgotten rather than forgiven. There would be no honorary Bafta. His late success with *Zulu* allowed its producer, Stanley Baker, to clean up: enough to buy a white mansion near the racecourse in Epsom. Charlie Richardson, South London businessman, scrap-dealer and torture buff, came along to South Africa for the ride. Location hunting doubled with the acquisition of mining rights.

Baker, according to Losey, possessed 'dark, wavy hair and a great deal of arrogance and machismo'. The machismo was evident (and approved by the locals) at my Dalston viewing. *The Criminal* is built around it. But the hair, by 1960, had gone, replaced by a brush-over, patent-leather skullcap. Being in the criminal life was all about style, the Look. No self-respecting face ever wore a flat cap like the one Stanley sports when he walks out of the prison gates. The Kingsland Road Italian suit, the narrow horizontal-stripe tie, yes. But the cap was in the wrong movie. It belonged on the Wakefield terraces of *This Sporting Life*. The London Look imitated George Raft or Ray Danton. Dirk Bogarde, Baker's great rival, was characteristically feline about the Welshman's first day on the set of Losey's *Accident*. 'Hideous toupee, thick stucco make-up. Stanley spent hours curling his eyelashes. After that he was marvellous.' The American critic Manny Farber pegged *Accident* as 'the most elegant infighting . . . a symphony in Bogarde–Baker nuances around the cooking and eating of an omelette.'

The Criminal is a 'baroque realist' prison drama with a vestigial heist plot tacked on. The romance element, involving a bemused Margit Saad, is a smokescreen to ameliorate the testosterone stink, the banter and bonding of this alternative seminary. Saad's prison visit, in nun-like white trenchcoat, is a Bressonian insert: austere Catholic geometry in a bleak winter room. A confessional in which nothing is confessed and the visiting room is positioned as an antechamber of hell. The fractured continuity of The Criminal stems from the thirty-five minutes hacked out of the delivered cut. But even this works in Losey's favour: life outside the prison walls is an hallucination, the women have no more reality than the pneumatic pin-ups taped to the trustee's wall. The coming-out party, the fin-tailed Detroit motors, the good-time girls, are all part of a lifer's wet dream: a fantasy stitched out of James M Cain and David Goodis, Mickey Spillane slush from the library cart. America is the Technicolor cartoon: the bite of language, the brutality of the urban landscape. You can't imagine the anti-hero of a Westerby novel lying on his narrow bed reading one of Westerby's own books.

The budget for The Criminal, as David Caute points out in his book on Losey, was £60,000. (Not much more than the amount lifted in the film's racetrack robbery at Hurst Park.) Caute is very good on contracts, budgets, expense accounts. He understands that film production is essentially a machine for manipulating credit (like the present fashion for stealing bankable art). The old legends of Mafia laundries are all true, but that's just the start of it.

There's so much going on off-screen that it's astonishing how well The Criminal coheres. I remembered it as a London film: a deserted park, a Soho café with posters for Tommy Steele and Cliff Richard, American cars in empty British streets. Oblique prompts give a fictional gloss to Baker's admiration for Albert Dimes, veteran of a notorious potato-knife duel with Jack Spot in Frith Street. Gangland figures like Dimes are ghosts out of Gerald Kersh's novel *Night And The City*, which was filmed with some panache by Jules Dassin (a long-term Losey rival). Dassin could do heists, the plotting, the slow build-up, the real-time suspense. Losey couldn't be bothered. When he slummed, he wanted it known that he was slumming. The escape from the prison van, carried out by a solitary heavy (the notably sculptural and long-coated Nigel Green), is so fantastic that the final reel becomes a posthumous dream. The wilful suspension of disbelief, the absurdist comedy, prefigures the sorry saga of the Kray Twins springing Frank 'The Mad Axeman' Mitchell from Dartmoor. Film crime and true crime indulge in a cosily cannibalistic relationship (copyright: Edgar Lustgarten). Both are extensions of place. They define the city as a quest for the perfect location shot. The most convenient parking place. The hippest off-piste restaurant. A release print is never more than a memento of a much more complex nexus of rivalries, love affairs, money rows, betrayals, inventive methods of subverting the original novel or screenplay and its manifold revisions.

Pause for a moment to inspect the team photograph of Soho Rangers FC: grinning recidivists in borrowed shorts (borrowed from much smaller men). Stanley Baker is the sponsor and manager (he's nicked Nigel Green's camelhair coat and trilby). Albert Dimes has his arm around 'Mad' Frankie Fraser. There's the scrap-dealer and freelance dentist, Eddie Richardson. Eddie was the brother of Charlie who was involved with the *Zulu* adventure: land speculation, mining rights, misunderstandings with hitmen. (A small part for Nigel Green.) There's nothing more showbiz than a gangland funeral. Two hundred mourners trekked into Kent to see off Albert Dimes. Baker paid his respects with a magnificent floral tribute. Ron Kray sent a monster wreath: 'To A Fine Gentleman.'

Dimes – mother Scottish, father Italian – came to Saffron Hill in the Thirties. The influence of the Sabinis (an inspiration for Graham Greene and *Brighton Rock*) was still felt; four streets, a delicatessen, an ornate church. Bannion's rival in prison is an Italian (played by Grégoire Aslan). His name is Frank Saffron. Bannion's 'B' Wing is token Irish (any Celt will do). When he faces a punishment beating from the fearsome O'Hara (Neil McCarthy), the big Paddy enquires: 'Are you an Irishman at all?' And then, grinning like an earth-mover, he rolls up his sleeves. His cellmate Flynn (Tom Bell), ribs bruised and battered by Stanley, takes down a crucifix from the wall. When there's a bit of business to enact, Saffron gets word to Bannion. 'See you at Mass, Johnny.'

The Criminal was unlucky enough, in terms of reviews, to be released a day after *Saturday Night And Sunday Morning* with its obvious literary pedigree and gritty 'northern' realism (actually Nottingham). But Losey's film carries more intriguing baggage: a proper respect for Hollywood prison dramas (with their ambiguous politics) and echoes of European art cinema (the snowy death-in-the-fields of Truffaut's *Tirez Sur Le Pianiste*, which opened in the same year).

Even through the smoky fug of Dalston, it was evident that *The Criminal* was immaculately shot in harsh black and white. Robert Krasker's photography made Losey's film look like the culmination of a series of British realist dramas directed by the likes of Endfield and Val Guest. Baker appeared in most of them, sometimes a driven copper with a bad marriage, sometimes a villain: two sides of the same coin. *The Criminal* predicted, in its use of a specific sub-culture, future projects such as *Performance* and *The Long Good Friday*. The relationship between Baker, Losey and Dimes would be reprised, and mythologised, in the later transactions of James Fox, Donald Cammell and David Litvinoff. But it's always the topography that gets skewed: Cammell talks about being led deep into the 'East End', when he means the Old Kent Road. The London of Johnny Bannion that I'd extrapolated from my Dalston viewing now seemed more distant in time than forty years: a winter of the soul. I held on to the provisional poetry of locations within a few minutes of Merton Park Studios. Five men meeting at a bandstand. Distant church bells. (A Losey obsession, which he dated, erroneously, to Rome, Venice and *Eve*.) An ugly bridge across an unseen river. A signature double-decker bus barely registered among back-projected traffic. (The contrary of Hitchcock's ironic exploitation of postcard views: most known, least seen. Most sinister. A tradition that runs through to Patrick Keiller.) Losey's London is factored from location-hunting excursions. The last flicker of consciousness in a snow-covered field. Bannion, cradled by his nemesis, Mike 'The Snake' Carter (Sam Wanamaker), mutters an Irish act of contrition, through a Jewish mediator, to a cold English landscape. Wellington boots, spade and a thin Italian suit. Earth hard as concrete. A dying vision of suburban pastoral through which the M25 orbital motorway will eventually rumble.

Scenes that take place beyond the Piranesi-theatre of the prison are unreal. That's where most of the cuts took effect. The actors are in different movies. Jill Bennett (once Mrs John Osborne) appears, fragmented through a Cubist kaleidoscope, at Bannion's coming-out party. And is immediately ejected. The gangland bash begins to feel like a wrap party for exhausted cast and crew at the end of a difficult shoot. Personal baggage infiltrates the fiction. Bennett (a former Losey lover), the script suggests, is an addict. The film offers no convincing evidence of this. Her performance is robotic, unmotivated: an Antonioni sleepwalker who has wandered onto the wrong set. It reminds me of Osborne's turn in *Get Carter*, his ability to produce sexually-neutral spite and malevolence. Sam Wanamaker's villain, gloves and ivory cigarette-holder, is the template from which Osborne's lethargic gang boss is printed. (Wanamaker was preoccupied with reviving that authentic fake, Shakespeare's Globe Theatre.)

The engine of *The Criminal* is the maggot cathedral of the prison. Its arched roof, its mean windows. A set was contrived in which Krasker, by the use of mirrors, achieved a vertiginous depth and constriction: with verticality, the hierarchies of a closed world, achieved by sweeping crane shots. Which combine, effectively, with affectionate close-ups of the best British and Irish character actors doing the business (being themselves). A master class in budget film-making. Making the most of the accident of an approved script; Jimmy Sangster's formulaic pap impregnated by Alun Owen's active sense of ritual, his relish for Liverpool-Irish language.

A mongrel Catholicism, drawing on Brendan Behan's *The Quare Fellow*, tempers Losey's narcissistic non-conformity. (Owen would return to play an Irish priest in *The Servant*, with the deranged prison warder, Patrick Magee, as his bishop.) Owen's theatre-workshop bias carries over into the banter, the jigs, the nursery rhyme chants and riots of *The Criminal*. Losey's brief exposure to Brecht – a chamber production of *Galileo* with Charles Laughton – complements Owen's experience with Joan Littlewood at the Theatre Royal, Stratford East. (Owen also worked as a stooge for Arthur Askey.)

The screenplay is shapely: from Kenneth Cope's return to prison, a humiliated informer, through to Baker's final transfer to an easier regime: after he has been set up, betrayer of the riot. 'Bannion's let the screws in. Bannion's let the screws in. Bannion's let the screws in.' Baker walks away, against a chorus of derision, severed from the only community in which he could function. The real world now belongs to a new breed of criminal, the organisation man. 'Our mutual friend in Highgate.'

Here, sweating, grimacing, are the gargoyle faces of the new British theatre. Kenneth J Warren (approved by Pinter). The growling Beckettian, Patrick Magee. Murray Melvin (soon to feature in Tony Richardson's film of Shelagh Delaney's *A Taste Of Honey*). Brian Phelan, the psychotic Pauley, would later appear in the Losey/Pinter collaboration, *Accident*. John Molloy (as Snipe) looks very much like Beckett himself: hatchet cheeks, electric-shock hair, eyes that have caught fire and can't be put out.

After London, the film school in Brixton, I moved to Dublin. In the pub we listened to extras who claimed to have done time in

The Criminal. They recollected the experience as a 'Stanley Baker picture'. (Old lags paid to play old lags.) Losey barely registered, a distant presence. The prison sequences, they insisted, memories floating free, had been shot in Ireland. Kilmainham? No shortage of heritage prisons in the Emerald Isle. Once again, as with the Fu Manchu series produced by Hammer Films, a mythical London becomes Dublin. Granite standing in for yellow stock brick. Anywhere is everywhere. Baker, by unsupported rumour, was fingered as the banker behind the Great Train Robbery. He produced Peter Yates' film, *Robbery* (1967). If these whispers had any substance, Johnny Bannion would become 'our mutual friend from Highgate'. The man with the white mansion and the racehorses.

Back in London, lodged in Hackney, where I would remain for the rest of my sentence, I learnt that we had a local celebrity, a writer who was working with the Beatles and Dick Lester. He'd written the script of *A Hard Day's Night*. His name was Alun Owen. A proper share of the credit for *The Criminal* should go to him. Losey's career inflated, then stalled; good money, bad debts. He drank too much and made peevish phone calls about pigeons and loutish behaviour in Chelsea streets. He believed that he was being overcharged by Harrods. Owen, respected but largely reforgotten, got to live for a time in De Beauvoir Town – before Hackney became a satellite of Moscow, an off-shore investment for Saudi princelings. Before the diamond geezers, admired and supported by Stanley Baker, left town. And films about heists became vanity projects, zippy and post-ironic, made by advertising men and unstoic comedians.

Iain Sinclair